FOREVER... ISABELLA... FOREVER

Emmy's Story, Part 8

by
Kenneth Lee McGee

To Family and Friends

I would like to thank Denise and Stephanie for their support and for sharing their knowledge and opinions. Without their help, this book would not have been possible.

I want to thank (and it's long overdue) Cathy Miller for suggesting WriteOn Joliet to me back in 2013. Joining that group changed my life, or at least my skills as a writer. Thank you, Cathy.

I want to thank the people from my church who have graciously allowed me to include fragments of their lives as inspirations.

A special thanks to Sue Midlock for creating the cover. Check her out on Facebook. She does an amazing job.

I want to thank my wife Sheila for going through the books and making suggestions.

Chapter One

"Hey, Kristen. What's up?" Emmy Colasanti-Colwell asked.

"I'm late, and it's all your fault," Kristen Randolph shouted over the phone.

"What do you mean? It's still early. We have plenty of time to get to church." Emmy knew exactly what Kristen meant and giggled.

"You know what I mean," Kristen said sarcastically.

"How is that my fault? I think it's physically impossible."

"You been pushing for us to have another baby, and now I'm pregnant," Kristen grumbled. "I saw my doctor yesterday. I'm due April twentieth, so it will be kinda like the difference between Zach and the girls. This time I want a girl."

"Kenny says he doesn't care one way or the other, but I think he's really hoping for a son. How did John take the news?"

"He's thrilled. He called his parents right away."

"Did you tell Tony?"

"Didn't have to. John told him. He also called my parents. He's more excited this time than he was for Zach."

"Are you thinking about hiring a nanny?"

"Yes," Kristen said.

"No way! You can't have Mary." Emmy shook her head even though they were talking on the phone. "I'm not letting her go."

"We have actually talked to Donna French. She's looking for a new position, so I think we could hire her right away."

"I've heard good reports about her, but what about her kids?"

"What about them?" Kristen dropped the phone. "Sorry."

"What are you doing? Will she have to bring them with her?"

"Daniel is in school and Isobel will start first grade in the fall. It will work out perfectly."

"Yeah, if you don't mind the kids picking up her British accent."

1

Later, Emmy grabbed her wireless mic, looked out over the sanctuary from her position on the platform just before the service started, smiled and whispered to no one in particular, "Well, I'll be!"

"What is it?" Liz Hammond asked as she braided her long blonde hair around a finger. "Were you talking to someone?"

"Do you see Randy Braun?" Emmy leaned closer to Liz and pointed.

"Yes, but who is that with him, and who is the little girl?"

"That's Randy's older brother Christopher, and the little girl just has to be his daughter Elena. I haven't seen Christopher for a few months. I'm surprised, but thrilled, to see him in church. He's on my prayer list." Emmy closed her eyes and bowed her head as Chase Hillman began the service with a prayer. *I'm going to sit with Randy and Christopher since Kenny didn't make it home in time for church.*

After the worship team finished singing, Emmy hurried back into the sanctuary. Randy saw her coming so he and Vanni scooted over to allow her to sit between himself and Christopher.

"I'm so happy to see you, Christopher," Emmy whispered as she took his hand. "Is this really Elena? You are so grown up."

"She's almost five, Emmy. Where's Kenny?"

"They had some trouble getting away last night. He didn't get home in time to come with me. I texted him and told him to stay home and sleep. Are you busy after church?"

"I have Elena with me." Christopher looked at Randy.

"Her uncle Randy could watch her if you guys want to grab lunch and catch up on old times," Randy whispered.

"Thanks, Randy," Emmy said. "Where is Stephen?"

"In the nursery with all the other babies. The church is going to have to expand that section if everyone keeps having babies."

"I didn't see the twins in the nursery today. They're not sick, are they?" Vanessa asked.

"No, they're fine. They had a sleepover with Kenny's parents last night and were going to church with them."

Emmy hung out with Randy, Christopher and Elena after

2

the service. Randy introduced his brother to his friends and Dr. Behren, the senior pastor at Crest Ridge United Nazarene.

Kristen walked over and stopped in front of Christopher but left space between them. "I thought that was you. It's good to see you. How have you been?"

"Good. Yourself?" Christopher asked while shifting his weight back and forth and glancing around the room. "How's John and your son?"

"Good. John is down in Bourbonnais for training camp. Zach is in the nursery. I need to grab him."

Though we once dated, our lives have traveled down separate paths, Christopher thought as he gazed into Kristen's warm, blue eyes.

"I gotta run. It was good to see you, Christopher." Kristen glanced at Emmy and then quickly left.

"Elena, are you ready to spend some time with Uncle Ranny and Aunt Vanni? We can have ice cream and McDonald's for lunch, and then we can watch TV all afternoon," Randy said while grinning at Christopher.

"Just wait, little brother," Christopher warned. "Stephen will be old enough to spoil before you know it."

A few minutes later Emmy and Christopher were standing outside with no one in hearing distance.

"Where should we go?" Emmy asked. "Do you have any preference?"

"I would suggest Darby's, but you might not want to be seen there with me. Mr. Darby might not like that."

"He won't know," Emmy said.

"Why? Did something happen to the old guy?" Christopher asked.

"Nothing bad. He finally sold the business to Danny, and he and his wife retired to Florida."

"Good for him. What about Danny? He knows you."

"Danny never works on Sunday. I think it's safe for us to go there."

Christopher took a step toward Emmy and grinned. "I see you're still keeping your hair short."

3

"I like this better than having it halfway down my back." Emmy looked around the parking lot and asked, "Where's your car?"

"I rode with Randy. I guess we'll have to use yours. Are you driving a fancy sports car or a BMW or something expensive?" he teased. *I wonder if Kenny still drives that old Civic? He should be driving a Ferrari like other famous rock stars.*

She pointed. "That's my ride over there. It was kinda expensive if you ask me, but it's just a GMC Envoy. Nothing too fancy or sporty about it."

"Would I be safe to call you a future soccer mom?"

"I won't slug you in public, but I might when we're in the truck."

"Should you call Kenny and let him know where you're going? I don't want to get you in trouble."

"You won't. Kenny knows all about my crush on you, but I told him that I don't feel that way anymore." She opened the Envoy, and they hopped inside. "Does that disappoint you?"

"Would it be okay if I say yes just to lessen the blow to my ego?"

She started the Envoy. "I suppose so. You're still very handsome and charming, but you don't quite look like a surfer dude anymore. It won't be difficult for you to find another woman. There are plenty of single women at church."

"Are you going to play matchmaker for me?"

"No need. They will line up for a chance to be with you."

"Thanks, Emmy. That certainly helps restore my shattered ego."

She pulled into the lot at Darby's. "Hang on a sec. I have to tell you something. I'm expecting again. I'm due in March."

Christopher took her hand. "Congratulations, Em. I'm happy for you."

"Thank you." She smiled and grabbed her purse.

"Will you let me buy lunch?" Christopher asked as he looked around. "This place hasn't changed much in thirty years. Mr. Darby always kept the place looking good, and I see the

4

parking lot has been repaved recently. It's the best place in South Hampshire to get a burger and fries."

"You better buy me lunch," she insisted. "Just because I don't have a schoolgirl crush on you anymore doesn't mean you can get away with treating me like one of the guys." She ran up to the front door and waited for Christopher to open it for her. "Thank you, Christopher," she said and then giggled.

"You're welcome, Emmy."

He placed their order while she found a booth. He brought the food over and slipped onto the red vinyl seat across from her.

"Chili dog with cheese and onions, large fry and root beer. Something tells me you've ordered this before."

"You know Kenny and I used to live on Fifth Street, right?"

"I seem to recall that." Christopher took a bite of his burger while Emmy stole one of his fries. "You have your own."

Her blue eyes sparkled as she remembered coming to Darby's with Kenny when they were kids. "I used to steal Kenny's fries a lot."

Christopher looked at the photos on the wall above them. "That's Fridays At Five, right? One of the early gigs."

"It was actually the second one. It was at Larry's Uptown Grill. This is our favorite booth."

"Then the little girl in the picture is you."

"Do I really look like a little girl? I was fourteen," Emmy asked and then took a bite of her chili dog.

"You look very young but very pretty."

"Liar! You're just trying to charm me."

He laughed. "Old habits die hard."

They caught up on old times as they ate.

"Finished?"

"Yes, but could you refill my root beer, please?"

"Sure, Em." Christopher dumped their tray, refilled their drinks and came back to the booth.

"Okay, now tell me about you and Victoria and Elena. She looks adorable by the way," Emmy said seriously.

"We never should have been together in the first place. I realize that now."

5

"I know she wasn't faithful to you, but were you faithful?"

He managed a quick smile. "You don't pull any punches, do you?"

"Don't see the point."

"You want the truth, huh?"

She nodded without saying a word.

"No, I wasn't. Happy?"

"I'm not happy about the situation, but I was pleased to see you in church."

"I know Randy and Mom and Dad have always prayed for me."

"You're on my list, too."

"Thanks, I think."

She took his hand in hers. "I know you grew up in the church, so you know what you need to do."

"Emmy, are going to try to convert me right here in Darby's?" He looked around. "Don't I need to be in church for that?"

"Nope!" she said as she grinned. "You can accept Jesus into your heart wherever you are. Both Tony and I accepted him by the side of our bed."

"What?"

She bit her lip. "I didn't mean it like that! I meant our separate beds. Mine at the house, and he was at his dorm."

"Were you with him?"

"I was, but not like you're thinking. It was after his accident."

Christopher grinned.

She smacked his hand. "You're teasing me. Have you already heard this story?"

"You told Randy, and he mentioned it to me. I just wanted to see if I could embarrass you."

"I suppose just a little, but the fact remains that you can accept Him anywhere."

"Will you be upset if I don't pray, or whatever, right here?"

"I won't be upset, but you shouldn't put it off too long."

"I would feel more comfortable making that decision in a

6

church," he said while listening to the sounds of the crowded building.

"Does that mean you will be coming back?" Emmy took another drink of her root beer and smiled at a couple walking by with a young daughter.

"I might. There's this cute singer that I like to hear."

"Stop flirting with me," she said. *I like it, but it's wrong.* "Do you still share custody of Elena?"

"No, I should have told you earlier. I have full custody now. Victoria lost her job because she failed a mandatory drug test. The third one in six months. I took her to court and the judge, who was female, blew her top at Victoria. She can only see Elena with me."

"Then you really need to make sure you bring her to church."

"Randy and Vanni can bring her."

Emmy shook her head. "You're her father, so you need to bring her. That way you can hear that cute singer." *Shoot! I hope that didn't come out wrong.* "We should head back. I have to take you home."

They slipped out of the booth, Christopher held the door open for her and they walked outside.

"You drive a hard bargain, Em," he said. "I was going to ask earlier. Is Kenny playing with the worship band?"

"He hasn't been because of the current tour, but he will probably start playing again when it's over. He likes to be able to sit back and just play his guitar." Emmy touched her face as the hot August wind blew her hair around.

"I didn't really know him at school, but I certainly knew of him. He still seems like a regular guy even though he's a rock star."

Emmy laughed. "He's a dork! And I mean that in the best way. If all of the fans around the world knew him like his friends in SoHam, they would understand why I call him that."

"I've often wondered how he can walk around SoHam and not be hassled by fans and the paparazzi," Christopher said as he opened the Envoy door for her.

"It happens occasionally, but most of the time he can

wander around without being bothered. He used to drive his Civic, so no one would think he was anyone famous."

"Did he get rid of it?"

"He gave it to our nanny to use. Mary Michaelis. She goes to North Park College. Now he's been driving the Odyssey." Emmy rolled her eyes. "I should call it the dork-mobile."

"Oh, I'm sorry, Em. It must be difficult to deal with a rock star who pretends to be a soccer dad."

Christopher jumped in and Emmy pulled out of the lot.

"Where to?" Emmy asked as she floored the Envoy.

"Would it be too much if we stop and pick up Elena?"

"Not at all."

"Do you remember the old house by North Park?"

She giggled while she moved around a car actually doing the posted speed of forty. "I remember the party house."

"We did have a few parties there."

"Stop thinking about the time I was there. Nothing happened between us."

"I know, unfortunately." He leaned against the door as she took a corner at full speed. "Elena and I are renting a place in Timberline Heights."

"I used to live in the Heights."

"I know. I love that neighborhood. I might try to buy the place. The owners have expressed an interest in selling."

They picked up Elena and headed back toward Timberline Heights.

"Did you have fun with Uncle Randy?" Christopher asked. "What did you have for lunch?"

"Uncle Ranny told me not to tell you that we went to McDonald's. I had nuggets and a milk shake."

"How does your tummy feel?"

"Okay. Can I have a snack when we get home?"

"We'll see, baby."

"Which street?" Emmy asked as she turned into the Heights.

"Ottawa."

"You're kidding! I lived on Hickory. That's just a block

8

over. Jeff and Frances, from the band, have a beautiful home in the Heights. She grew up there, and after they got married, they bought this big old three-story place and totally refurbished it."

"I think I read about that in a magazine while I was wasting time at an architect's office."

Emmy drove past the old place on Hickory. "That one. Two seventeen. I worked with the guy who lives across the street. His name is Ethan Hanks and his friend Fernando Ramos lives in that one," she said as she slowed down. "Not that you would care."

She drove past Fernando's place, and then made her way over to Ottawa.

"That one right there, Em."

She pulled into the driveway. Christopher hopped out and helped Elena jump down.

"That car seat was too small," Elena complained. "It was for babies."

"I'm sorry I didn't have a booster seat for you, Elena. I'll make sure I buy one."

Christopher walked around to the driver's side. Emmy rolled down the window and watched Elena run up the wooden front steps and grab a small bicycle.

"I don't suppose it would be proper to invite you in by yourself, huh?"

"Maybe another time." Emmy put her elbows on the door and her face in her hands. "I really need to get home."

Christopher put his hands on the door and leaned close to Emmy.

What would you do if I kissed you right now? He thought about it as he looked into her sparkling blue eyes.

"Will I see you at church next Sunday?"

He smiled as he backed up. "Are you going to be singing?"

"Yes."

"Then we'll be there." He looked at Elena riding her bike on the sidewalk.

"No training wheels, huh?" Emmy asked.

"She made me take them off because she's a big girl now."

9

Chapter Two

The temperature already topped ninety degrees without even the hint of a breeze when Reed Shafer arrived at the church at seven thirty Tuesday morning. He unlocked the door and turned off the alarm. He flipped on the lights in the foyer, walked over to the sanctuary doors and peeked inside. *Good! They got all the chairs out of there. Thank you, Jess and Joe.* He heard a motorcycle and turned around.

"Morning, Pastor," Reed said as Dr. Behren walked in wearing faded jeans and a t-shirt a moment later.

"Good morning, Reed. It's going to be another scorcher."

"I do believe it's going to be hot all week."

"Russ and Tyler should be here soon." Dr. Behren pointed outside and chuckled. "Reed, look! I told Russ I was going to ride my bike, and he said he would ride his, too."

They watched as Pastor Russ Benson hopped off of his bicycle, leaned it against a handicapped sign and locked it.

"That's a sweet ride!" Dr. Behren smiled as Russ entered. "How many horses under the hood?"

Russ chuckled. "One if the wind's behind me. Dana told me you meant a motorcycle."

They watched as Pastor Tyler appeared on top of the rise between his home and the church.

"Sorry I'm late, but the traffic was horrendous," Tyler said and then chuckled. "Whose bicycle? Oh, never mind."

"I thought I could use the exercise," Russ explained.

"You might want to bring it inside," Reed suggested. "It will be safer. Kids in Crest Ridge have been known to steal road bikes."

Russ brought his bike inside, stashed it in a maintenance closet and then joined the others in the sanctuary. "Where are all the chairs? I thought we would have to move them."

"I had the guys do that yesterday," Reed said and then pointed. "They are in that room behind those double doors."

"I've never been in there. I guess I should check out the building more thoroughly." Russ opened the door and peered

10

inside. "Wow! That's a lot of chairs."

Ten minutes later a cargo truck and an old pickup pulled into the lot.

"That must be the carpet guys," Reed said. "I'll let them in."

"Do you think they will be finished by Thursday?" Tyler asked. "There's only three guys."

"I think they will surprise you."

"What about Vacation Bible School? Will they be using the sanctuary?" Russ asked.

Dr. Behren shook his head. "They planned to just use the educational wing and the gym."

Tyler chuckled. "Plus, VBS is next week."

"I knew that." Dr. Behren laughed.

After being introduced to the staff, the three men started working. Dr. Behren, Russ and Tyler watched for a few minutes.

"They are super fast," Tyler acknowledged.

"Well, I've got work to do," Dr. Behren said. "I'll be in my office for an hour and then I'm going to St. Bart's to visit Mrs. Southmire. Her blood pressure is higher than a kite again."

"I talked to Liz yesterday," Emmy said while toweling off after her shower. "The new carpeting is installed."

"How does it look?" Kenny asked as he shaved.

"She said it's lighter than the old carpet, and it really smells like new carpeting."

Kenny turned his head toward her. "Is that kinda like a new car smell?"

"Be careful! You might cut yourself."

Kenny looked at his razor. "It's electric. How can I cut myself?"

"You're the dork. You figure it out," Emmy said and then giggled.

"You're gonna get it, Em." He picked her up, carried her to the bed and set her down gently on her back.

She grinned up at him. "I like that look."

"What do you mean?"

"You forgot to shave this side." She touched the left side of his face.

"I was interrupted by a beautiful woman." He kissed her belly.

"Stop that! I just took a shower, and we'll be late for church."

Kenny grinned later as they pulled into the church parking lot. "See! We're not late, Em."

"Only because we're not singing today."

Kenny patted her leg.

"Wipe that silly grin off your face. Do you want everyone to know?" Emmy said as she unbuckled Isabella. "Will you get the diaper bag, please?"

Kenny helped Heather out of her car seat and set her down. She promptly ran around the front of the Odyssey.

"Heather Rose! Stop this instant!" Kenny hollered.

She froze.

"How many times have I told you not to run in the parking lot. There are cars everywhere."

"Come and walk with Mommy, sweetie. Daddy is right." Emmy held Isabella's hand as they walked up to the building, but Heather stubbornly refused Emmy's other hand.

"Mary! Mary!" Heather squealed as she got closer and saw Mary waiting. She ran to Mary and jabbered. "Daddy yell! Daddy yell! I hold you."

Mary picked up Heather and looked at Emmy. "Did she take off running again?"

"Yes, I would spank her butt if I thought that would do any good." Emmy walked into the foyer and glanced down. "This is a lot lighter than the old carpet."

"Good morning, Emmy. What do you think?" Cam Frees asked and then adjusted his Buddy Holly style glasses.

"Hey, Cam. I like it."

"Some of the older people have remarked about how it might show dirt."

"Then maybe we should all have to take off our shoes."

During the video announcements, the congregation howled

12

as they watched a sped up version of the carpet guys working.

"They are really quick, Em," Kenny whispered.

" You do realize..."

"Gotcha!" he said. "I'm a dork, not a doofus. There's a big difference."

As they were leaving, Emmy overheard two of the older ladies from the church complaining.

"That carpeting won't last five years," Mrs. Dewey said as she shook her head and tapped her cane on the floor.

Mrs. Thompkins nodded. "I heard the board had to pay extra for the foyer."

"I wonder how much that cost. I suppose Dr. Behren will be asking for more money. Doesn't he know we live on fixed incomes."

"I heard Stella Rosek talking to Doris Smith. Her husband is the treasurer. She said the carpet was paid for by a young couple in the church."

Emmy looked up at Kenny.

He put a finger to his mouth. "It wasn't that much, Em."

"Why are we having potluck today?" Kenny asked Emmy as they got ready for church the following week. "I thought it was usually the second Sunday."

"It usually is, but the board changed it because of Bible school, or something. Are we going to stay? We didn't last month."

"We should."

"But I didn't make anything," Emmy said as she shook her hair. *I still love this style. I don't have to do anything but brush it out.*

"I'll drop you off and run to the store to grab something. I'm not playing with the band today," Kenny said.

After the service, while heading toward the fellowship hall for the potluck, Emmy heard someone call out her name. She turned around and smiled. "Christopher! I didn't know you were here."

"I came back today. Sorry I missed you singing last Sunday. I heard about the potluck and decided to eat here. How could I pass up free food?"

"Hello, Elena. How are you today?"

Elena hid behind her father.

"You don't need to be shy around Emmy. She's Daddy's friend."

Emmy squatted down to Elena's level. "That is such a pretty dress."

Elena moved closer to Emmy. "It's my princess dress. Daddy bought it for me. He braided my hair for me, too."

"He did?" Emmy looked up at Christopher.

"Vanni did it. I wouldn't have a clue, and I don't have a girlfriend if that's what you're wondering."

"Just checking."

"Are you alone?" Christopher asked.

"Kenny is getting the girls from the nursery." She looked down the hall. "Here they come."

Christopher watched as Heather and Isabella walked down the wide hall with Kenny.

"They are so big now, Em."

"They're nineteen months. They move so fast and are talking more."

Kenny walked up to Christopher and offered a hand. "It's good to see you. I missed you at church a couple of weeks ago."

"Emmy told me about the tour."

"Yeah, that was a rough weekend. I didn't get home until Sunday evening. She said you guys went to Darby's. I still love eating there." Kenny looked down at Elena as she talked to Heather and Isabella. "Is this Elena?"

"Yes, she's almost five now, and it looks like she has two new friends."

"Ah! There you are!" Mary came rushing up to Kenny. "I got caught talking to one of my professors from North Park."

"Christopher, this is Mary Michaelis, our nanny. This is Christopher and Elena Braun."

"Hi, it's a pleasure to finally meet you. Emmy has told me all about you," Mary said.

"Really?" Christopher looked quickly at Kenny. *I hope she*

14

didn't tell you everything.

"Come on! I'm hungry." Emmy waved for them to hurry up. "Kenny would you find a table, please?"

"No need," Randy said as he walked up to Emmy. "We have a spot for all of us. That is if you don't mind sitting with us instead of Kristen and Sloane."

"We can do that. I don't think they were staying. I think the guys are coming home from Olivet today. Training camp is over."

Tony Bertucci and John Randolph played professional football for the Chicago Bears.

Fifteen minutes later the whole group was sitting down and eating. The twins were in highchairs, and Elena was having fun helping them eat.

"Is anyone using these chairs?" Liz Hammond asked.

"No, please join us," Emmy said while shaking her head. "Have you met Christopher and Elena?"

"I introduced him to Pastor Tyler two weeks ago, but not Liz," Randy said.

"I'm Liz." She smiled as she and Tyler sat across from Christopher. "You have an adorable daughter. I was teaching her Sunday School class today, and she was well behaved."

"Not all of the kids that age are," Emmy said. "I'm thinking of two in particular."

"Emmy! You don't know the whole story," Kenny chided.

"I saw you playing the bass," Christopher mentioned to Tyler.

"I'm really just filling in until someone better comes along. We lost our longtime bass player to retirement and grandkids."

"Don't believe him, Christopher," Kenny said. "He plays the keyboards and cello. He picked up the bass real quick and is getting better and better."

Tyler chuckled. "I have been lucky. Kenny has taught me a few things about playing that I never would have picked up on my own."

"Who was the guy playing lead guitar?" Christopher asked as he scooped up the last of some potato salad. "Um, this is really good. Who made it?"

15

"Ross Knapp," Emmy answered.

"A guy made the potato salad?"

"No! He's the guitar player. I'm not sure who made the potato salad," Emmy said and then giggled. "And the guy who played the acoustic guitar is Liz's older brother Larry Kimmerle. He and his wife Allie just moved to SoHam." She turned her head and asked, "Randy, have you seen Larry on campus?"

"We did run into each other this week," Randy said.

"Anyway, Larry stepped right in. Boyd Goldman and Perry Johnstone from The Only Hope were helping out, but they're going to be touring this fall."

"Without you, Emmy?" Christopher asked.

"Yes, thank God! The tour we just did was enough for me. Taking the girls along was a lot more stressful that I had imagined. Mary is back in school, and I could never go on tour without her."

Christopher smiled at Mary, and she smiled back. A little shyly, though.

Emmy caught the glance between them. *Oh, no you don't, Christopher! Mary is much too young and innocent for you.*

"Please tell me you don't have my brother for any classes," Christopher said as he kept smiling at Mary.

"I haven't so far, but I might down the road."

As they were cleaning up, Emmy pushed Christopher to the side.

"What is it, Em? Did I do something wrong?"

"I saw the way you were smiling at Mary. Don't you dare ask her for a date." Emmy poked a finger in his chest while frowning up at him. "She is much too young for you, not to mention too innocent to resist your charms."

"You managed to resist my charms," Christopher said.

"That's different." Emmy bit her lip.

"How old is she?"

"Twenty and you're too old for her." Emmy squeezed his arm. "Oh, my God! You're thirty."

"Wait a second. I don't turn thirty until November."

"You're going to be thirty! You're an old man."

"Do I have to remind you that Kenny is my age?"

"He's almost a year older. He turned thirty in January."

"Okay, I admit I'm too old for Mary, but I do think she's a beautiful young lady."

"So you won't... you know?"

"I promise, Em. Elena takes up all my free time. I haven't been on a date in ages."

"I need to get going, Emmy. Will you be okay?" Mary asked as she hugged Isabella one more time the next morning.

"I will be fine. I can handle them by myself. I am their mother, remember?" Emmy said. "But I'm glad you spent the weekend with us instead of in Howe Hall. Have fun at school." Emmy thought about Christopher and added, "Just beware of the older guys."

"Emmy! I'm not ready for a serious relationship. I want to get my degree first."

"What about Christopher?" Emmy asked. "I saw you smiling at him yesterday."

"He is hot, but he's too old for me."

"Good! I'm glad you realize that," Emmy said and then grinned. "He is still hot though, and don't you dare tell Kenny I said so."

"It will be our secret, Em," Mary said and then laughed.

"I'll see you Saturday afternoon. Say hi to your family for me."

Kenny Colwell and the other four members of Fridays At Five arrived in Memphis on the last day of August.

"Hi, Em, I just have a few minutes to Skype before we start. I am so glad that this tour is ending. Just tonight and then the SoHam show tomorrow. I miss the girls so much even though I get to see them every week. How are you feeling?"

"Pretty good. I'm not having any morning sickness at all. I have to see Dr. Walsh on Tuesday."

"When will we know what we're having?"

"Soon. Be patient."

They Skyped for a few more minutes.

"I gotta go, baby. Memphis is clamoring for us to start the show."

"I'll see you when you get home. You can wake me up if you want."

"Oooh! That sounds like fun," he said.

Kenny arrived home and snuggled up to Emmy. He nudged her a couple of times, but she didn't wake up. He decided to let her sleep.

"What time did you get home? Why didn't you wake me up?" she asked in the early morning.

"I thought you might need your rest more than... you know."

"You're still my favorite dork." She rolled over and kissed him. "Uh! I can hear Heather already. She never wants to sleep late."

"I need to be at the stadium around four for the soundcheck, but then I can come home until around eight. Andy doesn't want us to be back until then. He knows we are all kinda worn out right now."

Emmy laughed as she got out of bed and thought about her distant cousin, Andy Walker. "Don't tell me he's mellowing in his old age. I might have to find a new manager if he is."

"I think he's as tired of touring as the rest of us. He said he's going to rent a remote cabin in the Upper Peninsula and become a hermit for the next month."

"What about his house? Did you promise to take care of it for him?"

"It's just down the road, Em. It's not like he's in San Diego anymore."

Emmy grinned and said, "Tell him that while he's gone I'm going to put pictures on his bare walls. I might even install carpeting all over his house."

"I'm tell him, Em."

That afternoon Kenny told Andy what Emmy said as the band went through their soundcheck.

"You tell your little wife that if she touches my walls, I will

18

book her for one night stands on opposite sides of the country for the next year. Don't even get me started on carpeting. I hate it."

Kenny laughed.

"Did you tell Andy?" Emmy asked when Kenny walked into the kitchen later.

"I did, and he said to go ahead."

"Get out! What did he really say?" Emmy sat at the kitchen desk and sorted through the mail.

"It was something along the lines of your next tour being all over the country." Kenny opened the fridge and grabbed a bottle of water. He closed it hard enough that two of the magnets fell to the floor.

"Wait until I see him. I'll set him straight about that."

Kenny picked up the magnets and replaced them. "Is this new artwork?"

"The girls were coloring yesterday. Do you like?"

He laughed. "Maybe in a couple of years they will learn to stay in the lines."

Fridays At Five traditionally either ended their summer tours with a show at the South Hampshire Memorial Stadium, or they scheduled a show for the Fourth of July. It was their way of giving back to the local fans who supported them in the early days.

As Kenny left the stage later that night, he turned to his cousin and longtime guitar tech, Frankie Hanna, and said, "Well, that's another one in the books. What are you going to do until the next one?"

"Nothing. Absolutely nothing. I'm going to spend a month at my cabin in Wisconsin and go fishing."

Kenny walked along with him. "I didn't know you knew how to fish."

"I don't, but I figured the fish might like that."

Chapter Three

"I talked to Diane earlier this evening. She and the boys are going to Disney World sometime after the holidays," Patricia Colasanti said to her husband, Raymond, as they sat in their recliners and watched TV.

"She should do something like that. She can afford it. Emmy takes her kids all over the place."

"That's different. Emmy takes them along on her band tours. She doesn't go on many vacations. Maybe we could take a trip somewhere. We have enough money in the bank to fly anywhere we want. We could even go to Italy. We used to talk about going to see if we could find our relatives when we were younger. Now that you're retired, we could do it. What do you think?" She waited for an answer. "Are you listening to me? What do you think about..." She glanced over to her right. "Raymond, are you all right?" Patricia asked as he slumped over in his recliner and clutched his chest. "Ray!"

He looked up and shook his head slowly.

"I'm calling 9-1-1." Patricia jumped up and ran from the living room into the open kitchen area. She grabbed the phone off of the wall, punched in the numbers and waited for a response.

"What is your emergency?" The calm voice asked.

"My husband is having a heart attack..."

The paramedics arrived at the Colasanti home in the gated, retirement community of Hampshire Glen three minutes later.

"He's in there." Patricia pointed down the entry hall.

"Don't worry, ma'am. We'll take good care of him."

Patricia grabbed the phone as the paramedics checked her husband. She dialed Diane's number.

"Hi, Mom. What's up?"

"Come over here right now! Your father is having a heart attack."

"Did you call 9-1-1?" Diane asked as she raced into the kitchen and grabbed her keys.

"Yes. The ambulance is here now. I need you to take me to St. Bart's."

"I'll be right there." Diane hung up and turned to Fernando Ramos.

"I heard. I'll stay here with Carson and Caden. You take care of your mom."

"Thanks! You're a good friend. I'll owe you."

"What are friends for?" he said while running a hand through his jet-black hair.

Diane ran out to the car. She raced across the river to Hampshire Glen, picked up Mom and made it to the ER section of St. Bart's a few minutes after the ambulance.

"Wait here, Mom. I'll find out where he is." Diane found an empty chair in the crowded waiting room. "Sit here and don't move."

Patricia stared at a little old white-haired lady in a wheelchair. *You look familiar, but I can't remember why.*

Diane talked to a lady at the desk.

"The doctor is with him already. You should have a seat, and he will come and talk to you as soon as he can."

Diane walked back to her mother.

"Where is he? Can I see him? I should be with him," Patricia said as she wrung her hands.

"The doctors are with him, Mom. We just have to wait. I'm sure Daddy will be all right."

"What if he's not? What if he dies and I'm not with him?"

"He's not going to die," Diane said with more assurance than she felt.

Mom looked at Diane. "You are such a good mother to your boys. I used to worry about you so much, but you have turned out all right."

"Thanks, Mom."

"Where are the boys? Who's watching them? You didn't leave them with that jerk ex-husband of yours, did you?"

"No, Craig is still living in Toledo as far as I know. My friend Fernando took us out for dinner. He was still there when you called, so he offered to stay."

"Your friend?"

"Yes, Mom. He lives in the Heights, too. Emmy knows

21

him. Where is Emmy, anyway?"

"I didn't call her yet," Mom confessed.

"What!? Why not?" Diane yelled. "She needs to know Daddy is here."

"I was afraid she would get too upset. She's just a kid."

"For crap's sake! She's not a kid, Mom. I'll call her."

Mom looked at Diane again. "I forgot. Emmy's all grown up now, isn't she?"

"Yes, she is." Diane took out her cell phone and dialed Emmy's number as she stared at her mother. *Are you in shock or something?*

"Hey, Diane! I was just thinking about you. What's up?"

"I'm at St. Bart's with Mom..."

"Is she all right?"

Diane looked at her mother. "Maybe, but it's Daddy. He's had another heart attack. Possibly. The doctors are checking him out now."

"I'll be there ASAP!"

"Don't drive like a maniac," Diane said, but Emmy had already hung up.

"Kenny!" Emmy shouted. "Watch the girls. I'm going to St. Bart's. Mom and Daddy are there."

She rushed out of their house in Bristol Ridge before Kenny could even respond.

"I'll take care of the girls, Em," he said as he saw the Envoy disappear down the driveway, "and I'll say a prayer for your parents."

He saw Emmy's phone on the island and checked for Diane's number.

"Emmy! Are you on your way?" Diane asked.

"She is. This is Kenny. She left her phone here. What's going on, Diane? Is there anything I can do?"

"Hi, Kenny. Mom called me and said that Dad had a heart attack. We're waiting to talk to a doctor."

"How's your mother doing?"

Diane stood up and walked a few feet away. "I'm not sure. It could be just the stress of this, but maybe not. I asked her if she had called Emmy, and she said she hadn't because Emmy was just a kid and it would upset her. It was like she really thought Emmy was still a little kid."

"Have you ever noticed anything else like that?" Kenny recalled an incident but didn't tell Diane.

"She does forget things from time to time. We were shopping last week, and she wanted to head back to Raynor Park after we were finished."

"Emmy said that she asked her how her day at school was."

Diane said, "Emmy hasn't been out of college too long."

"True, but your mother was asking about her day at Robert T. Colwell Elementary."

"Now that is weird!" Diane saw a doctor approaching. "I'll call you back. I think one of the doctors is coming."

"Are you Diane Colasanti?"

That's right. I did change my name. It's not Garrett anymore. Sometimes I forget. "Yes, that's me." She stared at the doctor who appeared to be in his early thirties. *You look familiar, but I can't remember your name.*

"Your father has been moved to CICU. Cardiac intensive care. He is stable for now, but all indications point to an acute myocardial infarction. In simple terms, your father has had another heart attack."

"Can we see him?"

"They are moving him now. It will take about twenty minutes before you can see him."

"Where will he be?" Diane asked as she saw her mother coming.

"Third floor," he answered as he walked away.

"Diane! What is it? Who were you talking to?" Patricia asked.

"That was the doctor who examined Dad."

"Where is your father? I'm missing my shows."

You might be missing all of them, Mom. Diane knew. "Let's sit down and wait for Emmy."

Five minutes later Emmy burst into the ER.

"Over here, Em!" Diane waved.

Emmy sprinted through the waiting room, dodging people along the way.

"Where's Daddy? Is he all right? Can I see him?" Emmy bit her lip as she looked up at Diane.

"They're taking him to the CICU on the third floor. They think he's had another heart attack," Diane explained as she hugged Emmy. *My God, Em. You do seem like a kid.*

"Emily, why are you here?" Mom asked. "You should be at home."

Emmy looked at her mother and then back at Diane. "Is Mom all right?" Emmy whispered.

"I'm not sure. Come on. Let's go up to three and wait there."

An hour later a nurse approached them. "You may see him now, but, please, just for a few minutes."

"How is he?" Diane asked.

"He's mostly out of it, but he is doing much better. He may not respond to you, so don't be alarmed at that. I assume you know about the IVs and the monitor leads, since he's been here before."

Diane led the way as they followed the nurse.

"Raymond, your family is here to see you," the nurse said, but he didn't respond.

Emmy reached for Diane's hand. Diane squeezed it. *It'll be all right, Em.*

"Mom, why don't you sit by Dad." Diane took control of the situation. "Em, you stand by Mom and take care of her. I'm going to talk to the nurse."

Diane talked to the nurse for a few minutes and then returned.

"We should go back to the waiting room and decide what we're going to do," Diane suggested.

"I'm going to spend the night here," Emmy insisted.

"Good. I'm going to take Mom home," Diane said. "I'll spend the night with her."

"Who's watching the boys?" Emmy finally remembered they wouldn't be with Craig.

"Fernando took us out to dinner tonight. He offered to

24

watch them. I should call him and let him know what's going on."

"I didn't know you were seeing him. How's he doing?"

Diane rolled her eyes. "We're not dating, Em. He's still a friend. Sometimes he watches the boys for me."

"It's all right if you date him." Emmy found a comfortable position in her chair. "Sure, he's older, but he's a good guy. He would probably make a good father."

"You used to call him grandpa," Diane said and then laughed.

"We did tease each other a lot. Do you ever see Ethan Hanks?" Emmy asked.

"Last month. He came with us for dinner. He even brought a date."

"You said you and Fernando weren't dating."

Diane sighed then said, "We aren't, and don't try to pry into my private life."

Emmy grinned and then asked, "Is he still a good kisser?"

"I'm gonna smack you, Em."

Diane left an hour later and took her mother home.

"I'll stay here tonight and take you back in the morning. Would you like some coffee or something, Mom?" Diane searched until she found the coffee. "Mom, why is your coffee in the microwave?"

"I didn't put it there. Your father must have," Mom said.

"Yeah, whatever. I'm making some. Let me know if you want a cup." *Great! Dad is going to die from a heart attack and Mom is going senile. I suppose it will be my job to take care of them. Why did I have to be the oldest. I can't believe she stills thinks Emmy is a kid.*

Two weeks later Raymond was ready to leave the hospital and return home.

"We're going to miss you around here, Raymond, but don't come back to see us," one of the nurses said as he was being transported downstairs in a wheelchair.

Unbelievable! Diane smiled insincerely. *Do you really say that to all your patients?*

25

Dad waved. "I appreciate all that you've done for me."

"Were your nurses nice?" Diane asked. *Or were they sadistic witches who waited until you were finally asleep and then came in to check your vitals?*

"For the most part they were nice. There were a couple I didn't much care for. I saw a guy who was a nurse one day."

Dad, you were in intensive care for a week. You probably don't remember any of them. Diane walked along side the orderly. "I'll get the car."

"I'll stay with him until I see you." The orderly stopped the wheelchair and smiled. "Take your time." *The longer I take with him, the longer I have before I have to wheel some other old fart around.*

Raymond managed to get into Diane's car on his own. "Where's your mother? Why isn't she here to pick me up? Did she forget?"

"Dad, have you noticed Mom forgetting a lot of stuff lately?" Diane asked as she pulled onto Joseph St.

"Hmmmph! She sometimes forgets to turn off the light before she goes to bed, and I have to turn it off for her," he said while struggling with his seatbelt.

Diane clicked the belt in place and then asked, "What do you mean? Aren't you sleeping in the same bed?"

"Not any more. I've shared a bed with her for an eternity. She snores louder than a jet. We've got two empty bedrooms, so I'm using one."

"Does Emmy know about this?" Diane asked as she stopped at a traffic light. "If she doesn't, you shouldn't tell her."

"I don't know, and I don't care. At least I'm getting a full night of sleep. I'm surprised the neighbors haven't complained."

"I'm sure she can't snore that loud," Diane said. "I slept over there one night, and I never heard her."

"Did you sleep in the same room?"

"No way! I slept in the other bedroom with the door closed," Diane admitted. *Okay, so I heard her.*

"Can we stop for a pizza and beer? I haven't had a good pizza in weeks." He pointed to a pizza joint as Diane drove past.

"You're a real riot, Dad."

"All right. I'll settle for a burger and fries."

"Not a chance!" Diane shook her head. "Your arteries are so blocked already. You need surgery."

"Never gonna happen. I'm not letting some doctor open me up and put pig arteries in me."

"What are you talking about?" Diane asked.

She crossed the river and turned into Hampshire Glen. She pulled up to the security shack and rolled down her window.

"I'm bringing my father back from St. Bart's."

The guard leaned down and looked at Raymond. "It's good to see you back. The guys at Miller's Bar were worried about you." He stepped back into the small building and pressed a button to open the gate. "Have a good day." He smiled at Diane and waved.

Diane stayed long enough to get her father situated.

"I'll talk to you tomorrow. Mom, you have to make sure he takes his meds every day. They are in this thing that looks like a carton of eggs."

"I can take care of him. I have been for almost fifty years now."

Yeah, I'll tell Emmy to stop by and see you tomorrow. Diane headed home.

"What the devil was that noise?" Something woke Patricia up from a sound sleep around midnight. "Ray, get up. I think someone's in the house." She reached out to wake him and then swore. "I forgot you're in the hospital."

She got out of bed, and realized the light was on. She stepped out into the hall and saw a light on in the other bathroom. She paused. "Ray, I can hear someone groaning." Cautiously, she crept down the hall. She reached the doorway and peered inside. "Ray! What the..."

She could see a gash on his head and he appeared to be unconscious. She dialed 9-1-1 and explained the situation. The same paramedics arrived and once more transported him to St. Bart's.

"What is it, Mom?" Diane answered the phone. "I was just getting ready for bed."

27

"Your father fell, and he's going back to St. Bart's."

"Call, Emmy! I can't ask anyone to come and watch the boys this late at night." Diane hung up and fell back onto the bed. *What could it be now?*

X-rays revealed a fractured hip in addition to the slight concussion Raymond received in the fall. He was admitted to St. Bart's again.

"What did the doctor say?" Diane asked when she saw Emmy the next morning.

"He broke his hip, but they won't need to do surgery. He has a concussion, but that isn't too serious. His heartbeat is erratic and his blood pressure is sky high."

"So, in other words, he's screwed," Diane swore.

"Don't say that! He will be all right. It will just take time." Emmy stressed by waving her hands.

Nine days later, Diane and Emmy argued with their mother.

"He can't go back home! You can't take care of yourself much less take care of Dad," Diane yelled as she pounded on a countertop.

Mom poured herself a cup of coffee. "Where is he supposed to go? The hospital is kicking him out. They said it was because of the therapy or something."

"He needs to go to a nursing home until his hip is healed," Emmy said as she watched Mom put five spoonfuls of sugar in her coffee.

"We can't afford a nursing home," Mom said. "They will take our house away." She took a sip of coffee and made a face. "Something's wrong with the coffee pot."

"Your insurance will cover it for a while. We already checked," Diane said.

"And if he's there longer? What then?" Mom crossed her arms over her chest. "Do you expect me to live on the street?"

"Emmy and I have agreed to cover whatever medical expenses there are."

"How?" Mom poured the coffee down the sink. "You don't

28

have a job, and Emmy is still in school."

"I'm out of school now, Mom," Emmy said calmly.

Mom looked at her for a moment. "That's right. I forgot for a second."

"We visited the Astoria Estates Care Center, and that's where he's going."

"Is it nice?" Mom asked.

"It's the best one in SoHam, Mom. He will get the best care we can afford," Emmy assured her.

"I know you girls think I'm losing my mind, but I'm not. It's just been the stress of taking care of your father." Mom poured herself another cup of coffee. "I do sometimes forget things, but look at your grandmother. She's almost a hundred, and she still lives by herself."

"She does, but she has someone who comes in every day to cook and clean," Emmy explained.

"How can she afford that? She has some money, but she's not filthy rich."

Emmy and Diane looked at each other as they thought about the money in the trust set up by their paternal grandfather.

"Let's just say Grandma doesn't have to worry about money and leave it at that," Diane said.

Emmy remembered the times Grandma Isabel helped her and Diane out over the years. *The least we can do is take care of you now, Grandma.*

On Friday Raymond was moved to Astoria Estates via ambulance. Emmy and Diane met the ambulance and stayed while he was settled into his private room.

"What do you think, Dad?" Diane asked.

He glanced around the room from his bed. "Turn on the TV. At least I can kill time watching it."

"You are going to be undergoing some therapy while you're here. You won't be lying in bed all day. As soon as you can, you're going to get on your feet and walk."

"How the hell am I gonna walk with a busted hip? I'll be lucky to get around in a wheelchair," he complained. "I need some

29

more painkillers. Every time I move I get these stabs of intense pain. I need a beer."

"Great attitude, Dad." Emmy flipped through the channels. "You can watch ESPN."

He waved his hand. "Bah! I don't like sports."

Diane laughed. "You like betting on sports."

"The Bears are off this week, but you can watch the games if you want. We could even watch them together." Emmy sat in a chair and watched *Sports Center*.

"Are you still going to the games?" Dad asked.

"I don't go to every one like I used to, but I try to watch if I can."

"You always were into sports," Dad remembered. "Your mother used to worry about you playing with the boys. She was afraid you would get hurt."

"Didn't you worry about me?" Emmy asked.

He laughed. "Nah! You were a tough little kid. I figured you would hurt the boys more than they would hurt you. I remember when you punched the Newton boy."

"Yeah, she was a little troublemaker," Diane said while looking over the dinner menu. "Look. You get a choice of either a ham slice or a chicken breast tonight. Which would you prefer?"

"I don't care. I probably won't eat anything. The food here will probably be as bad as the hospital crap."

"Okay, so you're getting the ham. It comes with mashed potatoes and mixed veggies. Bon apetite!"

Diane and Emmy sat down and talked for close to an hour while their father slept.

"That's it! I'm outta here, Em. Tell him I said goodbye." Diane pushed back her chair and the scraping noise woke her father.

"Are you leaving?" he asked.

"I've got to get home. Mom was watching the boys, and I'm sure she is worn out by now. I'll see you tomorrow." Diane waved goodbye and left.

Emmy talked to him for five minutes.

"I could stay a little longer, Dad, but I told Kenny I would make dinner tonight." She kissed him on the forehead and waved goodbye. "I love you."

"Love you, too, little one," he said.

Emmy walked down the hallway toward the front desk. She passed an open office and heard a man talking on the phone. When he laughed, she stopped in mid-step. *Holy crap! I know it can't be, but that laugh sounded familiar.* She backed up a step and peered into the office.

The man put down the phone, looked up and froze. "Holy... sausages!" he exclaimed and turned in his chair.

"Holy... cigar smoke!" she exclaimed.

For a second, neither one moved.

Then he stood up and took a step toward the end of his desk. "Is that really you, Emmy?"

"Yeah, it's me," she said and took a step toward him.

"This is like surreal," he said while moving around his desk. "Am I dreaming?"

"What are you doing here, Rory?" She rushed forward and stared up at him. "I haven't seen you for like ten years."

He smiled and then put his hands on her shoulders. "Let me look at you."

They stared into each other's eyes for ten seconds.

"You don't look any different than the last time I saw you."

"Don't I look a little older?" she asked as she grinned. "You look older, but better if you don't mind me saying so." She patted his stomach. "You've put on a few pounds, and your hair isn't as long or greasy looking."

"You do look a little older, but your eyes still sparkle just like they used to. I'd recognize your voice anywhere."

"I was walking past and heard you laugh and instantly thought of you. I don't know why."

"Have a seat, Emmy. Or do you need to leave?" He pulled up the chair from the desk beside him.

"I have a few minutes, but I have to get home to make dinner."

He sat on the front edge of his desk and looked at her wedding ring. "Mom told me you married Kenny Colwell from the neighborhood. Do you have any kids?"

"I have two beautiful twin girls, and I'm expecting another one in March." She patted her tummy.

"Good for you." He looked at her belly and grinned. "How does it feel to be hitched to a celebrity?"

She giggled and then said, "You know he's just a regular guy. I call him the dorkiest rock star ever."

"I caught one of their shows in Atlanta a few years ago. I thought about trying to get backstage to talk to him, but I didn't want to cause any trouble."

"You should have told one of the guys who you were. They could have gotten word to his assistant or someone. Frankie Hanna would remember you from the old days."

"Is he still working as a roadie?"

"He's Kenny's guitar tech. He doesn't do any of the hard work anymore."

Rory smiled at her without saying anything for a time.

"What?" she asked and then bit her lip.

"God! You are so pretty, Em. Still just as tiny as ever, though."

She smacked his knee. "Thank you, I think."

"So, why are you here? Did you tell me already?" he asked and then moved back to his chair behind his desk.

"Daddy was admitted today."

She explained everything that had happened to her father lately.

"I see," he said as he checked his computer.

"How long have you been here and what do you do?" Emmy asked.

"I'm one of the physical therapists. Well, I'm kinda in charge of the physical therapy here, but I still work with patients." He checked a computer printout. "Hey! Your father is on my list. I'll be working with him." *Crap! I wonder if he still holds a grudge.*

"That's great!" She checked the time. "I really should run, but I'll be back every day. Maybe we can grab lunch and catch up on everything, huh?"

32

"I'd like that, Em." He stood up and walked around the desk. "I'm actually working tomorrow until six. Stop by and I'll make time to talk."

She stood up, bit her lip but then hugged him again. "See ya, Rory."

He stepped out into the hall and watched her walk away. *I'm sorry that your father is here, but I'm glad I got to see you, Emmy. I was hoping to run across you one of these days. SoHam isn't that big of a city.*

Emmy returned at ten thirty the next day and spent an hour with her father. He didn't mention seeing Rory, so she didn't either. *I wonder if you will even recognize him or remember him. I hope you don't mistake him for Owen. Rory was kinda nice to me. Owen was a jerk. Shoot! I shouldn't speak ill of the dead.*

She squeezed his hand. "I'm going to go. Diane said she would bring Mom over later this afternoon. Love you!" She tentatively approached Rory's office, knocked on the open door and peered inside.

Rory saw her, smiled and said, "I saw your father earlier and talked to him about his therapy."

"Did he recognize you?"

"He didn't give any indication that he did. I even told him my name. Just Rory, not my whole name."

"I was afraid he would remember Owen and think you were him."

Rory chuckled. "I've suffered a few times because of my late brother's activities."

She bit her lip but then asked, "Are you busy, or do you have time to talk?"

"I have an hour for lunch. Wanna grab a bite here, or get some real food? There's a Burger Bob's three blocks away. I suggest Burger Bob's."

"Sounds good. I'll drive."

"Give me one minute to let someone know I'm leaving."

"I'll get my Envoy and pull up front."

Emmy pulled up to the front doors and Rory climbed in.

33

"I thought you would be driving some fancy luxury car since you're married to Kenny."

"Ha! He drives a minivan. I told you he was a dork."

"Did you tell him you ran into me?"

"I did, and he said to say hi. He should I should invite you over for dinner. Would that interest you?"

"Let me think about that. He might want to shoot me." Rory grinned and then pointed. "Turn right out of here. Burger Bob's is on the right."

"He doesn't know about everything we did together." Emmy bit her lip. "I can't believe I ever did some of that stuff. Daddy would have killed me if he knew."

"He would have killed me not you, Em. Besides, we didn't do anything too serious compared to Owen and Diane."

Emmy pulled into the parking lot. They went inside, ordered and found an empty table in the back.

Rory watched as Emmy said a silent prayer.

"Did you say one for me, too?"

"Yes, it's safe for you to eat." She popped a curly fry into her mouth. "Okay, so tell me everything you've done for the last ten years. I want to know it all."

"Well, let's see. Ten years ago I got out of bed, brushed my teeth, and then I ate..."

"No! All the important stuff." She touched his hand and then giggled.

"Okay, Mom said she ran into to you at a gas station a few years ago."

"It was in '03 just before I got married. She told me you had to get married, but that you settled down. You were trying to be a good father, and you were even going to church every week."

Rory laughed for a moment. "Mom actually said that?"

"Yes. Why? Isn't it true?"

"I did have to get married, but, sorry, Em, I never set foot in a church. Mom probably said that because she thought it might sound good. Owen is dead. Amy's divorced. Again. I guess she wanted something to go right."

"Are you still married?" Emmy asked.

"Nope! The marriage didn't last a full year. We are officially divorced, and I haven't seen the kid for several years."

"That's terrible."

"It's not as bad as it sounds. Or maybe it's worse," he said and then took a drink.

"What do you mean?" she asked as she opened a packet of ketchup and poured it on her fries.

"The kid wasn't mine."

"What?" Emmy exclaimed. "Are you sure?"

"I didn't do a paternity test, but shortly after he was born he had to have some blood work done. I'm type O negative, which I guess is kinda rare. Ian was B positive or something. The doctor said I couldn't be the biological father."

"So, she was cheating on you the whole time?"

He nodded. "Appears so. We split up shortly after that and eventually I got a divorce. She moved to somewhere in Texas, and I haven't seen her since. I did love Ian, and I probably would have forgiven her, but she figured out who the real father was and got back together with him. I thought it would be best for me to disappear from his life."

"I'm so sorry, Rory. Diane divorced Craig because he cheated. Numerous times," Emmy said, took a sip of her drink and then asked, "Why didn't you come back to SoHam?"

He shrugged. "I figured there was nothing left for me up here."

"That wouldn't have been true, Rory," she said softly as she touched his hand and bit her lip.

"I did think about you, Emmy. There were several times when I thought about coming back and looking you up. But after Mom moved away, I didn't really have a reason to come to SoHam. Amy didn't want to see me. I told her I was back, but she didn't care. Then I found out you were engaged, so I didn't want to interfere."

"I'm so sorry, Rory," Emmy said as her heart raced.

"How is Diane? Does she still live in SoHam?" Rory asked between bites of his Deluxe Cheeseburger.

"She lived in Ohio for a while but moved back." *I'll let*

Diane tell you about her life if she wants. I'm sure you will run into each other.

"I guess we have something in common. Diane and me, I mean."

"Yeah, just not something good," Emmy said and then laughed. "When did you become a physical therapist?"

I actually finished high school in Georgia, and then, a year or two later, started taking college courses part-time."

"That's how I first started. I worked full-time and took night classes. After I got married, I went to school full-time for three semesters," Emmy said.

"I worked my butt off. I worked full-time and went to school for three years. I earned my degree and got a decent job."

"When did you move back here? Did I ask that already?"

"End of July. A little over three months ago. I had been working in St. Louis, but I decided to come back here. The pay's better."

"I worked for Robertson Industries for a few years, but now I just take care of the babies."

Rory shook his head. "That's not totally true. I saw your CDs in the store the other day. You're a singer just like Kenny."

"Not quite."

"But you do sing. I bought one of the CDs. Not exactly heavy metal, but you have a great voice."

"Thanks, Rory." *Maybe this isn't the time to mention why I sing, but I will say a prayer for you.*

"Do you ever go back to the old neighborhood? I checked your father's address. They moved, right?"

"I bought them a place in Hampshire Glen. It's a senior citizen community."

He raised his eyebrows. "You bought it."

"I'd rather not go into the details."

"Okay. I won't pry," he said. "Raynor Park?"

"Kenny's parents still live in the same house."

"Does that place still look as good. It's really old, right?"

"Still looks great after a hundred and thirty years. Give or take." Emmy thought about the carriage house. "Have you ever been inside the house or the carriage house out back?"

"Nah, never. I've seen the carriage house, of course, but never been invited in." He finished his burger. "Where are you guys living? You don't have to tell me if you don't want me to know. I'm not going to pester you, Em."

"We have a place in Bristol Ridge." She bit her lip. *Should I describe it to him? Will he think I'm bragging?*

"Not sure where that is, but I bet it's a lot nicer than Raynor Park. Your house was pretty small. At least I lived in a two-story."

"Amy told me that house belonged to your grandparents, and your mom moved in after she got divorced."

"Yeah. Mom didn't stay there too long."

"Where are you living, Rory?" Emmy asked as she finished her fries and glanced around the restaurant.

"For now, I'm renting a one-bedroom apartment three blocks from Astoria Estates. Nothing fancy, but I can walk to work. Saves me gas money."

Emmy looked at Rory. "Do you think Daddy will recover? He's had two heart attacks, and he's refusing to have heart surgery to repair his blocked arteries. It's like he wants to die."

Rory looked away. "Damn, Em. That's rough. I didn't know."

"He's a stubborn old man, but he did cut back on his drinking. He should quit all together, but I think all he drinks is one or two beers a week. A bit of wine, too."

"He should recover from the hip injury with no problem. I'll make sure he doesn't just lay in bed and waste away."

"I appreciate whatever you can do. I should take you back. Thanks for lunch."

"No problem. If we do it again, you can buy."

"Deal!" she said.

Emmy dropped him off. She rolled down her window and hollered, "I was serious about the dinner invite, Rory. We can talk about it later."

Chapter Four

"Hey, Tony, what's up?" Emmy put her phone on speaker mode as she changed Isabella's diaper. "Did Sloane have the baby?"

"Not yet, but I am taking her to St. Bart's. She's been in labor for three hours. I think we're cutting it close."

"Do you need me to watch the kids?" She pulled Isabella's pants up, playfully swatted her bottom and sent her on her way.

"No, Mama's here. She's got it under control."

"What's his name gonna be?" Emmy asked trying to be sneaky.

Tony laughed. "You're gonna have to wait just like everyone else, brat."

"Be that way! I won't tell you what we're having."

"I already know," Tony said smugly.

"How do you know? Did Kenny tell you?" *If he did, I'm gonna murder him.*

"All right, so I don't know. Did you already do the ultrasound thing?"

"Tomorrow, so we don't know yet, either. We will tell everyone this time."

"Will you get off the phone and get me to the hospital before I smack you?" Sloane yelled. "The contractions are getting stronger."

"Bye, Em. I'll call you later."

"See ya." Emmy ended the call and hollered, "Kenny!"

"Hey, Em. Who was on the phone?" he asked over the intercom.

"Tony." She pressed the wrong button. *I hate this thing. I wish we had never installed it.* She stabbed at the buttons and finally hit the right one. "Tony. He's on his way to St. Bart's."

"He is? Is he hurt?"

Emmy rolled her eyes. "No, you doofus! Sloane is having the baby."

"I was pulling your leg, Em. I may be a dork, but I'm not a dumb dork."

38

"You're my favorite dork, Kenny."

"Shoot! Does that mean Heather has a poopy diaper, and you want me to change her?"

"You are a clever dork."

"Be right there."

Two hours later Emmy jumped up from the couch, pushed Kenny aside, raced down the hallway and grabbed the landline in the kitchen.

"Hello, did Sloane have the baby?" she asked breathlessly.

Pastor Tyler chuckled before he answered, "Uh, I don't know."

"Oh, I'm sorry, Tyler. Tony took Sloane to the hospital, and I thought it was him calling," Emmy explained. "How is Liz doing?"

"Okay, but she's complaining about her back."

"I can relate to that." Emmy sighed.

"Are you okay?" Tyler asked. "Liz wants to know. I want to know, too, but she's sitting on the couch and telling me to ask."

"Tell her I'm fine."

"I'm calling because Chase is on vacation this week, and we wanted to know if you were going to be able to lead worship this Sunday?"

"Yes, but could either you, or Cam, take charge of practice on Thursday? I'd rather not have to do that."

"No problem. I'll talk to Cam. There's a possibility I might not be there for practice. Liz thinks we will have our daughter that day. Please, send me a text or an email when you hear from Tony."

"Will do." *I wonder why Liz is thinking that. She hasn't mentioned having a c-section.*

Thirty minutes later, Emmy's cell phone rang. She grabbed it and asked, "What is his name?"

"Benjamin Alexander Bertucci. He weighs eight pounds, eleven ounces and is twenty-two inches long."

"Holy cow! He's half grown," Emmy teased.

"You're a riot, brat."

"Does he have hair? Is Sloane okay?"

"Yeah, you wanna talk to her?" Tony asked while glancing

39

over his shoulder. "She's feeding Ben, but she can talk."

"Let me talk to her. Congratulations, Tony."

"Thanks, Em. Here's Sloane."

Emmy talked to Sloane and learned that Lindsey was already at St. Bart's.

"Would you mind if I came up to see you? Kenny can watch the girls."

"I don't mind. Are you coming up to tease Tony, or to see Benjamin?" Sloane asked and then laughed.

"Both!"

"Come on up. Room 4010."

Emmy hung up the phone and found Kenny taking a nap in his recliner. She nudged his foot.

He opened his eyes. "What?"

"Were you asleep?"

"I was. Did Sloane have the baby?"

"Yes, could you watch the girls so I can run to St. Bart's? They're playing in their room."

"Sure. What did they name him?" he asked as he got up.

"Benjamin Alexander. I don't know where they came up with that name. I can't think of anyone in Tony's family with either of those names."

"Maybe it's from Sloane's family."

"I'll find out." She kissed him and headed out the door.

Emmy found an empty spot on the third level of the new parking deck. She took the elevator to the ground floor and hurried down the hall to the new main entrance.

"May I help you?" the volunteer asked without glancing up as Emmy approached. "Oh, hi, Emmy. Who are you here to see? I thought your father went home."

"He went to Astoria Estates, and I'm here to see a new baby," Emmy said with a grin. "Tony and Sloane Bertucci had a baby boy today."

The volunteer's eyes lit up. "The Bears middle linebacker?"

Emmy nodded. "We're old friends."

"Congratulations! I assume you know how to get there, right?"

40

"Yes, thanks."

"Have a nice day. May I help you?" she asked the next person in line.

Emmy took the elevator to the fourth floor and found room 4010.

"Knock! Knock!" She peeked around the corner.

"Come on in, Emmy." Lindsey waved goodbye to Sloane. "I was just leaving. I have to get back to school."

Emmy walked over to Sloane's bed. "How are you doing?"

"Not bad, but I'm glad I don't have to plow a field this afternoon." Sloane glanced over at Benjamin.

"Why would you ever have to plow a field?"

Sloane laughed. "It's just an expression Grandma used to say."

Emmy leaned over and cooed at Benjamin, wrapped in a blue blanket and sleeping in his basket. "He looks so cute with all that dark hair."

"He's content now, but when he gets hungry." Sloane shook her head. "He knows how to let me know."

"Where's Tony?"

"He went out to get some food from Darby's."

"Doesn't he like the hospital food?" Emmy asked with a straight face.

"Go figure."

"At least Darby's is close."

Tony walked in carrying a large bag and a tray with two soft drinks. "Hey, brat! I didn't know you were coming otherwise I would have got you a chili dog."

"You knew I was coming," Emmy said as she reached for the bag. "I love the smell of Darby's fries."

Tony held the bag over his head. "Just be patient, Em. Maybe I'll let you have a bite of one of my dogs."

"Creep!" Emmy wrinkled her nose at him. She set the tray of pop on the countertop and picked up the one with a straw inserted. "Is this one yours?" She held it out.

Tony set the bag on Sloane's tray, opened it and grabbed a dog. "Yeah, I've got a Coke and Sloane has Seven-Up."

41

Emmy took a sip of his Coke and set the Seven-Up on Sloane's tray.

"Gross! That was mine."

"Mine now," Emmy grinned.

"Fine! I spit in it."

Emmy shook her head. "Through the straw? I doubt it."

"You're a brat!"

"Creep!"

Sloane sat up higher. "Will you two knock it off before you wake up Ben? You're worse than the kids in my classes." She opened one of the remaining dogs. "Did you get me a regular one?"

"It must be the other one. I got two chili dogs and one with everything except onions." He pulled the rest of the food out of the bag. "You can have some fries, Em."

She grabbed a few fries and sat down with Tony's Coke. "Does Ben's name have any family significance, or did you just like the name?"

"I really like the name Benjamin," Sloane said between bites. "We thought about using Beckett as a middle name."

"Benjamin Beckett Bertucci!" Emmy said. "That's a mouthful."

"Alexander is Dad's middle name, and it was Grandma's maiden name," Sloane explained while handing her pickle slice to Tony.

"That's kinda like in Kenny's family." Emmy reached for more fries, but Tony swatted her hand away. "All the first born men have the name Robert."

"Did you go see your father today? Is he doing any better?" Tony asked.

"I saw him yesterday after church, and I'll see him tomorrow." *He has therapy tomorrow, so I'll get to see Rory again.* "Hey, do you remember Rory Porter from Roosevelt High? His family lived up the street from us for a few years."

"I think I remember the name. Did he have a sister?"

"Yeah, Amy, and an older brother named Owen, but he's dead." *No great loss!* "Rory is in charge of the physical therapy at

42

Astoria Estates, and he's working with my dad."

"Didn't Diane date one of the brothers?" Tony asked after swallowing his last bite of chili dog.

Emmy frowned and stole another fry. "Let's not talk about that."

Benjamin interrupted their lunch with a loud wail.

"Can I pick him up?" Emmy didn't wait for an answer. She swooped in front of Tony and lifted Ben out of his basket. "I bet you're hungry, little man. If you're like your father, you'll be eating all the time."

"Can I hold him?" Tony asked.

"No! You'll have lots of chances to hold him." Emmy turned her back to Tony.

Tony put his hands on Emmy's shoulders and peered down at his son. "Do you think he looks like me?"

"God! I hope not." Emmy glanced up at Tony. "I hope he looks like Sloane."

Sloane held out her hands. "He doesn't look like anyone yet. He's all red and his head is flat on one side."

Ben settled down as his mother nursed him.

"Are you gonna tell us the sex tomorrow?" Tony asked.

"And how many you're having," Sloane added.

Emmy nodded. "As long as the ultrasound shows it, but we've haven't talked about names yet."

"Do you know what Liz and Tyler are having? She's due this week, right?" Tony asked as he leaned over to watch Ben nursing.

"Will you back off, chili-dog-breath? I'm sure Sloane would like some space, and if you remember, Liz told everyone they were having a girl before her baby shower."

"Sorry, but I wasn't at the shower, and I don't have chili dog breath."

Sloane laughed and waved her hand. "Oh, yes, you do."

Kristen went with Emmy to her doctor's appointment the next day.

"Do I have to keep the sex a secret?" Kristen asked.

"No, we're going to tell everyone. Oooh! That tickles." Emmy giggled as the ultrasound technician smeared the jelly on her abdomen.

"It might feel cold, too," he said.

A few minutes later Emmy and Kristen were watching the computer monitor and saw something simultaneously.

"Is that what I think it is?" Emmy asked.

The technician smiled at her. "I believe it is."

"Krissy, we're going to have a son!" Emmy cried out and Kristen hugged her.

"Congratulations," the technician added.

Emmy giggled and then said, "Not us. My husband and I. We have two daughters and now we will have a son."

"I'm happy for you."

"Krissy, will you call Kenny, and let me tell him? My phone is in my purse."

"Sure, Em."

Kristen dialed Kenny's number and handed the phone to Emmy before he answered.

"How's it going, Em? Do you know already?"

"Do you remember that blue paint we liked for the..."

"For real? We're going to have a son?"

"Yes, the ultrasound is pretty clear about that," Emmy said and then laughed. "You can call your parents and send an email to whoever you want. Should I tell Krissy what we might name him?"

"You can if you want, but it won't be official until he's born."

"I'll be home soon. I love you, Kenny. Tell the girls they are going to have a baby brother." Emmy blew a kiss at the phone.

"So, what are you going to name him?"

"You know how Kenny has two middle names, right?"

"Yeah. Robert and Travis."

"Well, we are thinking about using the name Kevin Michael Robert Colwell. What do you think?" Emmy asked and then bit her lip.

Kristen repeated the name several times. "I like! It rolls off the tongue like royalty."

"You're a goof, but I still love you."

"Will you come with me when I have my next ultrasound?" Kristen asked.

"Sure." She glanced at the technician as he shook his head.

"Hey, Kenny! Did you check your email?" Emmy hollered from the kitchen as she checked her laptop two days later.

"Not yet, Emmy. Should I? Or will you tell me what's so important?"

"Liz had the baby this morning," Emmy hollered. "She was tiny compared to Ben. She only weighed six pounds and five ounces. Eighteen and a half inches tall. With just a wisp of blonde hair." Emmy read off the vital stats.

"What are they going to call her?"

"Baby Girl Hammond," Emmy teased and then giggled.

"No, for real."

"Natalie Margaret Hammond," Emmy said.

"That's a pretty name. Does that mean they won't be at practice tonight?" Kenny hollered back.

"Yeah, can you believe it? They're using having a baby as an excuse for skipping practice. I remember when I had Heather and Isabella I came home and mowed the yard."

"It was wintertime, Em," Kenny reminded her as he walked into the kitchen.

"I meant I shoveled the driveway."

Kenny walked up behind her, put his arms around her waist and kissed her neck. "You look very sexy this morning."

"Yeah, right. I haven't showered and I'm fat."

"You're not fat."

"Yeah, yeah, yeah. I've heard that before." She sighed. "What are you doing?"

He did his Groucho thing and said, "I think the girls are taking naps."

"Stop that!"

"Are you sure?" He wiggled his eyebrows again.

"Maybe."

A few seconds later, Heather screamed, "Mommy!"

45

"So much for those naps." Kenny sighed and kissed her again. "I'll take care of the little angels. I'm sure that scream woke up Isabella."

"Can I get a rain check on the other thing?"

"It might have to wait until tonight."

Emmy walked into the music suite on Sunday morning and saw Pastor Tyler shaking hands with the guys. She scurried over to see him. "Is Liz here? Is Natalie here?"

Chase shook his head and then said, "Liz is here, but they left the baby at home."

"Oh, I did that once, too. The girls were two months old, and I had to run to the store. I was ready to back out of the garage before I remembered them."

"I was kidding, Emmy," Chase said. "Did you really forget the babies?"

"No, silly, but it makes for a good story. Where are Liz and Natalie?"

"In the nursery," Tyler answered.

"Start rehearsing without me," she shouted over her shoulder as she ran out of the room. "I have to see the baby."

Emmy scooted around people as she hurried to the nursery. "Sorry!" she shouted after bumping into someone. *Way to go, Emmy. That was probably a guest, and I just ran him over.* She slowed down and spotted a group of women crowded around Liz in the hallway outside of the nursery. Emmy stood on her tip toes to try to get a look. *Shoot! I can't see her.* She shifted her weight back and forth. *Come on! I want to see the baby, too!* After an eternity to Emmy, or ninety seconds in real time, a path opened. Emmy shot forward and looked at Liz and then Natalie. "She is so beautiful!" Emmy gushed. "And so tiny. I have a hard time remembering when Heather and Isabella were this small."

Liz beamed with joy.

"How do you feel?" Emmy asked without taking her eyes off of the baby.

"I'm feeling better today. I actually got three hours of sleep last night."

46

Emmy stayed longer than she planned.

"I gotta get back to rehearsal, Liz. I'll talk to you later."

After the service Emmy and Kristen talked while heading to the nursery.

"I thought that was a really good message," Kristen said. "I've never thought of that verse in such a way."

"I'm not sure I've ever read that verse before," Emmy admitted.

"You've read the entire Bible, Em. Did you skip that chapter?"

"No, but sometimes I don't remember everything I've read. I used to read my Bible and have other stuff on my mind. Now I pray first to clear my head. I understand it better. Have you seen baby Natalie yet?" Emmy asked.

"Not yet, but maybe we can now."

They entered the nursery and Emmy saw Heather and Isabella standing in front of Liz as she rocked Natalie.

Isabella turned and saw Emmy. "Mommy! Look! Baby!"

"You need to be careful. She's only a few days old. Don't stand too close."

Liz looked up and Emmy and Kristen. "I wasn't supposed to bring Natty today, but I decided to take a chance."

"I couldn't bring the girls to church until they were almost a month old," Emmy said. She allowed the twins another moment to stare at the baby. "Okay, girls. We need to get home. Say goodbye to Natalie and Liz."

Heather and Isabella waved and blew kisses.

"I'll talk to you later, Liz," Emmy said.

"Hey, Em, what time is the game today?" Kenny asked later while he helped feed the girls in their high chairs.

"It's later because they're out in Oakland," Emmy answered as she cut up some chicken for Heather and Isabella. She set the plates down and warned Heather, "Here's some chicken for you and don't throw it at each other."

"Is Mary coming over today?" Kenny ducked as a piece of chicken breast flew over his head. "Stop that!" He swatted Heather's hand, but she just laughed.

47

"She's eating lunch with her parents, but she said she would stop by later."

Just before the game started, Mary stopped over.

"How are your classes going?" Kenny asked. "Come and watch the game."

"Forget that!" Emmy said. "Are you dating anyone special? Have you been out with Gary lately?"

"I haven't gone out for a couple of weeks. Unless going to a football game with a group counts," Mary revealed as she sat on the couch.

Heather and Isabella heard Mary's voice and scampered into the family room. Isabella carried Doll Kitty with her.

"Here you are!" Mary got down on her knees and held out her arms. "I have missed you so much! Let me give you both a big cuddle."

After talking to Emmy and Kenny about school, Mary took the girls upstairs to play.

Emmy got up from the couch. "They better find a way to generate some offense in the second half. A three all tie against the lousy Raiders isn't going to cut it."

"Are you hungry? I have a taste for a pizza," Kenny said as he headed to the kitchen.

"Should we order one?" Emmy asked.

Kenny looked in the freezer. "We've got a Home Run Inn pizza. Sausage and pepperoni. How about that?"

"Wouldn't you rather order one from Kerry Lynn's?"

"That would take too long. I'll fix this."

The third quarter was half over before the pizza was ready.

"I'll get it," Kenny said as the oven timer dinged.

"Call Mary and let her know it's ready," Emmy said as she concentrated on the game.

Kenny used the intercom to tell Mary about the pizza. He pulled the pizza out.

"Ow! That's hot!" He quickly set the pizza on the stove top. "These oven mitts are worthless. We need new ones." He cut the pizza and carried it on a platter to the family room.

"Oh, no!" Emmy jumped off of the couch and put a hand to

her mouth. "No! This can't happen."

"What is it? Did the Raiders score again?" he asked.

Mary and the girls joined them.

"No, John just got hurt." Emmy pointed as a replay appeared on the TV.

"Oooh! That doesn't look good." Kenny cringed as the Raider's safety tackled John.

"His foot was planted, and his knee kinda buckled," Emmy said as she watched the replay again.

The TV switched back to live action.

Emmy pointed. "Look! He's getting up."

They watched as number fifty-two helped John hobble to the sideline.

"Look, girls!" Mary pointed to the TV. "There's Uncle Tony and Uncle John."

Heather and Isabella stared at the TV but couldn't recognize them because they still wore their helmets.

Emmy grabbed her cell phone. "I better call Krissy. She will be worried if she saw that."

Kenny picked up Isabella. "Look! Tony just gave a thumbs up to the camera. John must be all right."

Before Emmy could call Kristen, her phone buzzed.

"Are you watching the game?" Emmy asked Kristen.

"Yes, do you think he's all right?"

"Kenny saw Tony signal the camera, so he must not be hurt too bad. It looked worse than it probably was," Emmy said.

"I always worry about him getting hurt. I'll be glad when he retires."

"I can understand, Krissy. I say a prayer for Tony and John before every game. They know that sooner or later they will have to stop playing. I'm glad they have the landscaping company to fall back on."

"They might never make a profit from it, but it will keep them busy," Kristen said.

"Yeah! About time!" Emmy screamed.

"What happened?" Kristen asked as soon as she could hear again.

"The Bears finally scored a touchdown." Emmy high-fived Kenny. "There's always Bertucci and Keasling Construction. They could both work with your father."

"John has occasionally talked about coaching."

"I asked Tony if he would ever think about that, but he said no way. I don't think he would have the patience to deal with it."

John didn't return to the field, but the Bears still won the game.

Tony drove John home from Halas Hall later that night.

"Did you call Kristen and warn her that you're using crutches?" Tony asked as he pulled into John's driveway.

"Yeah, I talked to her. I told her it's not too serious, but that I have to see Dr. Sadaharo tomorrow."

"I'll get your bag since you're crippled," Tony joked as he hopped out.

John struggled with his crutches, but managed to make it inside. "Thanks, I hope I never have to return the favor."

"Yeah, me, too." Tony carried John's gear inside. "Hi, Kristen. He's on his way in." Tony hooked a thumb over his shoulder.

"Do you think it's serious?" Kristen asked.

"He's in a heep of pain, but you'll have to wait and see what the doctor says."

After being examined by Dr. Sadaharo, The Bears placed John on injured reserve ending his season.

"I'm sorry, John," Kristen consoled him later at home.

"The doctor said I won't need surgery if I can do the rehab and let it heal. I've never been hurt before, and I feel like I let the team down."

"It's the nature of the sport. We will do whatever necessary to get you ready for next year."

John grinned.

Kristen rolled her eyes. "How can you even think about that now?"

"Sorry," John said. "Are we going to keep looking for a nanny?"

"I don't want to even think about that right now. I feel so bad for Donna and her kids. She lost both parents so close together."

"She has friends back in England. It's probably better that she's gone back home."

Later that night as Emmy lay on her back in bed, Kenny rubbed her belly.

"We need to talk about something, Kenny."

"What?"

"What Dr. Walsh said."

"Oh, you mean about not having any more babies, huh?"

"Yes. I know you have mentioned having a dozen, but that's...."

"I know that's not going to happen, Em. Your health is more important."

"We have a couple options." Emmy touched him and then giggled. "One of us has to get fixed."

Okay," Kenny said slowly.

"You could get snipped."

His eyes opened wide. "I'll do it if you want me to."

She looked into his eyes. "You don't really want to, do you?"

"Not really, but it would be the easiest solution."

She stared at him for a moment and then shook her head. "No, the problem is mine. I should be the one who gets fixed. What if something happens to me? You might want to have more babies."

"Nothing is going to happen to you, and I wouldn't want to have babies with anyone else."

"That's sweet of you to say, but you might change your mind," Emmy said.

"I suppose it is a remote possibility."

"That settles it. I'll get my tubes tied."

He sighed with relief. "That's a good idea. I like that option."

"Men are such wimps." She rolled her eyes.

Chapter Five

"Em, I'm supposed to meet the guys in fifteen minutes," Kenny hollered from the kitchen the next morning. "Heather, do not try to tip your high chair over."

Emmy walked into the kitchen while talking to Kristen on her cell phone. "Go ahead. I will take care of the girls. What time should I expect you home?"

Kenny grabbed his wallet, keys, put on his hat and coat and shrugged. "I should be home by six unless we are on a roll and decide to keep going."

"Hang on a sec, Krissy," Emmy said. She walked up to Kenny and reached up to kiss him. "At least you aren't in New York or Los Angeles."

"I promise to call if I'm going to be late," Kenny said as he ran out the door.

"Okay, I'm back," Emmy said as she stared sternly at Heather.

Heather frowned, but settled down in her high chair.

"John is in a lot of pain, but he doesn't want to take any painkillers. He's trying to be so macho," Kristen said.

"Tony tries to do the same thing, but he wimps out at the sight of a needle," Emmy said and then laughed. She opened the fridge to grab some milk. She used her knee to close the door and then yelled, "Heather Rose! Do not turn your cereal bowl upside down."

Heather and Isabella froze while looking at Emmy.

"I gotta go," Emmy said. "Call me later if you want to do lunch. I need to run to Sainsbury's sometime this week. We are almost out of everything."

Kenny pulled into the parking lot of the Steward Music Group building and jumped out of his Honda Odyssey minivan. He glanced at the other cars and saw Dave Persching's 1975 Porsche 911. "Maybe I should buy something smaller than a van." He dashed into the building, waved at the receptionist, turned right and headed down the hallway to Studio Two. He entered the lounge area and saw the rest of the guys.

Jeff Rawlings turned around, glanced up from the chord chart he held, frowned and then turned back around.

"I'm sorry I'm late, but the kids were not cooperating," Kenny said as he removed his coat and hat.

"We were just about ready to head inside," Jeremy Lenhart said. "We were going over the harmonies for "No Shortage.'"

Paul Joseph, the other guitar player in the band, nodded and said, "I couldn't hear my part, but I think I've got it now. Dave and I are going to switch because he can hit the higher notes."

Will Consoli and Stuart Lederer walked out of the control room.

"We're ready whenever you are," Will said.

Will had been behind the board for all of the Fridays At Five recordings, and Stuart for most of them.

"Let's get this show on the road," Jeff said.

The guys walked into the thirty by thirty foot room containing their gear.

"I saw the 911 in the lot," Kenny said to Dave. "When did you get it back?"

"I picked it up from the shop yesterday. It's running like a top for now," Dave replied as he sat down on his drum throne.

"Do you think Macy will ever let you buy a new one?" Jeremy asked.

Dave snorted and shook his head. "She bought a new Honda Pilot after the twins were born."

"Can you think of any other bands with two sets of twins?" Kenny asked the guys.

Jeff shrugged as he plugged in his bass guitar. "How would we know?"

"Just wondered," Kenny said as he looked at the rack of guitars Frankie had brought to the studio.

After warming up for thirty minutes to allow Will and Stuart to set some levels, the members of Fridays At Five began recording.

Two minutes later Kenny stopped playing. "I'm sorry, but this Telecaster is not the right guitar for this track. I'm going to switch to a Gibson."

"That's all right. My A string is out of tune," Jeff said.

Jeremy hit a chord on his Yamaha CP300. "I don't like this voice. Give me a second to find a better one."

Dave changed one of his crash symbols, and the band tried again.

When six o'clock arrived, the band was in the middle of laying down the tracks for "Everything About You" and didn't notice the time.

Emmy heard the garage door open at eight o'clock as she was wiping off the breakfast nook table. She tossed the washcloth toward the sink and walked over to the mudroom door.

Kenny slowly opened the door hoping to avoid detection.

Emmy faced him with her hands on her hips and said, "Six, huh?"

"I'm sorry," Kenny said as he set his wallet and keys on the kitchen desk just to his left. "We struggled to get going at first, but then we got in a groove and let the time get away. Am I in trouble?"

Emmy tried to keep a mean look but couldn't. She grinned and said, "You're not in trouble, but you better run upstairs and say good night. They won't go to sleep until you kiss them good night."

Kenny arrived home around three o'clock on the last day of November, walked into the family room and watched as Emmy played on the floor with the twins.

"I'm back," he said.

Heather and Isabella saw their father and raced to him while jabbering.

"Does this mean you guys are finished?" Emmy asked as she stood up.

Kenny picked up the girls and smothered them with kisses. "We're finished with the recording, but you know that doesn't mean we're completely finished."

"When are you going to start mixing it?"

Kenny set the girls down and answered, "Next week. It shouldn't take too long."

"Then we can work on finishing my CD, right?"

"Yes, we can concentrate on yours, Em."

"Did you talk to the guys at Prater-Saylor about the tour?" Emmy asked. "It's going to start in the summer, right?"

"June 4, I think. The dates are all set and tickets should go on sale in early January. The first show is in Dallas."

"Do you still want me and the band to play the Saturday shows?"

"I think it would be beneficial for you to gain the exposure. Your CD will be out by then, and this will be a good way to promote it."

"You sound like an accountant," she said and then grinned.

"Nothing wrong with trying to maximize the free publicity."

"I hope my CD is done by then."

Kenny watched the girls playing with their dolls and said, "I don't know why it wouldn't. We've got the demos done, and the lyrics are pretty tight. It won't take too long to finish."

"Did you guys decide to go ahead and release another CD in the fall?" Emmy asked.

"Yeah, but we still aren't sure of the title. All we know for sure is the word Chronicles will be part of it. We might want to add a couple more songs to it."

"Did you guys think about a two disc set?"

"We considered it once we realized how many good songs we had, but we decided against it pretty early. The songs are different enough to justify two CDs."

Chapter Six

Emmy had just returned from the nursing home and a doctor visit when she found Kenny on the phone in the kitchen.

"Do they have any idea what caused it?" he asked.

Emmy tossed her purse on the island and Kenny held up a finger for her to wait.

"Em, just got home, Dad. I'll fill her in, and we'll be right over. Talk to you in a few." Kenny ended the call.

"What happened?" Emmy bit her lip.

Kenny put his hands on her shoulders and looked into her blue eyes. "It appears that some kid, or kids, broke into the carriage house last night and started a fire. Dad said the place is gutted, but the walls are intact."

"No! That can't be."

"I'm afraid it is, Em."

"Who would do such a thing?" Emmy asked as she cried. "Was everything destroyed?"

"I'm afraid so."

"Our old couch is gone?" she whispered.

"I'm sorry. I know how much it meant to you." He held her close as she wept for a moment. "Luckily, no one was hurt, and, hey, the walls are still there."

"I want to go see it. I'll see if Krissy can watch the girls."

"I'm so sorry, Em. I know that place holds so many great memories for you guys." Kristen hugged Emmy as they dropped off Heather and Isabella. "You guys spent your wedding night there."

"The old couch is gone, Krissy. Everything else can be replaced."

John hobbled into the kitchen with Zachary in tow. The girls immediately started playing with him.

Kenny smiled at John and asked, "How's the hinge doing?"

"I'm lucky. I don't need surgery. How are you?"

"All right. I'm glad I moved all of my old gear out when we moved into the house. The only thing of real value was the old couch. It wasn't worth anything as far as money goes, but it had a lot of sentimental value."

"We'll be back as soon as we can, Krissy," Emmy said.

Kristen waved her hand dismissively. "Take your time. The kids will be fine."

Kenny pulled into his parent's driveway and saw his father talking to a man with a clipboard.

"Hi, son. This is Inspector Harmon from the arson unit."

"Hello, sir." Kenny shook his hand. "This is my wife Emmy."

"It's a pleasure to meet you, but I wish the circumstances were different. My daughters are fans of both of you."

"Thanks. Were you able to discover the cause?" Kenny asked.

"Definitely arson. The point of origin was in the northeast corner. The perpetrator used gasoline as an accelerator."

"The building might have been totally destroyed if the car and van had been inside," Mr. Colwell explained.

Kenny had parked behind his father's Accord. "Where is the old Odyssey?"

"In the shop. I was getting the oil changed, and they discovered I needed some other work done."

"I'm going inside to talk to Mom," Emmy said. "She wanted to know how Dad was doing."

"She's in the living room, Emmy," Mr. Colwell told her. "How is your father?"

"Getting stronger. He walked up and down the hall with his walker today," Emmy replied as she headed into the house.

"How soon will we be able to start the cleanup and rebuild it?" Kenny asked.

Inspector Harmon set his square jaw and rubbed his close-cropped gray hair. "My investigation will take a couple of days. After that, the place is yours. I'd hate to see the city lose another one of these old carriage houses. There aren't many left, and this is the third one to be torched this year."

"Do you have any idea who might be behind the crimes?"

"We have a list, but there is one person in particular we're focusing on. He's an old time arsonist who was released from

57

prison about eighteen months ago."

Mr. Colwell allowed a smile to cross his face. "In that case, we should take a look at the security footage."

"You have security cameras?" Inspector Harmon looked around. "Where? I didn't spot any."

"If you can't spot them, then our arsonist probably didn't either." Mr. Colwell smiled. "We have cameras that cover the entire lot. They're wireless and feed a hard drive in the house. Let's take a look."

They headed inside, and Mr. Colwell brought up the footage.

"There he is!" Kenny pointed.

They let the footage run.

"There he is coming out, and that's a good view of his face." Inspector Harmon clapped his hands.

"Is that your guy?" Mr. Colwell asked.

"You bet. That's him. Thanks to you, we will put him back inside."

"Do you have any idea why he does this?" Mr. Colwell asked. "He has nothing to gain."

"He just likes fire." Inspector Harmon shrugged. "Am I correct in assuming you plan to restore the old building?"

"Absolutely!" Kenny nodded emphatically. "We'll make it better than ever!"

Chapter Seven

"Did you have any trouble finding the place?" Emmy opened the garage service door and asked Rory on Saturday evening.

He smiled at her. "Not a bit. I didn't realize you lived in a gated community."

"I didn't mention it because it sounds like bragging." She bit her lip.

"Did you leave the driveway gate open just for me?"

"No, we don't close it very often," Emmy said. "Come on in. This is obviously the garage."

"Holy crap! Em, this is twice as big as my apartment." He looked around. "You need to buy more cars to fill it up."

"I might talk Kenny into letting me buy something smaller than the Envoy."

Emmy led the way up the stairs to the mudroom. "You can hang up your coat here," she said as she removed her comfortable tennis shoes.

"Do I need to take off my shoes?" he asked as he hung up his winter coat on a hook.

"Up to you. I like to run around in my socks, but it doesn't matter."

He removed his shoes and Emmy led him through the mudroom and into the kitchen.

Rory stopped and stared. "You have done all right, Em. I've never been inside a house this fancy."

"Ignore the mess on my desk. I was paying some bills," Emmy said as she pulled Rory along.

"It looks like a home, Em." He glanced around and spotted some crayons on the island and pictures on the fridge.

Kenny walked into the kitchen. "We look at it as an investment, but it is home. How are you, Rory?" Kenny offered his hand.

"Doing all right now," Rory said as he stared at Kenny. "It's been a long time since our days at Roosevelt High and Raynor Park."

"It has flown by."

"Emmy told me about the carriage house yesterday. Sorry. Kids?"

"No, it was an older man. Some kind of pyromaniac," Kenny said. "Would you like to meet the girls?"

"Is that all right? Are they still up?" Rory asked while he looked at Emmy.

"They're on their way to bed, but I told them they could see you."

"Why? They don't have a clue who I might be."

"I told them you lived close to Gra and Me-maw. Kenny's parents," Emmy explained.

Heather and Isabella were sitting on the couch in the family room as Mary read them a story.

"Mary, this is Rory. Rory, Mary, our nanny."

"It's a pleasure to meet you. Emmy told me you guys went to school together." Mary put her arms around the girls.

"We did for several years." Rory looked back and forth at the twins.

"This is Heather, and this is Isabella." Emmy sat next to Isabella.

"They are adorable, Emmy," Rory said. "Do they look a lot like you when you were their age?"

"Mom says they do. We don't have too many pictures of me as a little kid."

Mary put the book down. "Come on, girls. We need to go nighty-night now. Give Mommy and Daddy cuddles."

Kenny and Emmy kissed the girls good night.

"I'll get them to sleep, and then I'm going back to Howe Hall. We're having a party tonight to celebrate the end of the semester."

"Really? Will there be boys? Can I come to the party?" Emmy asked and then grinned.

"Just some of the girls. No guys. A pajama party of sorts," Mary explained.

"Thanks, Mary, and have fun."

Kenny gave Rory a quick tour of the main floor and the

60

basement while Emmy finished getting dinner ready.

"So, you can record everything right here?" Rory asked while standing in the control room. "Must be nice."

"We do use the studio over at Steward Music if we need more room. Like for a full string section. We tried recording strings here, but the acoustics are off just a bit," Kenny explained. "In any case, it beats having to spend a few months in New York or LA."

They left the studio and walked back toward the stairs.

Emmy met them at the bottom of the stairs and announced, "Dinner is ready. What would you like to drink, Rory?"

"What are my options? Do you still drink beer or wine?"

"Once in a while. We keep some in the house, but nothing hard."

"I'll have whatever you are, Emmy."

"Let's eat before it gets cold. I made mostaccioli, since you asked for pasta. We have a garden salad that Kenny put together, garlic bread and cauliflower. If you don't like cauliflower, I can make something else." Emmy led the way upstairs.

"That sounds delicious. I'm not a very good cook, so I eat a lot of frozen stuff. Prepared meals with lots of preservatives."

"Are we eating in the dining room?" Kenny asked.

"I thought we could eat in the breakfast nook since it's just the three of us. Is that all right?" She looked at Rory.

"Hey, I eat on my couch. It doesn't matter to me. Wherever is comfortable for you guys." Rory leaned over the stove. "Ah! A home cooked meal."

"Stop it." Emmy poked him in the side. "I'm going to open a bottle of wine, but I can only drink half a glass."

Kenny helped set the table. Emmy said a quick prayer, and they started eating.

"How did Daddy do today?" Emmy asked.

Rory held up his hand as he had a mouthful of mostaccioli. "This is really good, Emmy." Rory took a sip of wine. "He did all right, but he couldn't walk as far as the day before. He complained about his back. I told his nurse, and she gave him some extra pain medication."

"I talked to one of his nurses. She said he might be there for several months."

"It's possible. His heart is weak."

"He won't have any surgery. He is so stubborn."

Rory had seconds, and the guys finished off the bottle of wine.

"We have ice cream for dessert," Emmy said as she cleared the table.

"Could we save it for later, Em? I'm full," Kenny said.

"Sure. Let's sit in the family room and talk. I need to relax." She patted her tummy. "I can make coffee if you'd like."

"I'm good, Emmy, thanks." Rory followed Kenny down the wide hallway back to the family room. "I like the fireplace."

"We're going to use it more this year," Kenny said as he checked the logs stacked next to the fireplace.

Rory walked up to the stone fireplace and looked at the family photos on the mantle. "Very nice."

"Have a seat, Rory." Kenny pointed to one of the recliners that faced the fireplace and then sat on the love seat to Rory's left.

Emmy joined them in a couple of minutes, and the conversation turned to their days in Raynor Park.

"How old were you when you moved there?" Emmy asked Rory as she sat on the other love seat. She put her feet on the cushion and leaned back.

"Let me see." He tapped his chin. "Eleven."

"I was seven when we moved into the house on East Fifth Street," Emmy said. "You're two years older than me, so I would have been nine when we met."

"I guess, but we really didn't get to know each other until you were thirteen or so," Rory reminded her.

"Yeah, about the time Diane and Owen were sneaking around together."

Kenny listened as Emmy and Rory talked. After a time, he got up and added another log to the fire.

"I'm sorry to say this, but Owen was a jerk." Emmy held a throw pillow to her chest.

"He sure was." Rory looked at the fireplace and chuckled.

"I mean he was my brother and all, but he was a total... jerk. I wasn't exactly a choir boy, but he was worse. He would have ended up in prison if he hadn't left SoHam. Either prison, or some irate husband would have shot him," Rory said. "I don't suppose it matters now, so I can tell you guys." He hesitated for a moment.

"What? Tell us." Emmy encouraged him to continue with a wave.

Rory looked around the room and then said, "Owen was dealing."

"No! Really?"

"Yeah, he sold pot when he was at Roosevelt, but later he started selling coke. He got hooked up with some rather nasty characters," Rory said and then chuckled. "He was always a hustler."

"I remember when Emmy tutored you," Kenny said.

"She tried, but I wasn't interested in school at all. I was more interested in fooling around with girls."

Emmy laughed and threw the pillow at Rory. "You tried to get me in bed."

"I did not!" Rory looked at Kenny and shook his head. *Emmy, are you trying to get me killed? Why the hell would you say that in front of your husband?*

"You did so, but you didn't try real hard." Emmy grinned but then got serious. "You might be embarrassed about it now, but you kinda looked after me. Just like Kenny."

"You were hanging out with some people you shouldn't, Emmy. Older people. I didn't want to see you get hurt." He shifted his attention back and forth between Emmy and Kenny. He glanced at the children's books on the two rectangular coffee tables that separated the love seats. "You weren't like Diane and the people she and Owen hung out around."

Emmy looked at Kenny and then back at Rory. "I was kinda rebelling against my parents. I didn't want to be known as some perfect little angel who always did everything right."

"You weren't all that bad, Em. Not compared to some of the other kids at Roosevelt," Rory said.

"And I thought you were always a good girl," Kenny said.

"I was." Emmy bit her lip.

"Emmy!" Kenny said slowly. "You've told me some of the things you and Rory did. Are there more?"

Rory and Emmy looked at each other.

"What have you told him?" Rory smiled to cover his apprehension.

"I told him about John Grafton's parties," Emmy admitted. "A couple of them, anyway."

"I don't know if you've heard about those parties, but they could get out of control," Rory said.

"I heard all about them, but I never went to one. I was too much of a dork back then," Kenny said and then laughed.

"Don't worry, Kenny, you're still a dork," Emmy said. "You spent all your time practicing your guitar and writing songs."

"Grafton had a knack for getting lots of good looking girls with loose morals to his parties," Rory said, but then looked at Emmy. "I didn't mean to imply you were like that, Emmy. She went to some of those parties with me, but she never did anything other than maybe have a beer. I can't remember you ever smoking like the other kids."

"I've never smoked anything in my life," Emmy insisted. "I did drink beer with you, but Kenny knows that."

"Tell me something about Em that you think I should know," Kenny said.

"Don't you dare, Rory Porter. You can't have any ice cream if you tell him about the..." She didn't complete her warning.

"About the what, Em?" Rory appeared puzzled.

"Never mind. If you don't remember, I'm not going to tell you." Emmy pointed a finger at him. "Keep your mouth shut!"

Rory was quiet for a moment. Then he grinned at Emmy. "Do you mean the time you went with me, and I took some money from the cash drawer at that gas station?"

Emmy sighed with relief. *That wasn't what I was thinking about, but it's tame enough to tell Kenny.* "I hate you, Rory Porter! You promised me you would never tell a soul." Emmy threw another pillow at him. "Kenny, I didn't know he was going to do that. I swear it!"

"Em, I know you weren't always perfect. I knew it back then, but I still loved you." He stood up and joined Emmy on her love seat.

"She never did anything like Diane did," Rory mentioned. *Not with me, anyway. I don't know what you guys did.* "She talked about you a lot when we would hang out together."

Kenny looked at Emmy. "What kinds of things did you tell Rory?"

"Nothing derogatory," Emmy said. "Probably just stuff about music. I can't remember everything I ever told him."

"I had a crush on Diane, but she was into older guys. Emmy was kinda like a kid sister who just wanted to get away from her parents. She probably told you how she would sneak out the window, right?"

Kenny nodded.

"I know she would sneak over to your house. I saw you guys camping out in the backyard once."

"We did that a few times." Kenny nudged her and grinned.

Emmy bit her lip. "Nothing ever happened, Rory. I was to young to fool around. You might not believe me, but it's true."

"I know. Owen didn't think so though. I never told you, but we got into a fight once because he was talking about... doing the same thing with you that he did with Diane. I punched him out and broke a couple of ribs." Rory made a fist, punched his open hand and then shrugged. "Like I said. He was a jerk."

Emmy was quiet for a moment, but then blurted out. "One time Diane and I switched Mom's hair coloring. She ended up with orange-looking hair and didn't know why."

"You didn't!?" Kenny pretended to be shocked.

"Oh, be quiet. I know you're teasing me." Emmy stuck out her tongue at him.

"Did she stick her tongue out at you a lot, Rory?" Kenny asked.

"She did until I grabbed it one time." Rory made a snatching motion. "After that she didn't."

"Creep! You nearly pulled it out of my mouth."

Rory looked at Kenny. "What's the worst thing you ever

did when we were kids?"

"Ha! That's easy!" Emmy said and then got up and moved to the recliner next to Rory. She looked at Kenny as she put a hand on Rory's arm. "One time he skipped school and went into Chicago to a blues festival. He ended up sitting in with... Who was it?"

"Otis Rush and then Buddy Guy," Kenny said. "The school called my mom, and she covered for me, but I got grounded and couldn't play my guitar for a week."

"See what I mean, Rory?" Emmy whispered, "He's a dork."

"I'm ready for ice cream. How about you, Rory?" Kenny asked.

"Sounds good to me."

"Will you get it yourself?" Emmy asked. "And I'd like a bowl, too, please."

As Rory followed Kenny into the kitchen, Emmy stuck out her tongue. Rory tried to grab it as he laughed.

Kenny opened the freezer. "Looks like we have vanilla and vanilla fudge swirl."

"Vanilla fudge swirl sounds good," Rory said. He ran his hand along the granite countertops, checked out the cabinets and the view out the window while Kenny filled three bowls. "I'm assuming these cabinets are custom jobs. Am I right?"

"Yes, Emmy wanted the kitchen to be functional. There are all kinds of pullouts and stuff."

"I'm happy for her." Rory opened a drawer. "You know just as much. No wait." He waved a hand. "You know even more about her childhood than I do. My old man beat me and Owen. At least Emmy's old man never did that. He could be mean at times, but I know he loved his daughters. Especially Em. She was his favorite."

"Does he talk about them when you are around?"

"He talks about Emmy more than Diane. I still don't think he knows who I am. I've never told him my last name."

"What ever happened to your father? Is he still alive?" Kenny asked while pouring chocolate syrup on his and Emmy's ice cream. He then handed the bottle to Rory.

"Mom told me a few years ago that he was living in

66

Alabama with some woman. I haven't seen him for years, and I hope I never do. I might beat the crap out of him if I ever run into him."

"Kinda like that old Johnny Cash song, huh?"

Rory laughed. "At least he didn't give us girl's names. Rory and Owen are weird enough." He poured some syrup over his ice cream and handed the bottle back to Kenny.

"Hey!" Emmy hollered. "Did you forget about the ice cream?"

"Coming, Em," Kenny said and then rolled his eyes. "Pregnant women have no patience."

"I know everyone thought I was such a hard guy, but I always did like Emmy. She never treated me like an idiot. Some of the teachers thought I was stupid, but I just didn't care about school."

"I didn't know you as well as Emmy, but I never thought you were unintelligent. I assumed you were bored with school. I know I could have gotten better grades, but I was more interested in music. I suppose in a way, we were both rebellious students."

They walked into the family room. Kenny handed Emmy her ice cream, and he and Rory sat down.

"Were you talking about me? I heard my name a couple times."

"We were talking about how sneaky and rotten you were, Em," Kenny teased. "And I thought you were such a good kid."

"I had to be good around you and your parents," Emmy said between bites. "I didn't want to disappoint them."

"You never did, baby," Kenny said softly.

"Thanks for dinner and everything, guys," Rory said later as he got ready to leave. "I know I don't have to tell you what a lovely home you have. Big difference from Raynor Park, Em."

Kenny shook his hand. "I need to go check on the girls. Thanks for helping with Em's father."

"No problem."

"I'll walk you out to your car." She sat on the bench in the mudroom to put on her shoes

"You don't have to, Emmy. It's cold outside," Rory said as

he sat beside her while putting on his shoes.

"It's all right." Emmy grabbed her coat. She walked out of the mudroom and into the heated garage with Rory at her side.

They stopped by the service door.

"I meant what I said about being happy for you, Emmy. You deserve all of this after what you put up with. I used to get so pissed at your parents for treating you like crap at times. I expected it from my father, but you're a girl."

"Thanks for remembering." Emmy looked up at him and grinned.

He laughed. "I always knew you were a girl."

She bit her lip. "I know. Thanks for not telling Kenny everything."

"Hey! We never did anything to be ashamed of."

"Football," Emmy said.

They both remembered a certain pickup football game.

"The pickup game we played over at the grade school doesn't count, Em." *Kenny might have thought otherwise if he had been there.*

She giggled and then said, "It was supposed to be touch, not tackle."

"But it was so much fun to tackle you." He touched the tip of her nose.

She put her hands on his chest. "You wouldn't let any of the other guys tackle me."

"I guess I was a little protective of you. I thought maybe we would be... uh... more than friends when you got a bit older. But it didn't work out that way, did it?" *I never even got to kiss you.*

"No, but we talked about... Oh, never mind. I'll see you later. Maybe we can grab a quick lunch again."

"We can do that. Thanks again, Em." Rory smiled and stepped out into the cold air.

Chapter Eight

"Kenny, will you play Santa this year?" Emmy asked on Christmas Eve. "I'm too big to get down and crawl around the tree." She handed him another present. "This is for Heather."

He placed it on the left side of the tree. "It looks like Heather has more presents than Isabella. Shouldn't they have the same number?"

"The last two are Isa's." She pointed to two large gifts. "And I don't think they can count to a hundred yet."

"There's not that many presents, Em." Kenny tried to count the gifts.

"Maybe not a hundred, but there are too many." Emmy laughed but then added, "Seriously! You have to tell Andy to stop buying so many presents. Does he buy this many gifts for all the other kids?"

"If you mean the kids whose fathers are in the band, no, but none of them are family," Kenny said as he rearranged some of the gifts. "There all done. How does it look?"

Emmy bit her lip and a tear escaped and sprinted down her cheek.

"What's wrong, Em?" Kenny scooted over to the couch on his knees. "Are you all right?"

She wiped her eyes and sniffled. "I'm okay. I was thinking about a Christmas at home when I was eight, I think." She looked up at the ceiling. "Eight, or maybe nine, but around that time."

"What made you think of that Christmas?" He put his hands on her knees.

"We have a huge tree, and there are so many presents." She waved. "That tickles." She brushed his hands away, so he sat on the couch next to her. "Mom and Dad could never afford to buy much, and that year Daddy decided not to bother with a real tree. I can remember Mom yelling at him because she had given him money to go over to Miller's Bar. Remember that guy who used to sell Christmas trees in the empty lot next to the bar?"

"I remember it, Em."

"Instead of buying a tree, Daddy spent the money on drinks

for his friends. When he got back, Mom threw him out of the house and didn't let him back in for two days."

"I'm sorry, baby." He put an arm around her shoulder, hugged her and kissed her cheek.

"I am so grateful for everything we have, Kenny, but I would still love you if all we could afford was a tiny tree and only one simple gift for the girls."

For a moment they didn't say a word as they kissed and held each other close.

Kenny broke off the hug and whispered, "Does that mean that next year I can find a tiny little tree out back?"

"No way, buster! The girls will be more spoiled than ever by next year. You will have to build an addition onto this room just to hold the presents and a twenty-foot-high tree."

"Merry Christmas, Mom!" Emmy called her mother early the next morning.

"Yeah, Merry Christmas, Emmy." Mom glanced at the clock on her nightstand. *Why are you calling at six thirty?*

"What's wrong?" Emmy asked. "You don't sound very happy."

"I have a headache. I think I'll stay home today."

"Mom! It's Christmas. You can't stay home by yourself. Why don't you feel well?"

"My head hurts, and I'm tired."

"That's so lame. I'm coming to get you. We can stop to see Daddy, and then you're coming to our house."

"No!"

"Mom! I'm coming to get you, and you're coming with me. Get out of bed and get dressed," Emmy insisted.

"Fine, but I'm not staying too long at that nursing home. It's depressing and it smells funny."

"We won't have to stay too long, Mom." Emmy sighed and then shook her head.

They stayed at Astoria Estates Care Center for an hour because Emmy ended up singing Christmas carols in the dining room.

Several of the staff came up to Emmy afterward.

"Thank you so much. You helped brighten up their day," one of them said.

Emmy bit her lip. "I wish I could do more."

"Let's go, Emmy," Mom Colasanti said. "I will gt sick to my stomach if I have to stay here another minute."

Emmy kissed her father's cheek and said, "Merry Christmas, Daddy. I'll come and see you again tomorrow."

Mom and Dad Colwell came over for a late breakfast and to spend Christmas Day with the twins.

"Would you like some help with breakfast?" Mom Colwell asked as she inhaled the aroma from the stove.

"I got it, Mom. You and Dad can relax, or help Em and her mom with the girls." Kenny hesitated, but then asked, "Do you think we go crazy for Christmas? There are a lot of gifts under the tree."

"You might buy the girls too many toys. Why?" Mom Colwell leaned against the island.

"Emmy remembered a Christmas at her house." He turned down the heat on the bacon. "They didn't even have a tree."

"There were years when your father and I would be a little strapped for cash around Christmas, but we always bought you something and we always had a tree."

"I suppose we should just be thankful for God's blessings." He flipped the bacon and stirred the sliced potatoes. "We did donate money to the church for a charity drive. They buy presents for kids at the different shelters in town."

"You can't feel guilty about what you have, son. You've earned it, and you don't waste your money foolishly." Mom put a hand on his shoulder. "The eggs are burning."

"Shoot! Don't let Emmy know."

After breakfast, Emmy read the Christmas story from her Bible to the girls as they sat next to her on the leather couch.

"Did Jesus live in a garage, Mommy?" Heather interrupted.

"No, but He was born in a stable for animals," Emmy answered.

"Why?" Isabella asked.

71

"There was no other place."

"Why not?" Heather asked.

"Let me read some more, please."

"Why did strangers bring presents?" Isabella asked a minute later. "Didn't his mommy and daddy have any money?"

Emmy looked to Kenny for help. He looked at his parents and mother-in-law.

"Because Santa Claus didn't know where he was," Kenny said.

"Why?" Heather asked. "Did Rudolph get lost?"

"Santa Claus was late that year," he explained.

"Why? Did his sleigh break?" Isabella asked.

"I think that was it." Kenny shrugged.

"That was so lame," Emmy whispered after she finished reading.

"I did my best."

"You are a dork, but I still love you." She kissed him. "Now you have to wear the Santa hat and pass out presents."

Two hours later, they watched Heather and Isabella tear the paper off of the last present.

"What is it, Mommy?" Isabella asked.

"It's a dollhouse that your grandfather built," Emmy answered.

Isabella walked over to Grandpa Colwell. "Did you really?"

"Yes, I did. Do you like it?"

"It's bootiful! Thank you, Gra."

"You're welcome, sweetie."

"Hey, Kenny, Derrick called while you were at the office," Emmy told him as she emptied the dishwasher two days later.

"He did? What's going on?" Kenny put his arms around Emmy from behind and rubbed her belly. "Anything special?"

She held a casserole dish in her hands as she leaned back against Kenny and answered, "He and Amber are throwing a New Year's Eve party at the Keaslings. I told him we would be there. We haven't done that for a few years."

72

"Who's going to watch the girls?" Kenny asked while grabbing the casserole dish from Emmy.

"Mary agreed to watch them in exchange for an extra day off later."

"Doesn't she have any plans for that night?" Kenny asked as he set the dish on the counter. "Do you ever worry about her spending too much time here? Maybe she needs to spend more time with friends from college."

"She told me that she's not all that in to the partying they do at school. She doesn't like to drink, and she's not about to smoke or try any drugs," Emmy said as she handed Kenny a frying pan.

"That's good to know, but I'm sure there are other options. Not everyone at school is a party animal," Kenny said and set the pan on the island. "Do you ever regret not living in a dorm? You missed out on most of the social life that other kids experienced."

Emmy turned around to face him. "Yes, I wish I could have gone to all the wild parties and gotten smashed."

"You're being sarcastic, aren't you?" He put his hands on her hips.

"Ya think?" She laughed as she poked him in the stomach. "I doubt any of the other college kids got to travel the world with a famous rock band."

"You did get to do that." He tried to move his hands higher.

Emmy pushed his hands away and stepped aside. "Just because some of the kids in college are there just to party, doesn't mean that Mary is like that. She's more interested in the guys at church."

"There are plenty of them interested in her." He closed the dishwasher. "Maybe there's nothing to it, but does she kinda like Christopher?"

"I warned him not to get involved with her. There's too big of a gap in their ages and maturity."

"Okay, but have you talked to Mary about him?" Kenny asked. "I know sometimes young ladies are attracted to guys they shouldn't be."

"Mary's not me," Emmy insisted as she thought about who Kenny meant. "And you know I didn't give in to my desires."

"What about me?" Kenny looked stunned. "Didn't you have any of those desires for me?"

"That's different. I married you." She kissed him. "That makes it all right for me to give in to those wicked desires."

"Do you have any of those desires now?" He grinned as he grabbed her around the waist and stared into her sparkling, blue eyes.

She smiled back. "I certainly do. Do you think you could take care of them for me?"

"I can spend an hour or so trying." He took her hand and tried to pull her out of the kitchen.

"It won't take that long."

"We could try."

She let go of his hand and shook her head. "No, I mean it won't take you an hour to run to Darby's and pick up a chili dog for me."

"Oh." Kenny's shoulders slumped as he exhaled. "I get it. You have a craving for a chili dog with cheese and onions and you think that's wicked."

"You are so smart." She kissed him. "For a dork!"

He playfully swatted her bottom as she tried to get away.

"Root beer, fries and chocolate cake, please. I'm eating for two."

Chapter Nine

Tony Bertucci listened to the screaming fans in Soldier Field for a moment and then gathered his defense around him. "We know he's going to pass, so stay in your zones. I don't know about you guys, but I'm looking forward to a week off. My wrist has been killing me lately."

"Any chance of getting Randolph back for the playoffs?" Troy Apumalo asked. "We could use his help on offense."

"He's coming along, but there's no chance."

"Let's get this game over without anyone getting hurt," Aron Pelfrey said. "We need to be healthy for the playoffs."

"Sounds like a plan," Tony said.

The Bears beat the Saints by twenty-one points to clinch a first round bye and a chance for tired bodies to recover.

"Which maternity dress looks sexier?" Emmy walked out from her closet and held up two for Kenny to appraise.

"Hmmm, tough choice." He rubbed his chin. "The blue one is shorter, but the purple one really floats my boat. Wear the purple one."

"Why did I even ask? You do realize Diane gave me the purple one, right?"

"Did she?"

"Yes. She wore it the last time she was pregnant. It's really too big for me, but I do like the color and it looks brand new."

"You could buy some new maternity clothes if you want," he said.

"I kept all the stuff from last time. I never really expected to have to wear them again, but I'm glad I kept them. New stuff costs way too much, and you can only wear them for a few months."

"Maybe I should make sure you're always pregnant then."

"No way! I'm not Sloane. She loves being pregnant."

"What should I wear?" He checked the rack of clothes in his closet. "Should I wear a sport coat?"

"Sure. Oh, wait!" she exclaimed as she slapped her

forehead. "This isn't Halloween. You don't have to dress in a dork costume."

"So, I shouldn't wear a sport coat." He held one up to examine it. "Jeans and a button-down shirt okay?"

"Wear this shirt and a pair of black jeans." She searched for a certain pair. "These! They are nice and tight and make you look sexy."

"Are you making fun of me, or are you serious?"

"I'll never tell."

"We're going to head over to the party, Mary. Will you be all right?" Kenny asked later.

"I'll be fine, Mr. Colwell." Mary straightened his tie. "You look really sharp. Kinda like a song I heard."

"Do you mean 'Sharp Dressed Man' by ZZ Top?" he asked with a big grin.

"No, I think she means 'Man In Black' by that country singer." Emmy shook her head. "I told him not to wear a tie, but he won't listen to me."

"Tell me the truth, Mary. Don't you think I should wear a tie. It is a party for adults." He made a face at Emmy.

"Who is signing my paycheck?" Mary asked and then giggled.

"I am," Kenny reminded her.

"I think you look very handsome just as you are," Mary said with a straight face.

"Fine! If no one else is wearing a tie, I'll take it off."

"And throw it away?" Emmy asked.

"It's still a perfectly good tie."

"And thin black ties are sure to come back in style one of these days," Emmy said. "We won't be out too late, Mary."

"Have a good time."

After all the expected guests had arrived, Derrick brought everyone into the family room.

"I have..."

Amber coughed.

"Excuse me. We have an important announcement to share."

"Amber, are you pregnant?" Emmy asked.

Amber shook her head.

"May I continue, Em?" Derrick asked.

"Sorry."

Derrick took Amber's hand, and then held it out for everyone to see. "We are officially married!"

"What?" Kristen yelled. "Since when? You didn't tell me."

"We wanted to surprise everyone, little sister," Derrick said with a smile.

The ladies gathered around Amber as Derrick shook hands with the guys.

"Congratulations, Derrick." Tony slapped him on the back. "Did anyone know?"

"Just Mom and Dad."

"Where did you get married?" Emmy asked Amber. "And why did you choose a simple wedding band?"

"Dr. Behren married us at the church in a private ceremony. We didn't want a big wedding."

"So, who was there?" Kristen asked. "When did you do it? When did you finally decide?"

"We just wanted our parents to be with us, and we got married on Friday. We've been talking about it for several months, so two weeks ago, we got our license."

"Where did you spend your wedding night?" Emmy asked and then giggled.

"You are so predictable, Em." Kristen rolled her eyes and turned to face Derrick. "Where did you?"

Amber looked at the ceiling. "Here at home. We have the whole upstairs to ourselves, remember?"

"So, why the simple wedding bands?" Sloane asked.

"Just what we chose. No special reason," Amber explained.

Kenny asked Derrick, "Are you guys looking for a house?"

"Not really." Derrick shook his head and then smiled.

"What do you mean?" John wondered.

"Okay, I should tell you. Dad sold this house to me. They bought a place in Florida, and are planning to spend part of the year there."

"What?" Kristen exclaimed. "I've heard them talking about Florida, but why did they sell the house to you? Maybe I want it."

Derrick smiled and replied, "You already have an even bigger house, remember?"

"Yes, but all the grandkids are here," Kristen complained. "Don't they don't want to see the babies?"

"Of course not. You know how the cold weather bothers Dad. His hip hurts more in the winter," Derrick reminded Kristen.

"Where will they live when they're here?" Emmy asked.

"Here until they find a smaller place. They might buy a ranch in Hampshire Glen."

"They could be neighbors with Mom and Dad." Emmy smiled, but then bit her lip. "That is if Daddy recovers enough."

"He will recover, Em." Tony put his massive arm around her shoulders.

"He would make it easier if he would let the doctors do their jobs."

"He still won't consent to any surgery, huh?" Tony asked.

"He tries to justify it by claiming the surgery would kill him. He's just so stubborn." Emmy bit her lip. "Am I still as stubborn as I used to be?"

"You? Stubborn? No way," Tony teased.

Later, Kenny and John watched their wives dancing.

"They still dance pretty good for pregnant white women," Tony joked.

"Please don't tell me Sloane is pregnant again," John said as he frowned.

"Not yet. It's too soon. Ben isn't even two months old."

John laughed. "Kristen dances about as good as that actress on *Seinfeld*. What was her name?"

"Julia something," Kenny answered. "Kristen doesn't dance like that."

"She does when she's home alone," John admitted.

"How many kids are you guys planning to have?" Tony asked. "I want to have a dozen."

"You're crazy!" John shook his head. "Sloane will kill you first."

"Are you going to have more kids?" Tony asked John.

"Not if Kristen gets her way," John said and then shuddered.

"Why? What do you mean?" Kenny asked.

"After we know the baby is healthy and all, she wants me to get fixed," John said.

Tony looked shocked. "You aren't going to do that, are you? You're way too young."

"I actually think two kids is enough for us. How about you guys?" John asked Kenny.

"Since we never expected to have any kids, we feel so blessed we're going to have three. We haven't talked about having more, but Dr. Walsh is concerned about her having another baby. If her delivery is as difficult as the twins, we might do something about not having any more. I guess we will have to wait and see."

"You guys have heard about contraception, right?" Tony asked.

"Yeah, but... you know."

"Shush! Here come the girls."

"What were you talking about, Kenny? That's a guilty look if I ever saw one," Emmy said.

"Babies. We were just talking about babies, brat," Tony said as he grinned. "That and how funny you and Kristen look dancing."

"I assume Mama is watching the other kids, but where is Benjamin?"

Tony pointed up. "We brought over a pack-and-play thing. He eats every hour, so we couldn't leave him home."

"I want to see him." Emmy turned to leave the room.

Tony grabbed her arm. "He will be awake soon. Please, let him sleep for Sloane's sake. She is getting tired of getting up at night."

"Okay, I'll wait," Emmy agreed.

Derrick opened the champagne, and they toasted the new year.

"To another excellent year!" Derrick shouted as they counted down.

79

Kenny held Emmy close and whispered in her ear, "I still remember the first New Year's party we went to, do you?"

"Here at the Keasling's house?"

He shook his head as he grinned. "No, a few years before that."

"What are you talking about?"

"Don't you remember the year you came with us to Grandma and Grandpa's house, and we stayed overnight?"

"I was like nine or ten. What's that got to do with anything?"

"We were supposed to be sleeping, but we stayed awake. You snuck into my room, and we were talking. Then when it was close to midnight, we went out on the landing."

"I remember that. The landing was open to the living room. We watched the old people make a toast and kiss each other."

"Do you remember what you told me? I do."

"No, what did I say? How can you possibly remember?"

"You watched the couples kiss, and you said it was yucky, and that you were never going to kiss a boy."

"I was a little kid! What did I know?"

He smiled as he asked, "Do you remember anything else?"

She thought about it, and then poked him in the side. "That's when you kissed my cheek, and I wiped it off."

"True! But then you kissed my cheek."

"I did not!"

"Did so!"

"Not!"

"What are you guys doing?" Kristen shook her head. "It's New Year's. You're not supposed to argue."

"We were discussing an earlier New Year's party," Kenny explained.

Emmy stood in front of Kenny and put his arms around her waist. "He is claiming that I kissed him when I was nine."

Kristen's eyes lit up. "Nine? No way."

"Just on the cheek." Kenny kissed her cheek to show Kristen what he meant.

"Stop that!" Emmy said and then giggled. "Boys are yucky!

I'm never going to kiss one."

Kristen laughed as she shook her head. "You guys should go home. I'm sure this is some kind of foreplay. You are too weird," Kristen said and then walked over to hug Sloane.

"Did not," Emmy whispered.

Kenny rolled his eyes. "Whatever you say, Em. Whatever you say."

Twelve days later, Tony Bertucci walked over to shake hands with Len Hasselbeck as the final seconds of the Bears season ticked away.

"Tough game, Bertucci," Hasselbeck said. "Two freaky plays turned everything around."

"Good luck next week," Tony said and then looked around for other guys he knew. *Man! A tipped pass and a blocked punt both returned for touchdowns. What a way for the season to end.*

The Bears hope for a three-peat ended with a fourteen point loss to Seattle at Soldier Field.

John Randolph walked onto the field and found Tony. "I'm sorry, man. I think if I hadn't gotten hurt, I could have made a difference."

"Probably, but we can't control that. Every team has to deal with injuries," Tony said as he shook hands with some of the other Seattle players he knew.

"I know it sounds like a cliché, but there's always next year." John slapped Tony on the back and they headed to the locker room.

After church the next day, Emmy, Kristen and Liz decorated one of the Sunday School classrooms for the twins birthday party.

"I can't believe they are two already," Kristen said as she filled balloons with helium. "It seems like yesterday when you were in St. Bart's."

"Please don't remind me of that day." Emmy climbed a step-stool to hang a banner on the wall.

"I can do that, Emmy." Liz offered to help. "You shouldn't

be climbing in your condition."

"It's no big deal. I can do it." Emmy stretched her hands as high as she could. "Shoot! I'm too short. Maybe I will let you do it, Liz. You're taller than me."

"Everyone is taller than you, brat," Tony said as he stuck his head into the room. "Let me get that." He walked over, picked Emmy up, set her down gently and hung the sign.

Emmy bit her lip. "I'm sorry you guys lost."

"I'll get over it. Maybe when I'm old and gray."

Kenny wandered in and John arrived with Mama.

"Would you set up a table for the presents?" Emmy asked Kenny.

"Sure." He set up one of the new white plastic tables the church had recently purchased.

"I have the sign for that somewhere." Kristen looked around and pointed. "There it is. John, will you finish the balloons for me, please?"

"Are you saying I'm full of hot air?" He grinned while patting her belly.

Kristen kissed him quickly. "I didn't mean it like that, but if... "

"Yeah! Yeah!" Emmy handed the sign to Kenny, and he hung it over the table.

Tony read it out loud. "All gifts will be donated to the St. Bart's Children Center. That's kinda cool. Whose idea was it?"

"Mine. Why?" Emmy looked up at Tony. "Got a problem with it?"

"No." He put his hands on her shoulders and squeezed tenderly. "That's the section of St. Bart's where the kids with cancer are, right?"

Emmy nodded.

Tony kissed the top of her head. "You're a very special brat, Em."

She closed her eyes and whispered, "Thank you."

Mary brought the girls from the nursery. "They are changed and fed."

"Thanks, Mary."

Heather walked over to the table holding the birthday cake.

"Heather, please don't lick the frosting." Kenny lunged for her.

"Too late!" Tony laughed.

Guests soon started arriving and Liz explained over and over about the St. Bart's Center.

"You can place your gifts on the table."

"I bought this especially for the twins," one guest said. "Do you mean they are giving all the gifts away. Why?"

"Kenny and Emmy are donating all the gifts to St. Bart's. The children at the hospital will be so thrilled," Liz explained with a smile. "Please, help yourself to some cake and punch."

"They look adorable in their new dresses," one lady said. "I have always been able to tell them apart. You're Heather."

Isabella held Emmy's hand and shook her head. "I'm Isa."

"Are you sure?" the older lady asked.

Isabella grinned and nodded several times.

After the party Kenny, Tony, John and Pastor Tyler loaded up Kenny's Odyssey.

"It's a good thing you aren't still driving your old Civic," Tony said.

"Yeah, we would have to make fifty trips." Kenny closed the hatch.

Tyler accompanied Kenny to St. Bart's and, with help from hospital staff, brought in all the presents.

"Thank you, so much, Kenny." Sister Odelia patted his arm and smiled. "We will make sure all the gifts are given to children in need."

"You're welcome. Please let us know if you need anything more."

Tyler and Kenny headed back to the van.

"Do you think Heather and Isabella realized the gifts were for them?" Tyler asked as Kenny drove away.

"I'm not sure. We told them their presents were back at the house. We only bought one gift apiece."

Chapter Ten

"Who are we waiting for?" Diane asked as she and Emmy sat in a conference room at Astoria Estates Care Center.

"Dr. Bergman is on his way," the facility manager explained. "He will be here shortly."

"Would you like a glass of water?" one of the other staff asked.

"I could use something much stronger than water." Diane waved a hand dismissively.

"I'm fine," Emmy said. She sat next to Rory and asked, "How did Daddy do yesterday?"

Rory shook his head. "I'm sorry, Em. He wasn't able to get out of bed. Too much pain."

"The pain in his hip?" Emmy leaned closer to Rory.

"No, the pain in his chest. I'm not a doctor..."

"I'm sorry for my tardiness. I got stuck at St. Bart's for longer than expected. Thank you for waiting," Dr. Bergman said rapidly as he sat at the table and took a couple of minutes to look over Raymond's chart. He pushed his wire-rim glasses up three times as he read. "I'm not happy with his progress. He needs to have the surgery done. No, that's incorrect. He needed to have the surgery done two or three years ago. When did he have his first heart attack?" He checked his notes. "March of 2002. We can't change the past, so let's concentrate on today."

"What will happen if he refuses the surgery?" Diane asked.

"He will have another heart attack without the surgery. That's all there is to it. He likely will not survive another one."

Emmy grabbed Rory's hand and squeezed it without realizing it.

"Is there any way we can take the decision out of his hands?" Diane asked. "He refuses to surrender his power of attorney even though it's obvious he's in no condition to make his own decisions. Our mother is getting worse, so I have her POA for health, but that's beside the point."

The facility manager shook her head. "He's in bad physical shape, true, but mentally, he's still in good shape. I don't know how we can convince a judge otherwise."

Bam! Diane banged on the table with her fist and raised her voice almost to a shout. "How can you say he's in good mental condition if he refuses to have the surgery that could save his life?"

Emmy raised her hand.

"You're not in school, Emily," Diane said with a frown. "If you have something to add, just say it."

"Is there any guarantee he would even survive the operation?"

"No, of course not, Em. You can die from getting your tonsils out." Diane rolled her eyes. "But if he doesn't have the surgery, he will die for sure."

The discussion went on for another ten minutes.

"It is my suggestion that you seriously think about hospice care for your father," the manager suggested.

"Not as long as I'm paying for him to be here!" Diane said adamantly. "I'm not sending him somewhere to lay in bed until he dies."

"We can't do much for him at this time."

"Hell, yes, you can! You can keep trying the therapy, and I will find a way to get control of his health decisions. If he doesn't survive the surgery, that's one thing. But I'm not going to let him get away with not trying."

Dr. Bergman waved a hand. "All right. We will keep Raymond here. I suggest we meet again in two weeks." *You're wasting your money, but that's not my decision.*

The meeting ended and Emmy went with Rory to his office. He pulled over a chair for her.

"Diane is so upset. I've never seen her like that," Rory said as he sat down. "When we were kids, she hated him with a passion."

"I think that's why she's so upset now. I think she finally realizes she made mistakes and is trying to rectify them now before it's too late."

"I know you believe in the power of prayer, Em. You should double your efforts in that regard."

"I will, Rory. Thanks for everything you're doing." Emmy

stood up and hugged him. "I'm so glad you're here. It gives me some comfort knowing you are looking out for Daddy."

"I'm doing what I can, but it's really up to him, and God, I guess."

"I just got a call from Rory," Emmy told Diane on Monday afternoon eleven days after the meeting at Astoria Estates. "Daddy has pneumonia, and they took him to St. Bart's by ambulance."

"When? Why didn't I get a call?" Diane looked at the calendar on the fridge door. *February fourth. I hope he doesn't die today.*

"Rory said the ambulance was already there. At St. Bart's, I mean."

"All right. I'll get Fernando, or someone, to watch the boys and go right to St. Bart's." Diane hung up, called Fernando and explained the situation.

"I'll be there in three minutes. Are you going to leave now?" Fernando asked.

"No, I'll wait until you get here. I can't leave the boys alone. You know that."

"Just making sure you are thinking with a clear head," he said.

"I am. Just hurry up."

Diane let Fernando in the front door four minutes later.

"I'm sorry if I was rude on the phone. I really appreciate you taking care of the boys, and sometimes I take you for granted. Sorry." She kissed his cheek.

Carson came running to see Fernando, and Caden followed as fast as he could.

"Can we have some ice cream, Uncle Fernando?" Carson asked.

Fernando picked up Caden.

Diane frowned. "So you've been spoiling them with ice cream, huh?" She put a hand on his arm and squeezed it tenderly.

"Carson, you weren't supposed to let your mother know about the ice cream."

"Sorry," Carson said with a grin.

86

"Kenny!" Emmy waddled downstairs and into the studio where Kenny and the guys were recording their next project. "Kenny! You have to stop for a minute."

"What is it, Em?" He set his guitar down. "Are you having the baby? Is it time to go?"

"No, it's not that." She rolled her eyes. "It's Daddy. Rory called. He has pneumonia. Daddy, I mean. They are transporting him to St. Bart's. I need you guys to watch the girls until Mary can get here. I'm going to the hospital."

"Should I take you?" Kenny asked. *You drive too fast under normal conditions.*

"I can drive myself. I won't drive like a maniac."

"Did anyone call your mother?" Kenny shouted at her as she ran back up the stairs.

"I'll call her on the way."

"Don't call while you're driving!" Kenny shook his head. "But I know you will. So stubborn."

Jeff slapped Kenny's back. "She'll be fine. Should we call it a day and meet again tomorrow?"

"Yeah, I guess so. I'll call you guys if anything happens."

"Do you need some help with the girls?" Dave asked. "I know they can be a handful since they're walking."

"I bet it's not too long before they are running me ragged," Kenny said. "The gates I put up when they were smaller don't stop them anymore."

Jeremy asked, "How old is Emmy's father? I know he's in his late seventies."

"He's actually just seventy. He looks older, I know, but he just turned seventy," Kenny explained.

Jeremy put a hand on Kenny's back. "Please tell Emmy that we're praying for her father."

"I will. Thanks, guys. I appreciate the understanding."

Diane parked in the deck, raced inside and spotted Emmy talking to the volunteer at the front desk. "Where is he, Em?"

Emmy looked over her shoulder. "I'm trying to find out. I just got here."

"He's in room 8015. Do you know how to get there?" the

volunteer asked as she handed Emmy two visitor passes.

"Yes, thank you."

Emmy and Diane rushed over to the elevator bank.

"How did he get pneumonia?" Emmy asked as she stabbed the button for the eighth floor. "He seemed okay the last time I saw him. Rory didn't call me until today."

Diane frowned at Emmy. "What's going on with you and Rory? You guys are spending a lot of time together."

"No we're not!" Emmy said a little too loudly. "I only see him at the nursing home."

"Whatever! Just make sure you don't get too involved with him."

"In case you haven't noticed, I'm almost eight months pregnant. I'm not doing anything with anybody. So, how did Daddy get pneumonia so fast?"

"Probably from lying in bed all the time. He can be so stubborn."

"Are the nurses making sure he takes his medicine?" Emmy rocked back and forth as the elevator stopped at the fourth floor. "Sometimes he just pretends to swallow his pills."

"What are they supposed to do? Choke him until he swallows the stuff." Diane glared as the elevator stopped at the sixth floor and three more people got in.

Everyone got out on the eighth floor. Diane checked the signs on the wall. "It's down this way."

Emmy timidly followed Diane into the room. Diane walked over to his bed and stared at him.

"Why does he have that thing in his nose?" Emmy stood at the foot of the bed and pointed.

"That's oxygen to help him breath." Diane pulled a chair up close and sat while Emmy stood still.

"I know that! Why does he need it?" Emmy asked.

"It makes it easier. Are you going to sit down? Do you need to pee?"

"Not yet." Emmy pulled a chair up to the other side of the bed. *I don't like all those wires and tubes and machines.* She bit her lip as she looked around.

"His blood pressure is higher than it should be," Diane noticed.

"Is he taking medication for that?" Emmy asked.

"Who knows? The doctors are giving him so much crap. I doubt if they can even keep up with everything he's taking."

"Isn't that dangerous?"

"No kidding!"

They stayed for an hour, but Raymond never opened his eyes.

"Let's go, Em. He's not going to wake up." Diane scooted her chair back and stood up. "He's having a hard time breathing even with the oxygen."

Emmy leaned over and kissed his cheek. "Get well, Daddy. I love you."

"There's no need for all of us to be here all day," Diane said on Wednesday afternoon. "I'm going home to take care of the boys. I'll be back in the morning." She looked at Emmy. "Are you sure you'll be all right staying overnight?"

"I'll be fine. I'm going home, too. Kenny will come up to take Mom home later."

"Mom, are you awake?" Diane nudged Mom's shoulder.

"Yes, I was just resting my eyes."

"Did you hear what Emmy said?" Diane asked.

"Kenny will come and get me and take me home later. There's nothing wrong with my hearing," Mom insisted.

Emmy kissed both parents as Diane waited by the door.

"Call me if anything happens," Diane instructed her mother and headed to the elevators with Emmy. "How are we going to take care of both of them when they get really old?"

"We can't. I'm not sure if Daddy can go back to the house when he gets out of here."

"Hah! There's no way. He will be going back to Astoria Estates, and Mom may not be far behind."

Emmy returned to St. Bart's at ten that night.

Rory spotted her as she walked down the hall toward her father's room. "There you are, Em."

89

"Hi, Rory. Have you been here long?"

"Five minutes. I peeked into his room, but he's asleep."

"Did he seem to be breathing okay?"

"He's struggling, Em." Rory put a hand on her back as they walked into Raymond's room. *Actually, he's getting worse, but I don't want to tell you that.*

She bit her lip as she looked up at Rory. "I appreciate you coming up here to keep me company."

"No biggie, Em. I'm off for three days, so I have the time."

"You don't have to stay all night."

"Are you going to?"

"Yes, but I will try to sleep for a few hours. There's a couch in the waiting room down the hallway between this section and the older part. I figured I would crash there."

They stayed in the room with her father for two hours, but he didn't open his eyes.

"Emmy, why don't we grab something to eat somewhere and come back? You can use the waiting room couch to catch a few hours sleep. You need to take care of your baby." He patted her stomach.

"I'm not really hungry, but I could eat something. Could you run out and get a couple muffins at the Pantry Hut on the corner?"

"Sure. What kind?"

"I like blueberry ones," she said. "You probably don't know about me and blueberry pancakes, huh?"

"What do you mean?"

"I'll explain later."

Rory returned with muffins and coffee.

"I got decaf for you because of the baby."

Emmy checked the bag of muffins. She pulled out a blueberry one and smiled. "I always order blueberry pancakes. It drives Kenny nuts because he wants me to try something different."

"Okay," he said slowly and sat beside her.

"I guess it's only funny to us." She poked Rory in the side.

They sat on the beige couch, stared at the beige walls with

the boring artwork, ate the muffins and slowly sipped the coffee.

"I checked on Daddy while you were out. The nurse came in to check his vitals again and give him some medicine. He woke up for a moment but then went back to sleep. I told the nurse we would be in here all night. She agreed to come and get me if anything happens."

"Did she get on your case for staying overnight in your condition?"

Emmy shrugged. "She tried to talk me into going home, but you know me."

"Yeah, you're as stubborn as can be." He smiled and then patted her hand. "Did Kenny say anything about me coming up here tonight?"

Emmy bit her lip.

"Did you even tell him, Emmy?"

"I didn't mention it to him or Diane."

"Why not?"

"Diane told me I was spending too much time with you, so I didn't want her to know."

"We haven't seen each other that much."

"I know, but she remembers how I used to like you when we were kids. She thinks you were a bad influence on me."

"Just because Owen was a jerk doesn't mean I am," he said with a frown.

"I know. You were kinda nice to me when you weren't around your buddies."

Rory tossed the trash in the can and then sat back down. "I did treat you and other girls like... "

"Tramps?" Emmy interrupted.

"I would have used another word, but that sorta fits. I wanted to keep up my reputation as a hard ass, and if my so-called friends knew how I treated you when they weren't around, I would have been ostracized from the gang."

She laughed. "You weren't in a gang!"

"Not a gang like gangs are today, but we hung out together."

"Did you guys talk about all the girls you were messing

91

around with?" She grinned as she poked his arm. "I have to pee. Don't go anywhere. I want to hear your answer."

She returned in a few minutes.

"Are you all right?"

"Yeah. Pregnant women have to pee a lot."

"I know, Em. I did have a kid for a while."

She put her feet on one of the cushions and struggled to find a comfortable position. "So, did you guys talk about the girls, or not?"

"Yeah, we did."

"Did you tell them what we did together?" She bit her lip.

"Like what? What did we ever do that was so bad?"

"We played football together."

"You played football with lots of guys. You were a better athlete than most of us."

"Yeah, but I remember one game in particular." She put a finger to her mouth. "Do you know which one I mean?"

He thought about it for a few seconds and then smiled. "Geez, Em, you were what? Fourteen?"

"I think so. We played tackle football."

"Yes, I can remember what happened. We've talked about it before."

"No one had ever *tackled* me like that before." She used air quotes.

"We were just kids! It wasn't a big deal."

"Maybe not to you, but it kinda was to me."

"Did you ever tell Kenny about that game?" Rory asked. *I sure hope not.*

"He knows I would play football with other guys, but I never told him the specific details about that particular game. Would you be worried that he might hit you if he knew?"

"No, I'm sure he would probably laugh about it."

"You think he would laugh?" Emmy made a face at Rory.

"Oh, come on. It was cold that day and you were wearing several layers."

"On top, but I was only wearing my jeans."

"Can we change the subject?"

Emmy pointed at him and grinned. "I can't believe it! I'm embarrassing you over something that happened thirteen years ago. You were supposed to be such a ladykiller." She sat up higher. "The rumor was that you had slept with..."

"Hey! There were rumors about you, too."

"None of them were true, though."

"I know that, but there were a lot of kids who believed them."

"Yeah, because of Diane's reputation. I had to deal with the fallout of that all through high school." She tilted her head. "Were some of the rumors true?"

"You know they were, Emmy. I know I was a jerk."

"You weren't any worse than a lot of the guys. I can think of at least five girls from my class who dropped out to have babies. There were probably more that I never knew."

"I wonder what ever happened to that Delaney jerk. Do you know?" Rory asked.

"He ended up in jail for a time. He might still be there for all I know."

"Have you ever gone to any of the reunions or homecoming games?"

"No." She shook her head. "You?"

"No way! I did get an invitation once. Do you know that ten kids from my class are dead?"

"Not surprising. There were a lot of creepy guys in your class."

"Are you including me in that?"

"You know I never thought of you as a jerk. I knew that was only a facade. You were afraid to show your feminine side," she said and then grinned.

He reached over and tickled her kneecap. "I don't have a feminine side."

"Do you miss your brother?" She pushed his hand away from her knee, but then held on to it. "Or don't you even think about him?"

"We were never really all that close even before he moved out. After that, I didn't see him much. I didn't go to his funeral."

"Why not?"

He shrugged and let go of her hand. "Just didn't see the point. Mom didn't have a wake or anything. They just took the casket to a cemetery and buried him. I think a few of his friends showed up, but that was it."

"Other than your mom and Amy, right?"

"Yeah." He nodded. "I'd like to think that if I died, there would be a few more people who would care enough to show up."

"You aren't going to die for a long time, and you have friends."

"Not too many. I've been keeping a low profile since I moved back to SoHam."

"Well, I'm your friend," she said.

He saw a sparkle in her eyes. "I appreciate that, Em."

Diane arrived at seven the next morning and checked on her father. "You're awake. Do you feel better?"

He lifted his hand and made a so-so motion.

"Where's Emmy? Have you seen her?"

He shook his head.

Diane headed to the waiting room, peeked inside and saw Emmy's head on a pillow in Rory's lap. "What the hell are you doing?" she yelled loud enough to wake up both Emmy and Rory.

"What time is it?" Emmy asked and then yawned.

"It's after seven." Diane glared at Rory. "Why are you here?"

"He came to keep me company." Emmy sat up. "I'll be right back. Don't yell at him and don't you leave."

Diane didn't say another word as she stared at Rory. She waited until Emmy returned. "Are you going to explain this?"

"There's nothing to explain. Rory kept me company, and we fell asleep on the couch. He's not Owen! He's my friend."

"You need to go see Daddy." Diane put her hands on her hips. *Owen was a long time ago.*

"Is he awake?"

"Sort of."

"I should go, Emmy. I don't want to cause any trouble for

94

you." He frowned at Diane. *You never did like me, did you?*

"Oh, for cripes sake!" Diane rolled her eyes. "I'm sorry for assuming you would be like Owen."

"I never was as bad as him, but I wasn't a choirboy either."

"Yeah, I remember how you... Oh, never mind. If Emmy can forget about the past, so can I. Thanks for keeping her company." Diane held out a hand.

Rory shook it. "You look even better than I remember, Diane."

She pulled her hand away.

"Hey! I didn't say that because I'm making a move on you. I just wanted to compliment you."

"Good! Because I will never be anything other than a casual friend to you. It's not your fault, but Owen scarred me for life. I don't trust men much anymore."

"He did that to lots of people."

Emmy gingerly stepped into room 8015. "Are you awake, Daddy?"

He opened his eyes and held up his hands.

"Oh, Daddy, I've been so worried about you." Emmy took his hands in hers and sat on the edge of the bed and immediately set off the alarm. "I'm sorry. Did I do that?"

A nurse rushed in, checked Raymond and reset the alarm.

"I'm sorry. I didn't know."

"It's all right. Please don't stay too long. His blood pressure is high, and he's having more trouble breathing."

"I won't upset him. Promise." Emmy sounded like a child.

Thirty minutes later, Emmy tiptoed out of the room. She walked back to the waiting room.

"You're still here. I thought you would leave." She smiled at Rory and then looked at Diane. *Actually, I thought Diane would make you leave.*

Rory shook his head. "I wanted to make sure you were okay before I left. Are you?"

"I'm tired, and I need a shower... Oh, you want to know about Daddy, huh?"

"That, too."

"The nurse didn't want me to stay too long. I don't know if he's getting better or not. He looks so weak, and he looks like a really old man."

Rory opened his arms, and Emmy let him hold her. He looked at Diane.

"It's okay, Rory. You can hug her as a friend. Just not too tight."

"Emmy, could you blow these up for me?" Diane asked two days later. "I can't get them tied right."

Emmy opened the pack of balloons. "Sure, is six enough?"

"I want six balloons because I'm six now." Carson held up the right amount of fingers.

"What else would you like for your birthday?" Grandma asked.

Carson thought about it for several seconds. "I want to see Grandpa. Is he still sick? Is he coming to my party?"

Diane turned around in her chair. "I'm sorry, baby, but Grandpa is too sick to be here today. Did you say a prayer for him this morning?"

"Yes, I said a prayer for Grandpa and one for Toby's dog. He's old and sick, too."

"That was very thoughtful of you, Carson." Emmy handed him a purple balloon.

"Thanks, Auntie Em. I know your favorite color is purple."

Later, after the presents had been opened and the ice cream and cake eaten, Emmy, Diane and Mom sat at the table to relax.

"Carson, please don't knock Isabella over." Kenny picked her up.

"I'm sorry, Isa. I didn't mean to knock you down."

Emmy smiled. "He is getting so big, and he gets along with the other kids so well. How did you do it?"

Diane shrugged. "Got me."

"Who's taking me to St. Bart's tomorrow?" Mom asked.

"It's my turn," Diane said. "Hey, do you remember me talking about taking the boys to Disney World a couple of months ago?"

96

"I remember you mentioning it. Why?" Emmy watched as Heather stole a doll from Isabella. "Kenny! Make her play nice."

"I'm trying."

"Well, I booked it," Diane said.

"You booked what?" Mom asked.

Diane rolled her eyes. "A trip to Disney World."

"That's nice. Are you taking Emily? She's never been there and we promised to take her someday."

"I don't think I can go this time, Mom." Emmy looked at Diane.

"Told you so," Diane whispered.

"Your father wanted to go to Disney World, but we never made it to California."

"That's Disneyland, Mom. There's a difference," Diane said. "I'm not sure if we will still be able to go since Dad is so sick."

"Nonsense!" Mom waved a hand. "He's just got a bad cold. You go ahead and take your vacation. You work hard enough at that office all year long. They can get by without you for a week or two."

"Right, Mom." Diane sighed and let her shoulders slump.

"Caden is too young to get anything out of the trip," Emmy said. "He's not even two yet. He will get worn out by all the walking."

"That's what strollers are for, Em."

"How are you going to manage both boys by yourself?" Emmy picked at the remaining crumbs of cake on her plate.

"I won't exactly be by myself," Diane admitted. *Please don't ask right now, Em.*

Diane was saved from further explanation by Caden and Heather trying to play with the same stuffed animal.

"You have to learn to share, Heather." Emmy found another toy for Heather, who promptly threw it over her head.

"She's got a good arm," Kenny said and then laughed.

Chapter Eleven

In the early morning hours of Sunday, February tenth, Diane got the call she had been dreading ever since her father had been moved from the eighth floor to Intensive Care. She listened to the news without responding.

"I'm sorry for your loss," the detached voice on the other end said.

"Thank you," Diane responded. She closed her eyes and lay on her back. She waited for the tears to come, but they didn't. She looked at the clock on her nightstand. *It's too early to call Mom or Emmy. I'll wait until later. It's not like there's anything they can do.*

At six thirty Kenny realized the landline was ringing. He reached out to the nightstand, checked the caller ID, glanced at Emmy and answered the phone. "Hello, Diane," he whispered trying not to wake up Emmy. "Is it what I think?"

Diane cleared her throat. "I'm afraid so. The hospital called me a little before four. I didn't want to disturb you guys that early. Is she awake?"

"She's still out. I know she was up two or three times during the night."

"Yeah, I couldn't get back to sleep. I've done two loads of laundry and did the dishes. I even cleaned the bathroom. I've been sitting on the couch watching TV just to kill time," Diane said. "I stayed at St. Bart's until eleven last night, but I had to come home. I couldn't ask Fernando to stay any later. I thought Daddy would make it until this morning."

"Should I have Em call you when she wakes up?"

"Will you tell her, please?" Diane's voice finally cracked. "I just can't do it."

Kenny looked at Emmy and listened to her steady breathing. "Okay, I'll tell her. What about your mother? Have you called her?"

"I'm going over there as soon as Fernando gets here to watch the boys. I'm not sure how she will react. I need a drink. The next few days are going to suck."

"We'll come over as soon as I tell Em."

"Thanks. I appreciate that."

Kenny put down the phone and sat up. He looked down at Emmy and put a hand on her belly. He felt his son kick. He clenched his jaw to keep from crying. He didn't succeed.

She moved onto her side and stretched her arms above her head. She opened her eyes and looked at Kenny. "Did I hear the phone ring?"

He wiped his tears away, looked at her and took a deep breath. "I'm sorry, baby," he said after a moment.

She stared at Kenny and didn't move for a moment. "No," she whispered.

He pulled her closer.

"No!" she said as she threw her pillow toward the foot of the bed. "I'm not ready."

"You have to be." He held out his arms and she nestled against his chest.

"No, Daddy. Not yet."

He rubbed her back as her tears soaked his t-shirt. "I'm so sorry, Em." He bunched her hair together to keep it away from her face.

"I prayed for him to get better. I'm not ready to let go," she whimpered. "Why didn't God make him better?"

Shoot! What am I supposed to say? Kenny squeezed her tighter.

"When?" She asked a few minutes later as she wiped her nose on his shirt and sat up.

"Around four."

"I got up to pee around then. I can remember sitting on the pot and thinking about him. I said a prayer and started to cry, but then I was suddenly calm. I felt as though Jesus was letting me know everything was all right. It was spooky."

"You said when you talked to him Saturday morning, you asked him if he wanted to pray. I was surprised by his response, but I've never faced my own death before."

"He nodded his head, so I prayed for him. I asked him if he understood what I had prayed, and he nodded. I asked him if he

99

believed in Jesus and he tried to speak, but all he could do was nod." She bit her lip. "When Jesus was on the cross, he told that one man that he would be in heaven because he believed. Because of that I trust that Daddy will be there waiting for us."

"I think you're right, Em." *But he sure cut it close.* "I wonder why he changed his mind. Did he say? I mean, he must have known he didn't have long to live."

"No, and I can only think of one thing. All my prayers over the years made a difference."

Kenny squeezed Emmy's hand and stared at photos of the Dames-Blackburn funeral home founders on the wall as they sat in one of the offices on Monday afternoon.

"I almost hate to mention this." The director looked at Kenny and then back at Mrs. Colasanti. "But in view of who your son-in-law is, I feel it necessary." *I can tell you and your younger daughter have been crying, but your other daughter just looks pissed off.* "There is a chance that the press will, how can I put this?" He tapped his jaw.

"We don't want Raymond's funeral to become a media event," Mom said clearly surprising Diane. "What can we do to prevent that?"

The director lifted his eyebrows. "When we held the service for Clair Barclay, we used off-duty officers as extra security, but the Barclay family paid for that."

Emmy looked at Kenny. "Who?" she whispered.

"Damon Barclay's grandmother. Do you remember him? He married Diana Ahronson."

"Oh, those Barclays," Emmy said and then sniffled.

Kenny whispered, "Their family can trace their ancestors back to the Revolutionary War."

Diane rolled her eyes. *Who the hell cares?* "Fine, but where are we going to have the funeral?"

"Should we ask about St. John's?" Emmy asked.

Mom shook her head vehemently. "Ain't no way I'm letting that priest say a mass for Raymond. He's a complete jerk in my opinion. He never once bothered to come to the hospital."

"Where else could we have it?" Diane asked. "I suppose we could do everything right here."

"I have an idea," Emmy said.

Everyone looked at her.

"We could use our church. Pastor Dave did come to see Daddy several times."

"He seems like a nice enough man," Mom said. "But Raymond was raised Catholic. There's no way I'm having his mass at your church, Emily."

"It's large enough to handle the crowd," Emmy explained. "If there is one."

"I don't know if anyone will show up," Mom said. "Your father didn't have a lot of friends other than the guys at Miller's Bar, and I doubt if they will come to the wake if it's at a church."

Kenny looked at the director.

He cleared his throat and said, "We could hold the service here."

Mom looked to her right at Diane and then turned to see Emmy. "I've decided. We will have the wake and funeral here."

Diane waved a hand. "I remember when Grandpa died. Everyone in SoHam came to the wake. It dragged on for hours."

"That's different. Raymond is not his father," Mom said.

Emmy looked at her mother. "I remember the funeral, but not much about the wake."

"That's because you were only there for part of it, Em. You came home with us," Kenny said.

"I did?"

"Yeah, and we ended up playing football."

"Yes, and you scraped your elbow." Mom recalled that day perfectly.

Diane stared at Emmy and Kenny. "Can we concentrate on the moment, please?"

"Sorry," Emmy said.

Mom, Diane and Emmy decided to have the wake and funeral on Wednesday at the funeral home.

Mr. Blackburn shook hands with everyone and said, "I think having the funeral and wake here will work for the best."

"Thank you so much for taking care of the girls today. I know you're missing some classes," Emmy said as she hugged Mary. "We thought about bringing them to the funeral home, but Kenny decided that would be too much of a distraction."

"We will be fine here," Mary said as she tucked some stray hair behind Emmy's ears and looked into her red eyes.

"Does this dress look okay?" Emmy held up the black dress she planned to wear.

"It looks perfect."

"I wasn't going to buy a new one, but Diane insisted."

"Did Kenny buy a new suit?" Mary asked as she saw one on the bed.

"It's not new, but he's only worn it once before."

"Who's doing the funeral? Your father didn't go to church anywhere, did he?"

Emmy shook her head and waved her hands. "No, he was raised a Catholic, but stopped going years ago. I'm glad Dr. Behren agreed to do the funeral. Mom refused to even talk to the priest from St. John's."

"Are you going to say anything during the service?" Mary asked as she smoothed out Kenny's suit.

"No way! I would just start crying."

"Are you going to sing?"

Emmy nodded. "I have to. Mom wants me to sing 'Amazing Grace.'"

"Oh, God, Em. That will be so hard." Mary moved closer and hugged Emmy.

"Kenny told me to close my eyes, not look at the crowd, and concentrate on the words."

"Maybe you guys should sing together," Mary suggested. "That way when you start crying, he can take over. You know you're going to cry."

"Thanks for the vote of confidence." Emmy looked up at Mary for a brief second and then buried her face in Mary's chest and sobbed.

"It will be all right, Emmy," Mary said as she rubbed Emmy's back.

The wake started at nine and a few minutes later people began to trickle in. Some of Kenny and Emmy's friends from church came to pay their respects.

Diane watched as many of those people hugged Emmy carefully as if they were afraid to hurt the baby. *Why do those people seem so upset? They never knew him. How can they feel any emotion for someone they didn't know.* Diane forced a smile as more of Kenny and Emmy's friends offered their condolences. *Yeah, yeah, yeah. If one more person tells me he's in a better place, I'm gonna scream.*

A few people from the Raynor Park neighborhood stopped by and talked to Patricia.

"Who were those people?" Patricia asked about the last couple. "They looked familiar, but I don't know their names."

Diane whispered, "Those were the Fronczeks. They used to live next door."

Several men from the electric company entered dressed in their Com Ed work uniforms and shuffled up to the casket, paused for a moment and quickly moved on without speaking to anyone. One of them paused, looked at Kenny and nodded.

"Thanks for coming," Kenny said.

A few minutes later Emmy joined Diane at one of the two stands of photos. "Is that from when they got married?" Emmy asked. "I've never seen it before."

"Yes," Diane answered. She glanced over her shoulder as more people entered. *I don't recognize you. You must be from the church. Please don't come over and tell me how sorry you are.*

"It just looks like they're going to church or something. That's not a wedding dress," Emmy said.

"Grandma Isabel told me they got married at the courthouse. Didn't you know that?" Diane smiled as the people walked past.

Emmy turned around and allowed the ladies to hug her.

"Emmy dear, you shouldn't be on your feet. Why don't you sit with your mother?"

"Yes, dear. You look like you're ready to pop."

Emmy smiled and put a hand on her belly. "If I sit for too

long, he starts to kick."

Diane smiled again and waited for the ladies to move along. "I wanted to find photos of us as kids, but I only found one decent picture of all four of us." Diane pointed to the photo. "You must have been two at the most."

Emmy shrugged and then saw a photo in the bottom left corner. "That's my purple bike," she whispered, touched the photograph and tears immediately began to fill her eyes. "Daddy painted that for me when I was ten. I loved that bike."

Diane rolled her eyes. "Mom found it at a garage sale, and it looked hideous. It looked like green puke."

"Maybe, but I was the only kid in the neighborhood with a purple bike."

"I remember, Em. He took it away from you for a week because you crossed a street or something. Then he said you could have it back and you bawled like a baby because he painted it."

"I remember crying," Emmy said. "But I remember Daddy having tears in his eyes, too.

"Yeah, but he pretended it was no big deal. He would never let his emotions show." *I guess I inherited that from him.*

At eleven Mr. Blackburn walked to the front of the room and announced, "We would like to start the ceremony now, so if everyone would please take a seat." He escorted Mrs. Colasanti, Diane and Emmy to their seats in the front row and then nodded to Dr. Behren. A few minutes later Emmy walked to the front to sing "Amazing Grace" with Kenny at her side, holding her hand.

"Kenny, my heart is pounding and I can't breathe."

Kenny handed the microphone to her, coughed and whispered, "You can do this, Em. Take some deep breaths, close your eyes and start whenever you're ready."

She took a deep breath, looked down at her mother and Diane. *They are sitting like statues. How can they be so cold?* Emmy looked at Grandma Isabel in the row behind her mother and watched as Isabel dabbed at her eyes with a white handkerchief.

Kenny squeezed Emmy's hand. She looked up at him.

"I love you, m'lady," he whispered. "You can do this."

She squeezed his hand even tighter, turned to look at the

crowd and began, "Amazing Grace how sweet the sound..."

When she got to the fourth verse, she let go of Kenny's hand, raised her right hand into the air and sang strongly in her sweet voice, "When we've been there ten thousand years..."

"You did it, Em," Kenny said as they walked back to their seats in the front row.

"Is it all right if I cry now?" she whispered.

"You can cry all you want, baby," he said as he put an arm around her.

Dr. Behren read the eulogy he had prepared with help from Patricia, Grandma Isabel and Diane.

"I didn't know Daddy was a boxer," Emmy whispered to Kenny.

"I don't think he was a professional one, Em."

Diane poked Emmy in the side. "Ssssh! Listen and you might learn something else."

Dr. Behren continued, "In 1978 after nineteen years of marriage Raymond and Patricia became the proud parents of a baby girl. Diane Lynn. Then two and a half years later, another child entered their life." Dr. Behren looked down at Emmy, smiled and stroked his white goatee for a moment. "Emily Olivia," he continued a moment later. "We all know her as Emmy." He kept his composure and finished. He prayed and announced, "The family has requested that the graveside service be private. Please respect the family's wishes. They have invited everyone to the church for a lunch. "

Emmy made sure Kristen and Tony were coming to the cemetery. "You guys are family to me. Where is Mama?"

"Over there." Tony pointed to a plush couch along the wall.

"She has to come, too," Emmy insisted.

"Okay, Em. I'll make sure she's there," Tony said. He helped Emmy put on her coat. "You have to make sure he stays warm." He patted her belly.

Kenny drove his parents and Andy Walker to the cemetery in his Odyssey. Emmy rode behind the hearse with her mother, Diane and Grandma Isabel in the funeral home's limo.

"That was a nice service," Mom said. "Thank you for

singing that song. Someone sang it at your grandfather's mass."

Diane looked at Emmy and shook her head. "No way that happened. No one sang anything."

The driver parked the limo, and opened the door for them.

"Where do we go?" Mom asked.

Emmy and Diane each held onto Mom's arms. "It's there by the tent, Mom," Diane whispered.

Emmy looked up at the barren trees and saw the limbs move as a gust of chill wind whistled. She saw Grandma Isabel walking quickly toward the tent with her head up. "I'm going to make sure Grandma's all right." She let go of her mother and dashed ahead. "Are you all right, Grandma?" Emmy asked.

"I am fine, Emily. I'm not going to become emotional in front of everyone."

Emmy squeezed her grandmother's hand. "I know you and Daddy didn't always get along."

"I admit I always thought your mother made a mistake by marrying him even though she was expecting," Isabel said. "But it worked out in the end. I have you."

"You should sit here, Mom," Diane said after Patricia stood staring at the casket for a moment.

Isabel took a seat and motioned for Emmy to sit beside her.

Dr. Behren waited until the family was seated. He thought about the first time he met Emmy, smiled and began, "Sometimes a person's life is measured by the legacy they leave behind." He continued for a moment and then opened his Bible. "In the twenty-third chapter of the Gospel of Luke, we read starting at verse forty. 'But the other criminal rebuked him.' Meaning the other thief. 'Don't you fear God,' he said, 'since you are under the same sentence? We are getting punished justly, for we are getting what our deeds deserve, but this man has done nothing wrong. Then he said, 'Jesus, remember me when you come into your kingdom. Jesus answered him, 'Truly I tell you, today you will be with me in paradise.'" Dr. Behren paused and wiped his eyes. "I can assure you that as we speak, Raymond Colasanti is rejoicing with the angels in heaven." He dared not look at Emmy because he knew she was crying. "I'm not too proud to admit that I cried like a baby

106

when Emmy told me how her father accepted Christ this last Saturday."

Dr. Behren finished, walked over to Patricia and spoke to her for a moment. He shook hands with Diane and Grandma Isabel before he turned to Emmy.

"That was very nice, Pastor Dave."

"I hope I didn't embarrass you too much today."

She hugged him. "You didn't. Thank you for doing this for us. It can't be easy to do a funeral for someone you never really knew. We really appreciate it."

"You're more than welcome. I'll see you back at the church."

Mom took Diane's arm. They walked the few feet to where Raymond's parents were buried.

"Do you and Emmy ever come here?" Mom asked.

"I haven't been here since Grandpa died. I don't know about Emmy." Diane watched as Emmy talked to Grandma Isabel and Mama Bertucci. "It would be more in her nature to come and see them. That looks like an expensive headstone." Diane rubbed a hand along the top of the large piece of granite.

Mom nodded. "Bill Robertson donated the money for it, but no one is supposed to know."

"That sounds like something he would do," Diane said and put an arm around her mother.

Emmy walked over and put a hand on Mom's back. "What are you guys talking about?"

"Do you ever come to the cemetery?" Diane asked.

"I come out here on their birthdays, or as close to the day as I can. Why?"

"I just wondered," Mom said as she turned away.

Back at the church people waited in the fellowship hall for the family to return. Finally, Pastor Tyler received a call from Dr. Behren and then announced to the crowd, "They have just pulled into the parking lot. Please allow them to go first."

Mom saw how many people had gathered into the fellowship hall and whispered to Diane, "Do I have to pay to feed all these people? I don't even know them."

107

"No, Mom, you don't have to pay. Let me find you a seat." Diane led her mother and Grandma Isabel to the front table.

Emmy filled a plate for her mom and then went back to get some food for herself.

"Hey, Emmy! Are you getting seconds already?" Tony teased.

In spite of the seriousness of the day, Emmy smiled. "I'm eating for two in case you haven't noticed, dorkbrain."

"Brat!" he teased back.

Kenny smiled as he listened. *You guys are never going to grow up, are you?*

Emmy saw Rory after she and Kenny had finished eating. She walked over to him. "Thank you for coming, Rory."

He shuffled his feet nervously. "I haven't been in a church in years. At least I didn't get struck down by lightning," he joked, but then swore. "Oh, crap, Emmy. I'm sorry. I shouldn't have said that."

"It's all right. I know what you meant. You are welcome to come back anytime."

"Do you always sing on the stage?" He tried to loosen his tie.

Emmy straightened his tie. "If I'm here, I usually sing. Why?"

"You sounded like an angel, Emmy. I listened to you and I started to tear up. I had to clench my jaw the whole time you were singing to keep from crying."

"That's a very powerful song, and it's all right for men to show some emotion."

"I should go before Diane gets mad at me for being here."

"Nonsense," Diane said as she walked up behind Rory and Emmy. "You are an old family friend, and you can stay as long as you like."

He looked at Diane. "Do you mean that, or are you just being nice for today?"

"I guess I really mean it." She lifted her eyes to meet his and slowly smiled.

Chapter Twelve

"I still say Caden is too young for this trip," Emmy said as she slipped the van into a space between two small cars. "He's not even two yet. He won't remember it, and the walking..."

"Strollers, Em, strollers." Diane repeated while rolling her eyes. "Thank you for bringing us to the airport."

Fernando hopped out of his seat in the middle row. "You guys stay there until your mother comes to get you."

"We will, Uncle Fernando," Carson said. "Where are the airplanes? I can't see any."

"You will soon enough, little buddy," Fernando assured him.

Emmy checked the mirror before opening her door. "It's okay, but I'm still a bit upset that you and Fernando will be sharing a room."

"With my two sons, Em. That will make a difference," Diane said as she got out.

Emmy ran around the van and whispered, "It's still not right," as Fernando unloaded the luggage from the back.

"He loves the boys, and he's been such a help while Dad was sick."

"So you are rewarding him by sharing a bed?" Emmy scolded.

"I'm not discussing this with you. Are you going to help me get the boys out of the van, or not?"

"Yes, I'll help."

Carson unbuckled his own seat belt and got down from his booster seat without any help. "See! I can do it by myself, Auntie Em. Did I tell you we're going to see Mickey Mouse?"

"Yes, you did mention that a couple times."

Emmy got Caden out of his car seat and handed him to Diane.

"A couple thousand times." Diane sighed as she struggled to put Caden in the stroller.

Emmy hugged Carson. "You have fun and make sure you obey your mother."

"I will, and I'll be a good boy for Uncle Fernando, too."

"Hang on to your mother's hand. There are a lot of people in the airport, and I don't want Diane to get lost."

"I'll take care of her," Carson promised.

"Thanks for the ride, Emmy," Fernando said as he pushed the loaded cart. "I'll make sure Diane and the boys have a good time."

"I'm sure you will," Emmy snarled and put her hands on her hips.

"Hey! Lose the attitude, Emmy," Diane snarled back.

"Fine! Have a great vacation, Diane. Kenny will pick you guys up when you get back." Emmy kissed Caden and got back in the Odyssey.

"She sounded upset. Did you guys have an argument?" Fernando asked as he watched Emmy drive away.

"She thinks it's wrong for us to share a room. I tried to explain." Diane shrugged. "She can be so puritanical at times."

"I could always get a separate room," Fernando suggested as he led the way into the terminal. "We need to go to the right." He pointed.

"Don't be silly. I'm not going to let Emmy spoil our vacation." Diane held onto Carson's hand. *I knew it would be crowded, but this is ridiculous.* She took a deep breath and threaded her way between people.

"Did you tell her that we're just friends?"

"Is that all we are?" Diane asked.

"Maybe friends with a couple of special benefits." Fernando's eyes glinted, and, since he wasn't watching, he bumped into an empty cart.

Six days later, Kenny loaded the dishwasher as Emmy and Mary cleaned up the twins after dinner.

"What time are they getting into Midway?"

"They're supposed to land at seven thirty. Give or take a few minutes. Are you going to pick them up for me?" Emmy asked and then sighed. "Heather! Will you sit still and let me wipe your mouth? You have spaghetti all over your face."

110

"I'll pick them up, but I think you should go with me."

"No!" Emmy threw the wet washcloth at the kitchen sink, pulled Heather out of her chair and set her on the floor.

"You've been upset with Diane all week. You should come with me, so you can talk to her," Kenny suggested.

"I have to help Mary with the girls."

"I can get the girls ready for bed by myself," Mary said as she held Isabella.

Emmy frowned and crossed her arms over her chest. "I don't want to see Diane, and I might have the baby at any second."

"Emmy! She's your sister, and you're not going to have the baby yet."

Emmy put a hand to her belly and wiped her forehead with the other one. "Fine! I'll go with you, but I'm still gonna be upset with her. What kind of example is she setting for the boys?"

Kenny shrugged. "I'm not saying what she's doing is right, but she is an adult. Oh, did you talk to your mother today?"

"Yes, I called her back. She was wondering why Diane hadn't come over. I explained, and we ended up talking for almost an hour. It's weird but she seems to have accepted the fact Dad's gone a lot better than I would have thought. She likes being alone."

Kenny pulled into the cell phone lot a few minutes early. "This is a lot better than the old days when you had to circle around."

Emmy rolled her eyes and made air quotes. "In the 'old days' no one had cell phones, so a cell phone lot wouldn't have made much sense."

"Is he kicking? Is that why you're upset?" Kenny patted her belly.

"I'm sorry for being such a grump. I'm upset with Diane, but I'm also feeling like such a whale. I have to pee every five minutes."

"I hope not!"

"Okay, maybe I was exaggerating a bit and wipe that silly grin off your face."

Kenny's phone rang a minute later. "Are you guys ready?"

Diane replied, "We are still gathering up the luggage. I'll

111

call you back when we're outside. Is she with you?"

Kenny chuckled as he looked at Emmy. "She is, and she's still upset. I brought her so you guys could talk about this."

"Maybe." Diane hung up.

Ten minutes later, his phone rang again.

"We're ready."

"Be there in two minutes, Diane," Kenny said and then turned to look at Emmy. "Are you going to be civil to your sister?"

Emmy stuck out her lip and pouted. "Yes, I will be civil, but if she starts talking about what she and Fernando did, I'm going to explode."

Kenny pulled out of the lot and made his way to the arrivals area. *I don't think Diane will tell you anything about that, Em.*

"There they are!" Emmy saw Diane first.

Kenny pulled the van up to the curb and jumped out. "Hi, guys! How was Disney World?"

Carson handed Kenny a stuffed Mickey Mouse. "This is for the baby when he comes out of Auntie Em's belly. I bought it with my own money."

"Thank you very much, Carson." Kenny opened the sliding door and helped Carson get in.

Diane saw Emmy sitting in the front passenger seat. "I didn't know you were coming, Em."

Emmy forced a smile. "How was your trip?" she asked as she got out and tickled Caden.

"I'll tell you on the way home."

Diane put Caden in the car seat in the back row and made sure Carson was buckled in.

Kenny helped Fernando load the van."I think if we put this big suitcase here, we can fit this one on top." It took a couple of minutes, but they got all the luggage in the back.

"Em, would you mind if Fernando sits up front with me? There's more leg room up here."

Emmy glared at Kenny. "Fine!" *Fernando isn't that tall. You just want me to sit next to Diane so we can talk.*

Kenny merged onto Cicero Avenue with the other airport traffic.

"So, how was the hotel?" Emmy asked. *I might as well get this over.*

"Wonderful! We had a room facing the pools and a balcony."

"How were the beds?"

Kenny looked in the rearview mirror and frowned at Emmy.

"Listen, little sister, it's none of your business whether Fernando and I shared a bed or not." Diane kept her voice low, but the anger permeated the air.

"So you did, huh?"

"Emmy! You promised," Kenny reminded her.

"All right, I'll be civil. Tell me about the trip." Emmy made a face but didn't mention the sleeping arrangements again.

Diane went over the highlights of the week while Kenny and Fernando talked about music and then landscaping.

Diane looked over her shoulder and checked on the boys. "They're both asleep, Emmy."

"Good! Then we can talk."

"Fine!" Diane sighed. "Let me hear another lecture on how to live my life."

Emmy's shoulders slumped. "I'm turning into Mom, huh?"

"Yes, you are."

They looked at each for a few seconds and then both began to laugh.

"I'm sorry, Diane. I won't try to run your life."

"It's all right. I know you are concerned about me setting a good example for the boys. There were two king-sized beds in the room. It was a suite, by the way. I would get the boys in bed and read to them. I would stay with them until they were asleep."

"So, they didn't know you were sleeping with Fernando?"

"We would be up before the boys."

"Well, I guess that's better than... oh, never mind. I'm just glad you could get away."

"How has Mom been? Is she still having memory lapses?" Diane asked.

"She has actually been doing better. Now that Daddy is

113

gone, she has less stress in her life. She calls me every day and talks about Daddy, but it's not like she's obsessing about him. I went over there last Thursday, and we went through his clothes."

"What did she do with them?"

Emmy laughed and then said, "She gave them all to Goodwill, so she could get a receipt for her taxes."

"Why did you let her get rid of all of Dad's clothes?" Diane asked.

"Why would I stop her? I think it's better not to have them around for her to look at. It's not like we know anyone who would wear them."

Fernando turned in his seat. "I might have been interested in them."

"You wouldn't fit in any of his clothes," Emmy said. "You're shorter than Daddy."

He shook his head. "Not for me. For the theater group I joined. We might have been able to use something."

"When did you join a theater group?" Emmy asked.

"Last year. I've actually been in two plays."

"Why didn't you invite me to your plays?" Emmy asked. "Was it because they sucked?"

Diane came to his defense. "Actually, they were quite good. Fernando had the lead in one of them. He played Harvey in *The Rabbit's Revenge*."

"I could never be an actress," Emmy said.

"On the contrary," Fernando said. "You are a very good actress."

"What do you mean?" Emmy eyed him suspiciously. "Stop laughing at me."

"You are always trying to act like an adult, and sometimes you even succeed in convincing people you are one."

Kenny laughed. "I think he's got you there, Em."

"Ha! Ha! You guys are too funny," Emmy said and made a face at Fernando. "If you're ever in another play, I want to come and watch. I want to be able to boo and throw rotten vegetables at you."

"Then Fernando should be allowed to retaliate at one of

114

your concerts, Em," Kenny mentioned as he passed a group of trucks.

"You wouldn't let him do that, would you, Kenny?"

"He might think he has the right. Especially if you hit a sour note."

"I don't sound awful, do I?"

"No, Emmy. You have perfect pitch."

"Hey, Em, do you want to come and see the carriage house with me?" Kenny asked. He finished his coffee, set the cup in the sink and checked the time. "The furniture is supposed to be delivered between nine and noon."

"Will your mom and dad watch the girls?" Emmy asked as she entered the kitchen.

"Mom would be disappointed if you don't bring the girls."

"Give me a couple minutes to get them ready. Did the city do the final inspections?" She grabbed a fresh container of wipes and stuffed it into the diaper bag.

"Yes, the carriage house is better than ever," Kenny said and then grinned. "I think you will be pleased and even a little surprised."

"I know the insurance paid for most of it, but you still paid a lot out of your pocket." Emmy handed the diaper bag to Kenny. "I'll bring the girls out."

"I think you will like how it looks."

Twenty minutes later, Kenny turned into the long driveway, drove all the way to the back and parked in front of the restored carriage house.

"Did you notice that whoever's living in Mom and Dad's old house painted it and took down the fence in front?" Emmy asked as she slowly got out of the van. She looked up at the two-story brick building. "It doesn't look any different on the outside."

"I noticed the missing fence, but didn't see the house," Kenny said.

His parents scurried over to the van.

"Where are my little angels?" Dad Colwell beamed.

"Gra! Gra!" Isabella held out her arms to be picked up as

soon as Kenny set her down and she saw her grandpa. "Me hold you!"

Mom Colwell walked around the van to get Heather down.

"Me-maw!" Heather shouted and held out Doll Kitty.

"You brought Doll Kitty," Mom said.

"She insisted on bringing her, Mom," Emmy said. "How are you feeling?"

"Much better. The chiropractor said I was higher on my right side and that was causing the aches in my legs. How are you?"

"I'm all right. I hope he doesn't wait too much longer." She patted her belly. "I should have bought a new coat. I can barely close this one."

"Come on, Carter. Let's take the girls inside before they freeze. We're supposed to get three more inches of snow later."

Emmy smiled at Kenny. "Maybe we can build a snowman."

He stared at her for a moment. "More likely, you want to have a snowball fight."

"Either one will be fun."

Kenny's parents looked at each other.

Mom whispered, "Are you remembering the blizzard of 1990?"

"It did cross my mind."

"We had twelve inches on the last day of February. Emmy's parents were stranded and couldn't get home, so Emmy stayed overnight," Mom said as she helped Heather up the steps. "Today is the twenty-ninth. The last day of February."

"I forgot this is a leap year. Where was Diane?" Dad asked while carrying Isabella.

"She stayed with a friend for the weekend. I can't remember who."

"I remember the kids wanted to build a snow fort." He looked back in time to see Emmy throw a snowball at Kenny.

"You helped them build it. That thing was there for a month," Mom recalled. "I didn't think it would ever melt."

Dad laughed as he watched Kenny and Emmy. "They

116

wanted to spend the night in it."

Mom opened the back door. "And you were going to let them." She poked Carter in the side.

"I wasn't really going to let them, was I?" He tilted his head to help his memory.

"You were until I pointed out it was about twenty degrees outside."

"Stop it!" Emmy yelled as she waddled toward the house. "Dad, make him stop throwing snowballs at me."

Dad handed Isabella to Mom. "Take her inside. I want to have some fun!"

"Carter! What are you doing?" Mom rolled her eyes as Carter took the steps two at a time and gathered up some snow. "Emmy! Don't do anything foolish."

"I'll be all right," he said as Emmy hid behind him.

"Kenny is being mean to me," she said as she stuck her head around to locate Kenny. "He's hitting me with snowballs."

"Let's get him back," Dad suggested.

Mom watched out the breakfast nook windows as Carter, Kenny and Emmy threw snowballs at each other. "Girls, do you see what your mommy and daddy are doing?"

Heather and Isabella pointed out the window and squealed.

"That's all for me." Dad stood on the back steps and brushed off the snow. "Are you okay, Emmy?"

"I'm fine. That was fun!" She threw one last snowball at Kenny but missed. "I want to see the carriage house now."

She and Kenny held hands as they walked into the restored building. He kept his hands on her and followed her up the stairs.

"This looks like the same door. Is it?" Emmy asked as she stood on the landing.

"I found a similar one at that antique shop next to Paul's bookstore downtown." He opened the heavy door. "Are you ready?"

"I'm ready." She paused and held up her hands.

"What?" Kenny wondered.

"Aren't you going to carry me over the threshold like you did on our wedding night?"

"Will it hurt the baby?"

"No, silly."

He picked her up and carried her inside.

"Well, here it is!" He set her down and waved a hand to encompass the new space.

She took a few steps toward the kitchen area. "This looks great. Is that granite?"

"Yes." He smiled and took several steps into the great room. "How about over here?"

She walked into the room. "The new furniture looks perfect." She sat on the couch, rubbed a hand over the fabric and then looked up. "Where did you find those old beams? They look like they've been here for a hundred years."

"I found them at a farm in Indiana. They are the almost as old as the originals," Kenny said. "The planks for the floor came from an old mill in Kentucky."

"I like the skylight. It looks bigger than the other one."

He grinned as he nodded toward the other wall. "Anything else you like?"

Emmy looked around and did a double take as she spotted something unexpected on the other side of the room, tucked into the corner by the closet.

"Kenny! Is that our old couch? I thought it was destroyed in the fire," she asked as she got up.

He held her hand, and they walked over to the old couch. "It looks like the old one, doesn't it?"

"It does. But it's not, is it?"

"No, it's not the same one, but I found this online. The fabric is almost identical, but this one has more blue in it."

She sat down. "It doesn't sag like the other one." She pulled him down next to her.

"Do you want me to kiss you, Em?"

Her eyes sparkled. "Yes, kiss me, Kenny. Kiss me like it was the first time again."

He did his best.

They checked out the rest of the carriage house, and then headed back to the main house.

"What did you think, Emmy?" Dad asked while sitting in his recliner and reading his paper.

"It is amazing!" Emmy sat on the couch with Kenny. "I love the old beams and the new furniture fits the old style of the building."

"Did you like the old couch?" Dad asked.

Emmy blushed. "Do you know about the couch?"

Mom walked into the room. "Yes, dear. We know the story about the old couch." Mom grinned as she kissed the top of Emmy's head. "The girls are taking naps."

"The whole story?" Emmy bit her lip.

Dad set down his paper. "We know that's where Kenny first kissed you. Is there more?"

Mom sat in her recliner and looked at Emmy. "You don't have to tell us if it's too personal."

Kenny squeezed Emmy's hand.

"We used the couch the morning after our wedding night." Emmy bit her lip but then grinned. "We were married, so it was okay."

"It wasn't as comfortable as the bed," Kenny said.

Emmy poked him in the side. "They don't need to know all the details."

Dad picked up his paper and began to read.

Mom cleared her throat and asked, "Do you have any specific plans for the apartment?"

"I want to use it as a hideaway," Emmy said.

"What do you mean? It's right out in the open."

"Exactly!" Emmy waved her hands. "No one will ever suspect we're using it to get away from everything. It will be prefect. I want to use it to write songs, too."

"That sounds like a good plan," Dad said. "Just as long as you bring the grandkids with you."

Chapter Thirteen

"Kenny, wake up!" Emmy poked him in the side early on Monday morning.

"What is it, Em? Are you having the baby? Do we need to go to the hospital?" he asked as he jumped out of bed.

"I think I'm having contractions, but I didn't pack my bag yet." She swung her legs over the edge of the bed and sat up. "I need to get dressed. Can you hand me my sweatpants?"

He handed her the sweatpants she wore the previous day, and began packing an overnight bag.

"Kenny!"

"What? I'm packing."

"You're putting your clothes in the bag."

He looked at the clothes in the bag. "Oh, right. I need to put your stuff in here, huh?"

You're such a lovable dork. "That would be better." She grinned, but then bit her lip as a contraction started.

Kenny stopped packing the bag and stared at Emmy. "Are you okay?"

"That depends on what you mean by okay. Would you hand me the phone, please?"

He did that without any trouble.

Emmy called Kristen. "Can you watch the girls? I have to go to the hospital."

"I'll be right over!"

Kristen arrived, still in her pajamas and wearing one of John's coats, five minutes later. "You're early. You aren't due yet."

"Tell him." Emmy laughed and rubbed her belly.

This time Kenny didn't panic but delivered Emmy safely to the hospital. He calmly announced to the nurse. "I'm here with Emmy. She's having a baby."

Six hours later, he pulled into the garage.

"Why are you here?" Kristen asked as Kenny walked into the kitchen. "How are Emmy and the baby?"

"She's all right."

"And your son?" Kristen rolled her eyes when she realized

120

Kenny was finished talking.

Emmy waddled into the room and patted her belly. "He's still here. False alarm." Emmy plopped down on the chair by the kitchen desk. "I suppose we can think of this as practice for when I'm really in labor."

"What time is your doctor appointment, Em?" Kenny asked while grabbing a Coke from the fridge.

"I can't remember the time, but it's on the calendar," Emmy hollered from the family room.

Kenny looked at the calendar. *Nice picture of a mountain. I wonder where it is.* "Let's see, uh, March seventeenth at four thirty. That's today."

"I wasn't sure. I'll see if Mary can watch the girls."

Later that afternoon, as Emmy waited for Dr. Walsh to examine her, she felt a contraction.

The doctor walked in and smiled. "How are you feeling, Emmy?"

"Ready to pop. I think I'm having contractions, but they're not as strong as with the girls."

"Let's take a look." He examined her and then stood up. "Is Kenny with you?"

"Yes, he drove me. Why?"

"Do you feel up to a short ride?"

"Where to?" Emmy grimaced.

"St. Bart's. Your son is staring me in the eye," Dr. Walsh said with a smile. "He's ready to leave the womb."

"Now?"

"Pretty soon. I'll have my nurse call the hospital and let them know you're on your way."

Emmy lay her head back and sighed. "Let's get it over with."

A few minutes later Kenny helped Emmy into the Envoy. "Are you going to make it? Should we call an ambulance?"

"We're only three blocks from St. Bart's," she said. "I'm not calling an ambulance. I'll walk there first."

Kenny arrived safely at the ER. Two staff members met

them with a wheelchair.

"Are you Emily?"

"Yes, Dr. Walsh said it won't be long."

"We'll take you right upstairs."

Kenny handed the keys to the valet and walked along behind Emmy. They took the elevator to the fourth floor, and Kenny waited in the hall as the nurses got Emmy ready. Dr. Walsh arrived within minutes and examined Emmy again.

"How long have you been having contractions?" He appeared puzzled.

"Not more than two hours. Why?" Emmy asked.

"I remember your first delivery. It appears that this time you are going much faster. Your blood pressure is good. Your pulse is fine. You're dilated to an eight. I would venture to guess that your son will be here in under an hour. I'll tell Kenny he needs to get ready."

Dr. Walsh stepped out into the hall and told Kenny the news.

"An hour!" Kenny exclaimed. "What do I have to do?"

Dr. Walsh smiled, patted Kenny's back and said, "Not a whole lot. The nurse will take care of you."

The nurse handed Kenny the necessary gear and said, "Try to be quick putting this on. Your son's in a big hurry."

Dr. Walsh's estimate was close. Kevin Michael Robert Colwell was born at 5:29.

Kenny held him in his arms even before Emmy did. "He is amazing, Em. A little red and wrinkly, but absolutely perfect."

"Does he have any hair?" Emmy tried to see.

"He's got a full head of dark hair. Just like yours."

Eventually, Emmy got to hold their son. "I think he's hungry already."

Kenny slapped his forehead. "Shoot! I haven't called my parents or your mom or anyone."

"Then you better start making calls." Emmy smiled as Kevin Michael began to nurse.

By calling some people and texting others, the news spread rapidly. Mom and Dad Colwell were the first to arrive.

"Can I hold him, Em?" Mom asked.

Emmy handed him over.

"How much did he weigh? He is so tiny."

"Six pounds and five ounces. He's small but full-term. I imagine I will be able to come home Wednesday or Thursday."

"Are you still planning to have your tubes tied?"

"Yes. That's what we decided."

Kristen and Sloane arrived a few minutes later.

"Let me see him!" Kristen rushed to Emmy's side.

"Where are the guys?" Emmy asked. "Didn't they come?"

"They stopped downstairs to grab some food." Sloane shook her head. "They were actually excited to get hospital food."

"They're dorks!" Kristen said as she held Kevin. "He looks adorable. He has your nose, Emmy."

"Get out! You can't tell that already." Emmy pulled up her gown as Tony and John entered the room.

"See! I told you their burgers were good," Tony said between bites. "Hey, Em. How's it going?"

"You're a creep," she said but then grinned.

"Brat." Tony looked at Kenny.

"It's all right. She's doing great," Kenny said. "You don't have to pretend those burgers are good just to ease any tension about Em."

Tony and John tossed their burgers in the trash. "Thank God!"

"Were you worried about me, Tony?" Emmy bit her lip.

"What? No way! I knew you'd be fine." Tony patted her hand as he looked over at Kristen and the baby. "He's got hair."

"Do you want to hold him?" Kristen asked.

Tony waved his hands as he backed away. "No way! He's too tiny. I might break him."

Diane brought their mother, but they were only able to stay for thirty minutes. "I have the neighbor kid watching the boys, so we can't stay long."

Emmy and Kenny repeated the vital statistics several times over the three hours as more visitors arrived. By ten, everyone had left.

123

Kenny pulled a chair next to the bed. "Em, I know we picked out his name a while back, but if you want to make a change, it's okay with me."

"You mean change the Robert to Raymond, huh?"

Kenny nodded.

Emmy closed her eyes. "Kevin Michael Raymond Colwell. Kevin Raymond Robert Colwell. Kevin Michael Robert Colwell."

"Raymond Michael Robert Colwell," Kenny said softly.

"No! I hate that combination." Emmy shook her head emphatically. "I appreciate the gesture, and I know Daddy would understand, but let's leave it the way we planned. I'm not going to break the tradition."

Kenny kissed her just as Kevin Michael began to cry.

Emmy returned home Thursday after having her tubes tied.

"Come on, girls, you need to meet your baby brother," Mom Colwell said as she brought the girls into the family room.

Heather and Isabella climbed onto the couch and peeked into the tiny crib.

"Baby!" Isabella squealed.

Heather pulled off his blue cap.

"One baby?" Isabella asked.

"Yes, Mommy only had one baby this time," Emmy said. "His name is Kevin. Can you say Kevin, Isa?"

"Kefin!" Isabella said proudly.

Heather threw the blue cap back into the crib and then leaned close. "We wuv you, Kefin."

Emmy looked at Kenny and his parents. "Wow! Heather might actually be a good big sister."

"Today is Easter Sunday, Em." Kenny kissed her as they woke up. "Are we going to bring Kevin Michael to church with us? He's only six days old. Should we?"

"Liz brought Natalie to church just three days after she was born."

"Yeah, but..."

"I suppose we can leave him here. We'll only be gone for a

124

few hours," Emmy said without even a hint of a grin.

"But we can't... You stinker! You're kidding."

"You are my clever husband."

"You didn't call me a dork."

"It's still early," Emmy said as she headed to the bathroom. "Since we're not part of the worship team today, can we skip the Easter brunch and just go for the service?"

"I suppose it will be all right," Kenny answered.

Kenny helped the girls get ready and fed them breakfast as Emmy took care of Kevin Michael.

"Daddy! I want hoops," Isabella said as she sat in her high chair.

Kenny checked the pantry and brought out two other kinds of dry cereal. "We're out of hoops, but we have this." He let the girls choose and filled their bowls.

"I need more juice," Heather said.

He filled their cups with apple juice.

Emmy came downstairs with Kevin Michael in his carrier fifteen minutes later, looked at the girls and sighed. "Why didn't you put bibs on them? Look at their dresses." She set the baby carrier on the island. "They need to be changed. Watch your son."

Kenny checked the damage. "Sorry, I forgot. I'll clean up the mess."

"You got that right," Emmy said. She found clean dresses in the laundry room.

Kenny, Emmy and the kids arrived at Crest Ridge United Nazarene, and he took the girls to the nursery. Emmy carried Kevin, who was sleeping in his basket, in one hand and carried the diaper bag in the other as she headed toward the sanctuary.

"Would you like some help with that diaper bag, Emmy?"

She turned and smiled. "Why thank you, Christopher. I would appreciate the help. How are you?"

"Doing good. You?" He smiled at her and peeked at Kevin.

"Not bad. I managed five hours of sleep last night."

"Are you... you know?" he asked as he shifted his weight back and forth.

"Yes, I'm nursing him." Emmy grinned and held Kevin up

higher. "But I won't in the sanctuary in case you're wondering. I learned my lesson."

Christopher didn't understand, but didn't pry.

Emmy looked in the sanctuary. "It's already half full, and the breakfast isn't over. I hope we have enough chairs."

"I could always stand," Christopher said. "Where's Kenny?"

"He took the girls to the nursery. Where's Elena?"

"I brought her here early. She's with Randy and Vanni."

"Good! She should be in Sunday School."

"Aren't you going to tell me I should be in a class, too?"

"I don't need to. You already know."

Suddenly, a group of ladies noticed Emmy and the baby and rushed over. Emmy spent a few minutes telling them about Kevin Michael. She listened as the ladies commented about how adorable he looked.

The ladies moved on, and Emmy found seats close to where they usually sat. "Do you want to sit with us, Christopher?"

"Would you mind?"

"I'll make an exception this time," she said while taking Kevin Michael out of his carrier. She adjusted his blanket and then spotted Rory Porter on the other side of the sanctuary. "Can you hold Kevin for a second? I need to talk to someone."

Christopher didn't have time to refuse as Emmy hurried away. "Sure, Em," he whispered. Christopher held Kevin Michael and made faces trying to coax a smile from him.

A middle-age woman walked up behind Christopher and noticed the baby. "My! What a lovely child. Is it a boy or a girl?"

"His name is Kevin, and he's only a few days old," Christopher said. "But he's not..."

"It's never to early to bring your kids to church," the lady interrupted. "Where is his mother?"

Christopher pointed. "Emmy's over there talking to a friend."

The woman stared at Emmy. *I know her. She's the singer.* "Oh, I thought she was married to someone else."

"She is..." Christopher started to explain, but the woman

126

saw someone she knew and walked away. "... I'm just a friend."
Darn it! Sorry, Em, but I may have just ruined your reputation.

"It's so good to see you here, Rory," Emmy said as she hugged him.

"How are you, Em? How's the baby?"

"We are both good. Come and see him. He's over there with Christopher Braun." Emmy pointed and saw Christopher talking to a lady.

"Maybe I shouldn't."

"Of course you should. Christopher won't bite, and neither will Kevin," Emmy said and then giggled.

"How about Kenny?"

"He might bite, but not too hard."

Rory followed Emmy across the auditorium, and Kenny appeared at the same time.

"Are you going to be a CEO now, Rory?" Emmy asked.

"No, I'm just a physical therapist. You know that."

Emmy grinned and said, "I meant something different. A CEO is a person who only comes to church on Christmas, Easter and occasionally."

"Ah! I get it. I might be persuaded to show up a little more often."

"Kenny, I promised Mom I would come over this afternoon," Emmy said. "The kids are napping, so will you listen for them?"

"I'll listen, but I might take a nap, too," he replied. "Where did she go for lunch?"

"Some friends were taking her to Larry's Diner. She should be home by now."

Emmy drove to Hampshire Glen and used her remote to access the gated community. She opened the garage door and walked in.

"Mom, are you home?"

"I'm in the living room, Emmy."

Emmy joined her mother on the couch and asked, "How was your lunch?"

"We had a good time. The place wasn't very crowded when we got there, but it was packed when we left. I had ham and a sweet potato. It was good. I didn't bring anything home if you're wondering."

Emmy shook her head. "That's all right. I'm still full."

"Did you go to church this morning?" Mom asked.

"Of course, it's Easter," Emmy answered. "What are you watching?"

Patricia turned off the TV. "Not sure. I just turned it on out of habit. It gets pretty quiet around here without it. Your father would leave it on all the time."

"I know this is a silly question, but do you miss Daddy?"

"Certainly, but I'm adjusting. My neighbors call me, and we do things together."

"I'm glad you're not sitting around and moping. That wouldn't do you any good."

"Emily, your father and I were together for a very long time. It will take me years to fully get over him if I ever do. There have been a few times when I wake up during the night and forget he's gone. You know he was sleeping in the other bedroom, right?"

"Yes, I know. He couldn't sleep because of your snoring."

Patricia laughed. "He would complain about my snoring, and then complain because he couldn't sleep without hearing me snore. Go figure."

"How you ever thought about taking a short vacation to Florida?" Emmy asked while looking at the magazines on the coffee table. "It would be a lot warmer there."

Patricia stared at Emmy for a moment. "Are you asking if I want to go see your grandmother?"

"She is your mother," Emmy said. She adjusted one of the small pillows and turned to look at her mother. "Grandma would like to see you."

"Ha!" Patricia shook her head as she laughed. "Don't lie to me, Emily. You know better than that. We would be fighting within ten minutes. No way could I stay in her house."

"You could stay with Aunt Betty," Emmy suggested.

"You and Diane get along better than I ever did with my

sister, and you guys weren't exactly close," Patricia said.

"We get along a lot better now. We still disagree about things, but we don't fight too much."

"I'm not going to Florida so don't mention it again." Patricia grabbed the remote and turned on the TV. "I'm surprised you and Diane didn't murder each other. You would fight all the time when you were little. It got better when you were teenagers."

"Yeah, Diane was never home. She would sneak off with her friends."

Patricia smiled. "You were pretty good at sneaking out, too. We didn't say anything at the time, but we knew about the bedroom window."

Emmy bit her lip and then said, "At least Heather and Isabella can't do that unless they get a big ladder."

"Happy birthday, Grandma. How are you this morning? It's April fifth, and you know what that means." Emmy called her grandmother in Florida.

"It means I'm another year closer to one hundred. Did I tell you I plan to live to be a hundred?"

"Yes, Grandma, you've mentioned that a few times."

"Dear me, I almost forgot. That means this is your wedding anniversary, too. How long have you been married, Emily?"

"It's been five wonderful years!" Emmy exclaimed. "Did you get the pictures I sent?"

"Yes, I did. The girls are getting so big, and the baby is beautiful. You do know how to send the pictures using the computer, don't you?"

"I know how, Grandma."

"Then send them to my email account."

"I do. I just thought you might like to have a few real photographs, too."

"How is your mother?"

Emmy sighed. "She has good days and bad days."

"Don't we all. Don't we all."

Chapter Fourteen

"Kenny, do I have to go to your CD release thing? I'd rather stay home with Kevin and the girls," Emmy whined as she nursed the baby.

He kissed his three-week-old son. "I suppose you can stay home, but your new CD is set for release next month. You will have to go for that one."

"If I have to."

Kenny left for the Steward Music Group office, but was home two hours later. The band insisted on a smaller ad campaign for their new CD titled *Street Corner Gospel.*

"I'm home! Did anyone miss me?" He walked through the kitchen and into the family room. "Where is everyone?" He checked the rest of the main floor. *They must be upstairs.* He started to use the intercom, but decided against it. *They might be sleeping.* He checked the nursery first. *No one.* He finally found everyone sound asleep on his and Emmy's king-size bed. *Here you are.* He slipped into bed and snuggled up against Emmy.

"You're home early. How did it go?" she asked as she opened her eyes.

"Smooth and quick! Just the way press conferences should be." He made a flat motion with his hand. "I have some good news for you."

She turned over to face him. "What?"

"Do you remember the bet we made when the last CDs were released?"

"Vaguely. Did we ever agree on what the winner won?"

"I can't remember, but it's not important."

"What's the good news?"

"Drum roll, please!" He tapped the headboard.

Emmy rolled her eyes. *Dorkiest rock star ever.*

"*These Things Take Time* has now officially sold over a million copies."

"Get out!" She jabbed him in the stomach. "No way! Did you buy like a hundred thousand copies or something?"

"I bought ten copies when it came out, but that's all. You

130

are going to get a platinum record award at your CD release party."

"Unreal! Wait! Are they selling them for a dollar apiece or something?"

"No, regular price. Just think, you are one of only a few Christian artists to accomplish that. Even for secular bands, that's getting more difficult. Kids just aren't buying CDs the way they did in the past."

"I suppose in a few years they will be as obsolete as vinyl records are now."

"Actually, Em, vinyl is coming back."

"Why?" She patted Kevin as he stirred.

"Some audiophiles insist that vinyl sounds better."

"Good grief! I hope cassettes never come back."

Emmy and Kenny sat with Kristen in the sanctuary after the worship band finished singing.

"Krissy, why are you here? You should be home in bed." Emmy squeezed Kristen's hand. "You're ready to pop."

"I feel all right for someone in my condition," Kristen said. "It might be another week before she's born."

"I doubt it," Emmy said.

"Ssssh!" Tony frowned at Emmy. "Pastor Benson is getting ready to pray."

Emmy made a face at Tony, but kept quiet until after the prayer. "He's probably nervous since this is the first time he's preached on Sunday morning."

"Where is Dr. Behren?" Kristen asked.

Kenny answered, "He and Cathy are on vacation in Texas with Joey, Candice and the kids. They will be back next Sunday."

"How do you know they're in Texas?" Emmy asked while reading the church bulletin.

"Because he sent an email. Don't you ever check your email, Em?"

"Once in a while. I don't have time to sit and work on the computer all day. I have responsibilities. I have to take care of the babies and finish my CD."

Tony stared at Emmy until Sloane poked him in the ribs.

131

"What? I didn't say anything." Tony shrugged in protest.

"Just pay attention to Pastor Benson and stop worrying about Emmy."

After the service, Emmy, Kristen and Sloane headed to the nursery.

Sloane told Tony, "Will you find Peter and Dotty? Do you know which classrooms are theirs?"

"I know." *I think I know. I'll be able to find them.*

It took Tony ten minutes to find Peter and Dotty.

"Where have you been, Papa?" Dotty held up her hands to be picked up. "I colored this for you. Do you like it?" She held out the paper.

"It looks beautiful. Did you do it all by yourself?"

Dotty nodded.

"You stayed in the lines for the most part. I will put this on the fridge, so everyone can see it."

Peter saw Tony holding Dotty and ran up to him. "I don't like Sunday School. The teacher made us sing songs, and she took my football away."

"What football? I know you didn't bring one to church."

"I found one in the closet."

"You aren't supposed to be playing football in church."

"Why not? It's boring. Why can't I sit with you and Mommy in the big church?"

"Because you have to go to church with the other kids." Tony ruffled Peter's dark, straight hair. "You need a haircut. Maybe we can go tomorrow."

The ladies picked up the other six kids from the nursery.

"Mommy, Mommy!" Isabella shouted when she saw Emmy. "Kefin make poopy diaper, and she had to give him a fresh one," Isabella said and then pointed to the nursery volunteer. "She said it stunk to high heaven. Is that bad? I thought heaven was 'posed to be where Jesus lives."

"He does, Isa. High heaven is just an expression." Emmy picked up Kevin, and he started fussing.

"He's hungry." Isabella pulled Emmy over to a rocking chair. "Sit!"

132

Heather and Zachary tugged on the same stuffed lion. Zachary won the tug of war, and Heather promptly hit him.

"Heather! You have to share." Kristen pointed a finger and scolded her. "Sorry, Em. I shouldn't yell at her."

"It's all right. I know how she is." Emmy started nursing while Isabella watched.

Noemi Claire walked up and stood next to Isabella.

"Baby." Noemi pointed as Emmy covered Kevin with a blanket.

"Yes, he's Heather and Isabella's baby brother. You have a baby brother, too." Emmy pointed to the crib where Benjamin slept. Emmy watched as Noemi walked over to the crib. *You're younger than the girls and Zach, but you're bigger than all of them. Benjamin is big for a five-month-old, too. I suppose it's genetics.*

Kristen held Zachary's hand and walked up to Emmy. "Could I get a ride home with you? Tony and Sloane are stopping at the store to pick up Mama's birthday cake."

"Do you have a car seat for Zach?"

"Yes, you did drive the van?"

"Yes, it's too crowded in the Envoy. We can take you home. What time is Mama's party?"

"It's supposed to be at one, but who knows when we'll eat."

"How old is she?" Emmy asked just as Kevin spit up. "Thanks, buddy. I don't have anymore clean outfits for you in the diaper bag."

"I think she's sixty-four. Should I ask Sloane?"

"No, you can ride with us."

Kristen laughed. "No, I meant should I ask Sloane how old ... oh, never mind. I appreciate the ride."

"It's about time you got here," Tony said as Emmy, Mary and the twins walked into the kitchen. "Did you get lost? Where's Kenny and the baby?"

"No, doofus, we didn't get lost." Emmy made a face. "We decided to walk, since it's such a lovely day. Kenny is getting Kevin out of the stroller."

Tony laughed and asked, "How long ago did you leave?

133

Everyone else has been here for thirty minutes."

Kenny walked in carrying Kevin in his baby carrier. He lifted him up and set him down on the kitchen island. He shrugged. "It took a minute to figure out how to detach this from the stroller."

"Heather and Isabella had to examine every single plant on the way here," Emmy explained.

"Even the poison ivy?" Tony asked with a straight face.

"You don't have any poison ivy, do you?"

"He's pulling your leg, Em." Kenny picked up Isabella and set her on the island. "Let's take off your coat, Isa."

"You're a dork." Emmy poked Tony in the side and then waited. "Aren't you going to call me a brat?"

"Nope! I'm going to start something new. From now on, I'm going to treat you as an adult and not tease you like a kid sister."

"Yeah, that ain't gonna last," Sloane said as she carried a kicking and screaming Heather. "I found this one trying to carry Benjamin."

"Heather! You can't pick up the babies," Emmy scolded. "They are not Doll Kitty. They are real people and they break."

Mama walked up behind Emmy and put her hands on Emmy's shoulders. "You are still too skinny, child. Are you eating enough?"

"I'm trying." Emmy turned around and put her arms around Mama's ample waist. "I know it's not until tomorrow, but happy birthday."

"Thank you, Emmy. Now let me see that baby." Mama stood in front of Kevin and cooed. "I think he smiled at me."

"He can't smile yet. It was probably gas," Emmy teased and then looked up. "Marco! I didn't know you were here."

Marco held out his arms, and Emmy gave him a hug.

"I flew in for Mama's birthday, but I have to be back on Monday."

"What are you up to these days?" Emmy asked Tony's older brother. "How are Nancy and the boys?" *Your beard is bigger than ever, and you're getting really gray.*

"I'm teaching one class at Johns Hopkins, and spend the

rest of my week at Loyola, which is rather amusing because the two universities are arch rivals in lacrosse. I did finish my PHD."

"Do I have to call you Dr. Marco now?" Emmy asked and then giggled.

Later, after lunch, everyone gathered in the family room. Emmy held Isabella on her lap, while Heather sat on the floor with Peter and Dotty. Kenny kept a close eye on Kevin as he took a nap in his carrier. He talked to Daniel Keasling about the carriage house and thanked him again for the great work.

Kristen sat next to her mother. "Where are Uncle Carmen and Uncle Vincent? They should be here."

"They are still in Florida," Karla answered.

"I thought they usually came home for Easter."

"They would have, but Vincent was in the hospital again."

"What happened?" Kristen asked.

Karla leaned close and whispered, "Don't let Maria know, but the doctor thinks Vincent had a minor stroke."

"Is he all right?"

"I talked to your aunt Donna, and she said he is getting better. Carmen and Sharon are going to stay until Vincent can come home."

"What are you two whispering about?" Mama asked as she walked back into the room.

"Nothing, Maria," Karla said. "I know you were doing the dishes even after I told you not to." Karla frowned at her older sister. "Now sit down and rest."

"You have to open your cards and read them, Mama," Sloane insisted while bouncing Noemi Claire on her knee. "As you requested, no one brought presents to open, but you have a lot of cards."

"There better not be any money in these cards." Mama looked at Tony.

"I can't control what everyone does." He shrugged his wide shoulders.

Thirty minutes later, Emmy and Kristen were counting the money from the cards.

"Hey, Mama!" Emmy hollered. "There's almost a thousand

dollars here. What are you going to do with it?"

"Give it back! I don't need that much money," Mama answered.

"Can't do that," Emmy said. "We didn't keep track of where it came from. You will have to keep it."

Kristen suggested, "You could take a trip somewhere. You like to travel."

"I do like to travel, but I can't. I have all these babies to spoil," Mama said. "I suppose I could buy more toys."

"No, Mama!" Tony waved his hands. "No more toys. I keep tripping over them everywhere. Soon we will have to build an addition to house all the kids' toys."

"Are you all right?" John asked as Kristen winced.

"I'm fine."

Emmy saw Kristen's look and scooted closer. "Are you going into labor?"

"Not yet." Kristen managed a weak smile.

"I thought your doctor said you had another week."

"You, of all people, should know doctors aren't always right."

"Can you hold on until tomorrow? That way she will be born on Mama's birthday," Emmy said.

"I'm fine. I'm not going to have the baby for several days."

Kristen did manage to make it until until April twenty-first, but just barely. Grace Allison Randolph arrived at 12:13 and immediately expressed her displeasure.

"She sounds pretty angry," John said while rubbing the back of Kristen's neck.

"Are you going to tell Tony and Emmy?" Kristen held Grace to her breast.

"Yeah, they're still in the waiting room. The last time I checked, Emmy was calling Tony a dork for some reason." John smiled at his daughter and let her grab his finger.

"Go tell her that Grace and I are doing fine. She needs to get home to feed her baby."

John waited a few minutes. He walked into the waiting

room just in time to see Tony pick up Emmy and hold her head against the ceiling.

"Put me down, you dork!" Emmy insisted as she squirmed to get away.

"I told you I could still hang you from the ceiling," Tony said and then saw John. He set Emmy down.

Emmy slugged Tony's arm, but then noticed John. "Is she here?"

John nodded. "Grace is here, and they are both fine. Kristen told me to make sure you go home."

"Not until I see Krissy and Grace." Emmy grabbed her coat and purse, scooted past the guys and rushed down the hall to Kristen's room.

Kristen patted a spot on the bed next to her as Emmy rushed into the room. "She's sleeping, but you can hold her."

Emmy tossed her coat at a chair, set her purse on the counter and slipped in next to Kristen. "She doesn't have any hair."

"She has a little bit, but it's real light."

"Do you realize that Benjamin, Kevin and Grace were all born on Mondays? Why is that?" Emmy asked.

"I didn't remember that, but it does seem odd."

Emmy held Grace for a few minutes before kissing her and handing her back to Kristen.

"Tony, will you take me home, please? I'm sure Kevin is probably starving."

"Sure, but it will cost you, brat." Tony peered down at Grace and shook John's hand. "You're lucky. She looks just like Kristen."

"Hey! I thought you weren't going to call me brat anymore," Emmy said as she put on her coat.

"Whoops! I forgot."

"It's all right. I like it when you call me that. It means you really love me."

Tony rolled his eyes. "It just means I can barely tolerate you."

"See you tomorrow, Krissy." Emmy grabbed Tony's arm and pulled him out of the room. "Take me home, so I can go to bed. It's been a long day."

"Mama will be pleased to share her birthday with Grace," Tony said as they stepped into the elevator.

"It was good to see Marco again even if he had to leave so soon."

Tony laughed and then asked, "Did you notice all his gray hair?"

"I noticed that, and he sounds so much like an absent-minded professor. Do you wish he lived closer than Baltimore?"

"I know Mama would like it, but, to be honest, I think it's best that he lives there."

"So if you saw him all the time, you might have some squabbles. Is that what you're saying?" Emmy asked.

"Probably. We live in different worlds."

On Thursday morning, Tony drove John to the doctor's office for his procedure.

"Are you sure you want to do this?" Tony asked as he pulled into a parking space. "You're still young."

"We're sure we don't want any more kids. We just wanted to wait until Grace was born, just in case... you know." John unbuckled his seatbelt.

"Hang on!" Tony grabbed John's arm. "What if something terrible happened and you and Kristen would... you know."

"Tony, Kristen and I have discussed this for nine months. I'm having a vasectomy."

"Okay, I just wanted to be sure."

Sloane talked to Tony about having people over for dinner on Saturday.

"It's all right with me," Tony said as he ate breakfast.

"I want it to be just the adults. No kids, No babies."

"I understand. You need a break from the kids, so you can spend time with adults. Are you going to invite Emmy, or does she have to stay home?" Tony asked.

"You should get a new job as a comedian," Sloane said and the rolled her eyes. "I'll make some calls."

Sloane talked to Kristen, who agreed to come over. Then she called Emmy and explained the plan.

"I'm sure Mary will watch the girls, and I'll feed Kevin right before we come over. We could have maybe three hours of piece and quiet," Emmy told Sloane over the phone.

"Kristen is getting her parents to babysit, and Tony and I will make sure our kids are in bed, too," Sloane said.

"Are you all right?" Emmy asked. "You sound tired."

"I'm okay. See you tonight."

After dinner that evening, Tony and the guys sat in the family room and waited for the wives to join them. After watching *Sports Center* for a couple of minutes, Tony looked at John, who was sitting on the love seat across from the couch. "How is everything going? Any, uh, problems? Sloane wants me to get fixed now."

Sloane sat next to Tony on the couch. "I think it's time."

"For cripes sake, Tony. He just had a coupe of little snips done," Kristen said as she snuggled against John. "It wasn't a major operation."

Emmy sat on Kenny's lap in one of the leather recliners.

"Don't listen to her, Tony," John said as he winked at Kenny and Emmy. "It was so painful to have it done and don't expect to be able to have sex for like six months. It hurts to even move and forget about going to the bathroom. It's all I can do to keep from screaming."

"Tony, don't believe John," Sloane said and then frowned at John.

Kristen smacked her husband for trying to scare Tony. "I guess we won't be making love for six months since you've had such a painful operation."

"I'm feeling much better now, Kristen. I think we can make love any time you want." John put an arm around her and pulled her closer.

Kristen moved his arm and scooted away. "What if I don't want."

"Come on, Krissy, you know you love me and want to make me happy," John pleaded.

"My doctor told me I could start having sex again," Emmy announced out of the blue.

Everyone looked at her.

"Too much info, Em." Sloane made a face and then pointed at Tony and John. "Neither one of you will be needed for sex anymore unless both of you are fixed. I'm not getting my tubes tied like Emmy."

Tony looked at John and shrugged.

"Well, old buddy, I guess you'll have to take one for the team," John said.

Tony grimaced. "Does it really hurt a lot? I don't like needles."

"Nah! I'm just putting you on," John said because Kristen was still frowning at him. "I'm glad I did it because now we don't have to worry about getting pregnant again.

Emmy kissed Kenny, giggled, then said, "It's great! We can have as much sex as we want and never worry about me getting pregnant again."

"Will you stop that, brat, or at least find a bedroom. Preferably one of your own," Tony said.

Sloane stood up. "I'm pregnant again."

"For real?" Kristen asked.

"Yep! Again. That's why I want him to get fixed. This will be number five. I think that's plenty."

John and Tony stood up and high-fived each other. Emmy jumped off of Kenny's lap and gave Sloane a hug.

"Are you okay, Sloane?"

Sloane sniffled and wiped her eyes. "Yes, I'm fine. I want a large family, five kids is just perfect, but the thought of being pregnant again is getting me down."

Emmy turned to Tony and poked him in the stomach. "You need to get fixed and don't be a big baby about it."

"Fine. I'll get it done."

Sloane and Tony met with his doctor and scheduled the procedure for May fifth. On the morning before the appointment, Tony needed to take care of something for the major operation.

"Will you help me, Sloane?" he asked while holding a razor. "I'm afraid I will..."

Sloane laughed and then shook her head. "You are such a baby. I bet John didn't make Kristen shave his."

He handed her the razor. "Just be careful, okay?"

Sloane drove Tony to the clinic, and then home thirty minutes later.

"I'm sorry, Sloane, but I just couldn't go through with it. Will you keep it a secret for now?" Tony asked.

"It's all right. I know you don't like needles, but I never thought you would nearly faint."

"Please swear you won't tell Emmy or John," Tony begged.

"I won't tell John, but why would I ever tell Emmy?"

"She will tease me about having it done, and I don't want her to know I chickened out at the last minute."

Sloane grinned and then said, "And just think. I shaved you for no reason."

"Are you ready for bed?" Emmy asked later that night. "The house is quiet, so I'm going to bed."

"I'll be there in a sec. I want to check my email again," Kenny said while working on his laptop.

Emmy rolled her eyes. "You're always checking it. Are you having a secret online affair?"

"If I tell you, then it won't be a secret." He grinned and quickly scanned through his private email account.

"You're such a dork."

"It's a good thing I checked."

"Why?"

"Becky and Taylor had the baby today. A girl."

"We knew they were having a girl. What is her name?"

"Eve Robin. Robin is Becky's mom's name."

"That's kind of a cool name."

Kenny was replying to the email. "I'll let Becky know you approve."

"Don't you dare," Emmy said. "Just send them our congratulations."

Chapter Fifteen

On May eighth, Steward Music Group released *Strength,* the fifth CD by Emmy Colasanti. Emmy attended the press conference but felt awkward about the attention lavished upon her by the press.

"What should I do if they ask something personal?" Emmy whispered to Stephanie Grachan as the press conference began.

"Don't answer anything that makes you uncomfortable," Stephanie instructed. "Just because you are a public figure, doesn't mean they have the right to know details about your personal life. I'll be right beside you the whole time."

The first three questions were standard ones about the recording and artwork.

"Where did you shoot the cover?" a local DJ asked.

"On our deck, Perry. You've been there. Brady Robertson shot that for me. Didn't he do a great job?"

"What are you reading?" Perry asked.

"My Bible. When it's nice, I like to read it outside," Emmy answered.

"When did you come up with the title for the CD?"

"Towards the end. I was struggling to come up with some lyrics and read the verse in Psalms that says something about God arming me with strength and keeping my way secure. Then I just kept noticing the word strength in so many verses." She paused and then shrugged. "Voila, I had my title."

"How do you write your songs?" the next reporter asked.

Emmy said, "With a crayon. I find them all over the house."

That broke up the reporters and allowed Emmy to relax. The reporters kept their questions about the music, and before long, Stephanie signaled the end of the session.

"That wasn't too bad now, was it?" Stephanie asked.

"No, thanks, Stephanie." Emmy hugged her. "How are your boys doing?"

"They are growing like weeds."

"The same with the girls," Emmy said.

The ladies spent a few minutes talking about their families before Emmy left.

"How did it go?" Kenny asked.

Emmy waved a hand. "No biggie. Piece of cake. No one said anything about a platinum record."

Kenny shook his head and smiled.

Two days later, Emmy and Kristen were shopping at Sainsbury's. They had moved out of the produce department and into the bread aisle. Emmy let Kristen move ahead and then made a call.

"I gotta hang up. I'll see you at three thirty." Emmy quickly ended her call when Kristen returned after running back to the produce aisle to pick up a green pepper.

"Who were you talking to, Emmy?" Kristen asked as she tossed the pepper into her cart and crossed it off of her list.

Emmy bit her lip. "Just a friend." She checked the dates on two loaves of rye bread and put one back on the shelf.

Kristen walked farther down the aisle and scooped up two packages of hamburger buns. "Which friend?"

Maybe if I pretend I didn't hear the question, she won't ask me again. Emmy checked the label on a loaf of potato bread and set it on top of the rye bread.

"Who was it, Em?" Kristen asked as she waited at the end of the aisle.

"Who was what?"

Kristen rolled her eyes and waited for another shopper to move out of aisle two. "You know perfectly well what I mean. Are you trying to hide something?" Kristen picked up a large jar of Skippy Extra Crunchy.

Emmy moved past Kristen into the now empty aisle. She pushed the cart ahead, put her feet on the bottom rail and rode it until it stopped in front of the soup section.

"Will you stop that? You aren't a child anymore." *Even though you act like one at times.* "Who were you talking to? Who are you meeting later? I heard that part." Kristen caught up to Emmy and picked out several cans of soup.

Emmy saw that Progressive Kitchen soups were on sale, so she chose several cans.

Kristen pushed her cart against Emmy's. "Tell me!"

Emmy scowled. "I was talking to Rory if you must know."

"Rory! Rory Porter?" Kristen stared at Emmy.

Emmy turned her back. "Do you know any other Rorys?"

Kristen pushed her cart alongside Emmy's and grabbed Emmy's arm. "Why are you talking to him? Does it have to do with your father? If so, then I apologize for thinking otherwise."

"It wasn't exactly about Daddy." Emmy reached down for two cans of Dinty Moore beef stew.

"What is going on? Why would you need to talk to Rory again?" Kristen picked up one of the cans of beef stew from Emmy's cart. "This doesn't contain as much sodium as I would have thought. Is it good? I've never bought it before."

"I like it. Mom used to buy it a lot because it's cheap and easy."

"Would you grab one for me, please?"

Emmy did.

"Thanks, Em. I'll give it a try." Kristen set the stew in her cart, but then turned back to Emmy. "Tell me about Rory. I know you had a crush on him in high school, and I know he didn't exactly have the best of reputations."

"There's nothing to tell." Emmy turned away to inspect the different cans of tuna. "I didn't see him for like ten years until we ran into each other at Astoria Estates."

"Yes, and now that you've seen each other...?"

"I am married to Kenny!" Emmy tossed three cans of tuna into her cart. They bounced off the the side and ended up on her fresh produce.

"Yes! You most certainly are. I hope you won't forget that when you see Rory later."

They didn't speak to each other again until they got to aisle five.

"I can't remember if we have any crackers at home," Kristen said to gauge Emmy's mood.

"Then buy some! They don't cost an arm and a leg," Emmy

144

said as she picked up the house brand of saltines. *These are a dollar cheaper. I don't think the girls will mind.* Emmy set the crackers in her cart, looked at Kristen and bit her lip. "I'm sorry for yelling at you, Krissy."

"Apology accepted." Kristen tossed four different kinds of crackers into her cart. "I need cookies."

Emmy followed Kristen down the aisle. They both picked up three packages of Chips Ahoy.

"They're on sale," Emmy explained. "Cookies and milk are kinda healthy for you."

"If you want to believe that," Kristen said.

They each needed several boxes of cereal. They reached the beverage aisle. Emmy bought Dr Pepper

"It's on sale."

Kristen shoved two cases of Coke under the cart. "We like Coke."

Emmy checked the price but held her tongue.

They helped each other with the cases of bottled water, and then moved to the frozen section. By the time they left the frozen and dairy sections, both carts were overflowing.

"I'm meeting Rory at the Jimmy John's on the opposite side of the mall from the nursing home. We're just getting together to talk about old times," Emmy suddenly confessed.

Kristen pulled her cart to an empty space past a display of Twinkies and other assorted junk food. Emmy followed and grabbed a box of Twinkies.

"I don't buy a lot of junk food," she said when Kristen frowned at her.

"That's not why I'm mad." Kristen grabbed two boxes of Twinkies. "I am mad because you and Rory are sneaking around."

"We are not!" Emmy insisted.

"Does Kenny know you are meeting him?"

"Actually he does!" Emmy raised her voice. "How does that grab you?"

"Are you telling me the truth?"

"Have I ever lied to you?"

Kristen grabbed Emmy's hands.

"What are you doing?" Emmy yanked her hands away.

"Making sure you didn't have your fingers crossed, or something equally childish."

"I'm telling you the truth. I told Kenny that I might be meeting Rory later."

"How did he react? Was he thrilled?" Kristen asked. "Did you catch the sarcasm in my voice?"

"Do you want me to explain or not?" Emmy got behind her cart and gave it a shove to get it moving.

"Hold on!" Kristen stopped Emmy's cart. "I'm listening."

"Please, don't tell John or anyone, but I think Diane has gone out with Rory."

"What? I thought she and Fernando were dating? She did go to Disney World with him."

"True, but that was just to sorta pay him back for all his help with the boys." Emmy put her box of Twinkies back.

Kristen harrumphed, "She shared his bed as a reward? How sick is that?"

"I don't think it was quite as bad as you make it sound. Anyway, she and Fernando have gone out before."

"So, you are going to grill Rory to see if he and Diane are hooking up? Is that it?" Kristen put the box of Twinkies back onto Emmy's pile of groceries. "You know you want them."

"Yes, thanks. I do like Twinkies. Mom wouldn't buy them very often when I was a kid."

"So, if Rory and Diane aren't hooking up, are you?"

"What?"

"I'll be blunt. Are you and Rory going to fool around?" Kristen asked as she stared at Emmy. "And I'll know if you're lying."

"Yes," Emmy said.

Kristen did a double take. "For real?"

"Sure! Why not? I'll throw my life, career, reputation, everything away, so I can hop into bed with Rory." Emmy walked away leaving Kristen standing in shock.

After a time, Kristen caught on to Emmy's sarcasm. "Wait for me! I'm sorry for doubting you, Em. Will you forgive me?"

146

"I will forgive you if you pay for these groceries," Emmy said. "You can use my coupons."

"You should pay for mine. You guys make more money than all of us put together."

"We do..." Emmy started to protest, but then realized the truth of Kristen's statement. "Let's get home, so I can put these groceries away before they melt."

They got back, and Emmy helped Kristen carry her groceries into the kitchen.

"Thanks, Em. I can get them put away."

"I'll talk to you later."

Kenny helped Emmy with the groceries, and she told him about her disagreement with Kristen while they put the perishables in the fridge.

"She really thought you and Rory would do that?"

"I think so. She sounded serious. She wanted to know if you knew."

"Did you explain?" Kenny asked as he opened the box of Twinkies and tossed one to Emmy. "You shouldn't let the girls see these."

"I won't." Emmy grinned as she licked the filling out of her Twinkie.

Kenny finished his Twinkie and tossed both wrappers into the garbage can. "What are you going to do if Rory confesses to the crime of dating Diane?"

"Shoot him, of course," she said and then giggled. "He's supposed to be fooling around with me."

Emmy saw Rory inside the Jimmy John's when she arrived an hour later.

"Why didn't you order?" She took his hand in hers and smiled.

"I thought I should wait for you."

"Did you walk over here?" Emmy asked while perusing the menu board.

"Yeah, would you give me a ride home, please?"

"I will if you buy my sandwich."

"Deal." He knew he had enough cash.

"I'm kidding, Rory. This is my treat."

"I won't argue, Emmy. I know you can afford it."

The clerk smiled and asked, "Hi! What can I get you guys?"

"What would you like, Em?" Rory asked.

"A number five with chips and a drink." Emmy gave the clerk her order.

"And I'll have a number nine."

"Chips and drink?"

"Yes, please."

Emmy discretely handed Rory a twenty, so it would appear he was buying. Their sandwiches were ready almost instantly. They picked out their chips, filled their cups with pop and looked for a place to sit.

"How about back there, Em?" Rory pointed to the table in the back.

"That's fine."

Rory finished his larger sandwich and his chips before Emmy had eaten half of her sandwich.

"I think I'll save the rest for later." Emmy offered some of her chips to Rory.

"Thanks. Need a refill, Em?"

"Yes, Coke, please."

He refilled their cups and sat back down.

"I can tell you have something bothering you, Em. Care to spill it?"

"Are you fooling around with Diane?" Emmy blurted out.

He grinned, then said, "Not yet, but I'm working on it."

"Are you really trying to?"

"I think it's more a matter of her trying," he answered.

She took a long drink of pop before asking. "But you would be willing, right?"

He thought about it for a moment. *She's single. If you were single, I wouldn't be after Diane.* "I'm looking for a serious relationship."

"But you would sleep with her, huh?"

"We are both single adults, Em."

148

"The boys need a father. A father who is going to be there for the long haul. Know what I mean?"

Rory took a drink and then sighed. "Diane told me about Fernando. He would probably be a better father than me."

"He's old enough to be the boys' grandfather," Emmy said. "I like Fernando. Don't misunderstand me. He's a great guy, but he's too old."

"Diane doesn't think so."

"Don't get me started on that."

"You know I wanted Diane when we were kids, but she always shot me down," Rory said quietly as a customer walked past to use the restroom.

"Did you try harder with her than me?" Emmy asked bluntly.

"You know I did."

"So, I was just a fall back?"

Rory shook his head. "I never thought of you as someone to settle for. Believe me, Em, I would have gone after you if you hadn't been so young and so in love with Kenny."

"Do you mean that?"

"If you had been the slightest like Diane in that regard, I would have... never mind. Can we talk about something else?"

"Should I take you home?"

"Yeah. Do you need another refill?"

"I'm good."

They waved goodbye to the guy who took their order, walked out and climbed into her Envoy. Rory directed her to his apartment.

"You can park anywhere. There's no assigned spots."

She parked and followed him inside.

"Well, this is my humble abode. Not exactly what you're used to, Em." He took her jacket and hung it in the small hall closet.

She stepped into the living room. "It's clean, and it doesn't smell."

"Gee, thanks," Rory said and then chuckled.

Emmy grinned and then explained, "I was thinking about

149

the place where Craig and Diane lived. That apartment always smelled funny."

"Funny how?"

"Stale beer and pizza and I think Craig and his roommate smoked pot," she explained as she looked around. "You need some photos or something to make this place yours."

"One of these days. Have a seat, Em. The couch may be old and threadbare, but it's clean." He picked up an empty beer can and some junk mail.

Emmy took off her shoes and sat down.

"I'd offer you something to eat or drink but since we just came from Jimmy John's."

"I'm fine, Rory. Let's just sit and talk."

He sat at the other end of the couch. Emmy put her feet underneath her and faced Rory. "Did Daddy ever realize who you were?" She noticed a single picture on top of the TV.

"I don't think so. If he did, he never let on," Rory answered.

"I think he would have done something had he known." Emmy got up to look at the photo closer.

"Yeah, like try to murder me," Rory said.

"That's no laughing matter," Emmy said. "He didn't have any reason to hold a grudge against you. Owen, yeah, but not you." She picked up the photograph and stared at it. "This is you, Owen and Amy, right?"

Rory got up and stood beside her. "Yeah, it's the only picture I have of all of us."

Emmy set the picture back. "How old were you?"

"According to the writing on the back, I'm nine. Owen was twelve and Amy five."

"You look cute," Emmy said. "But you needed a haircut."

"Mom was always on my case about my hair. I think my hair was always longer than Kenny's, and he's the rock star."

They moved back to the couch.

"Do you remember when Mom made me take piano lessons, so I wouldn't always be playing football and stuff with the neighborhood boys?"

"Yeah, you whined about it, but you were pretty good. I

150

heard you practicing a few times."

"Did you ever play a musical instrument?" Emmy asked.

"Sure! All the time."

"What?" Emmy tried to remember.

"My stereo," he said and then laughed. "I don't have an ounce of musical talent in my body."

"God gave your body other talents," she said with a sparkle in her eyes.

He stared at her for a moment.

"We never did kiss, did we?" she asked. "I wonder why."

"I wanted to kiss you, Em, but you weren't interested."

"I was interested, Rory."

"You were only interested in Kenny. I'm assuming you let him kiss you."

"He was my first." She bit her lip.

"Are we still talking about kissing?"

She moved to the middle of the couch and didn't say anything for a few seconds.

"Have you ever... you know?"

She shook her head. "Just Kenny."

He's one lucky guy. Rory smiled.

"Can I tell you something I've never told anyone?" She moved closer to Rory until her knees touched his leg.

"Maybe you shouldn't, Em." He felt a surge of electricity course through his body. *If this is about some sexual thing, then I don't want to hear it.*

"Sometimes I think maybe I missed out on a part of growing up because I was never with anyone else." She looked into his eyes. "Kenny had another girlfriend. Becky. He met her in Los Angeles."

"Emmy, you don't have to tell me this." He felt a bead of sweat run down his back.

"I love Kenny, and I couldn't ever see myself with anyone else, but I have kissed other boys."

"Boys?"

"Young men."

"Please don't tell me who you've kissed."

151

She put her hands in her lap. "Tony Bertucci, Derrick Keasling..."

"Wait! Isn't he Kristen's brother?"

"Yeah, I went out with him before I met Tony."

"Did you ever kiss Todd Delaney? Tell me the truth."

"Yuck! No way!" She waved her hands. "I know he spread all kinds of gossip about what we did, but none of it was true."

"I never believed a word of it, Em."

Emmy leaned forward and, without hesitation, kissed Rory on the mouth for a brief second.

He scooted back against the arm of the couch. "Why did you do that?" His voice barely audible.

"I just had to know. I'm sorry, Rory."

"Are you really?"

She shook her head. "Do you want to kiss me again?"

"I want to kiss you very much," he said as he jumped up. "But I won't."

"Didn't you like it?" She bit her lip.

"That's not it, and you know it." He stood in front of her.

She sat up on her knees and took his hands in hers.

He squeezed her hands. "You are a very desirable woman, and if I was like Owen, I would carry you into the bedroom." He let go of her hands. "But I'm not Owen, and you're not Diane."

She sat back. "It was just a kiss, Rory."

"Just a kiss?"

She nodded.

"Geez, Em, you scared me. I thought.. well, with all that talk about you missing out on stuff because you've never slept with anyone but Kenny... I guess I got it all wrong."

She moved to the other end of the couch and motioned for him to sit. "If Kenny had stayed with Becky, I would be a different person today."

He sat down. "Can I ask you something really serious?"

"I was still a virgin when we got married. Barely."

"What?" He jerked his head. "No, that's not it."

"Ooops! I guess I thought. Never mind. What were you going to ask?"

"If I wanted to start coming to your church, would you be ashamed of me?"

"Never!"

"But I've done some terrible things, Em. I still lust after women. I've never paid for sex though, if you know what I mean."

"No, what do you mean?" She kept a straight face and pretended not to know. "Why would you have to pay for sex?"

"Come on, Em. I know you're not that naive." He saw her start to smile. "You're really funny. I'm tired of trying to find someone in a bar, or at work. I would like to find someone to love, settle down and raise a family. A family of my own."

"Not someone who already has kids?"

"I know you mean Diane. If Diane and I got together, fell in love and all that, I would want to have kids with her."

"Are you asking for permission to pursue Diane?" she asked with a serious expression.

He waited to see if she would laugh, but she didn't.

"If I need your permission, then, yes, I'm asking."

Now she grinned.

"You're too much! I can see why Kenny loves you."

"It's okay with me if you want to date Diane, but don't get her pregnant until you get married. I won't ask you not to sleep with her, though I don't think that's right."

"I get the picture, Em."

"Oh, my God!"

"What?"

"I just realized," she said and then grinned. "If you marry Diane, you will be my brother-in-law."

"That's usually the way it works, but let's not get ahead of ourselves. I haven't proposed... yet."

Chapter Sixteen

"Emmy, would you mind if I ate dinner with you guys today?" Mary Michaelis asked after church.

"I don't mind. You aren't going to eat with your family? You usually do on Sunday."

"I know, but I need to talk to you and Kenny about something."

"You know you're always welcome to eat with us. The girls think you are a big sister. Sometimes I wonder if they think I'm just a big kid, too," Emmy said.

As they ate, Emmy tried to draw Mary into the conversation. *You are being more quiet than normal. It must be something serious that you want to talk about.*

Kenny helped Emmy clean up the kitchen while Mary got the kids down for their nap.

"Do you have any clue what's going on with Mary?" Emmy asked as she handed Kenny the last plate.

He took it and dried it off. "Not really, but I'm wondering if it has to do with college."

Kenny finished drying the dishes as Emmy wiped down the countertop. They retreated to the family room and waited for Mary.

She tiptoed down the stairs a few minutes later. "They're sort of asleep, but Heather is being a real fuss butt. I tried to sneak away."

"She can fuss all she wants," Emmy said. "Sit down and talk to us. We're concerned about what's bothering you." Emmy patted a spot on the couch next to her.

Kenny sat in his recliner and set down the *Billboard* he had been reading.

"This semester has been a little rough for me." She waved a hand. "I don't necessarily mean my grades have suffered. They haven't, but in other regards. My social life is a mess and my spiritual life has slipped. Nothing drastic."

"That's good to know," Emmy said. "Not that your spiritual life has suffered, but that it's nothing drastic."

Kenny shook his head. "I think Mary knows that, Em."

154

"I have been thinking and praying about this for some time and I've made a decision." Mary folded her hands in her lap. "Please don't try to talk me out of it."

"You aren't quitting college, are you?" Emmy asked.

"Not quitting, but I'm going to take the fall semester off. I need a break."

Kenny sat up straighter. "Mary, I know there's something else behind this decision."

She looked at him and then back at Emmy. "You're right."

"What? Tell me." Emmy reached for Mary's hand. "It's not because of a man, is it?"

"No, of course not." Mary blushed and looked away. "It's because you guys are going to be so busy this summer and fall. You'll both be on tour at the same time, and you need help with the kids."

Emmy looked at Kenny and bit her lip. "We have been praying about what we would do about the babies. How did you know about the tours?"

"I've known for months. Your tours don't just happen overnight. They take months of planning. It's been on my mind all semester."

Kenny stood up. "You will be paid extra for both the summer and the fall tour."

"You guys pay me too much just to be the nanny. I don't expect more than that."

"You might not expect it, but you deserve a raise. It can be rather tedious on tour. You know how that goes."

"I know, but I couldn't let someone else take care of the girls and baby Kevin."

"What would we ever do without you?" Emmy hugged Mary and they both cried.

Fridays At Five still owned the warehouse they had purchased from Jeff's father years ago for rehearsals and storing their gear. Now that the Street Chronicles summer tour approached, the band used the facility to prepare. The stage was built. All the lights and pyrotechnics assembled. Everything to

155

allow the band to fine tune their performance was in place.

For only the second time in the band's history, the guys made a change in personnel. They borrowed Garrett Hainsey as a touring musician. Garrett's band, The Barefoot Prophets, one of the other bands on the Steward Music Group roster, was taking time off to allow Finley Husted, their drummer, to recover from a serious car accident.

"Welcome to the warehouse, Garrett," Kenny said as they shook hands. "Thank you for helping us out."

Garrett pushed his glasses back up on his nose and pushed his mop of dark hair out of his eyes. "I'm looking forward to working with you guys."

Kenny pointed at the stage where the rest of the guys jammed to get loose. "Are you ready?"

"I'm as ready as I'm gonna be." He held up his guitar case. "I have to admit that I'm a bit nervous."

"I don't blame you," Kenny said. "We're not all that good."

Garrett laughed. He knew everyone because The Barefoot Prophets had opened for Fridays At Five countless times.

After rehearsing for thirty minutes, Jeremy called for a break.

"Hey, Garrett, do you think you could help me out? Some of these songs are kinda difficult to duplicate with just one keyboard player. I know you play keys, in addition to guitar."

"What's the matter, Jeremy?" Jeff Rawlings, the bass player, asked as he grinned. "You've got two hands. Why can't you play two keyboards at once?"

"I can, but the Hammond B-3 is set up over there. My arms can't quite reach that far."

Kenny handed his guitar to Frankie Hanna, and walked over to the Hammond organ.

"I think P.J. and I can handle the guitar parts on the songs where Garrett is needed on keys."

"Where is the princess?" Andy Walker bellowed as he and Charles La Rosse walked up to the stage. "Is she being a diva again?"

Kenny shook his head. "No, but the only way she would

agree to tour with us was if we figured out what songs we needed her vocals and rehearsed them on Wednesdays. What can I say? She got three kids to look after."

"Tell her that she better be ready to work hard on Wednesdays," Andy said and then laughed. "Charles and I are going to grab some burgers. We need a dose of blue cheese. See you guys later."

By May thirtieth, the band's confidence and eagerness to get going soared in anticipation of the June fourth opening night in Dallas. Everyone felt comfortable with Garrett.

"Too bad we can't convince you to join up full-time," Jeremy told Garrett after the last rehearsal.

"I appreciate the thought, but I have to do my own thing. I've got so much music inside me, and I need an outlet for it."

"I understand totally. I've written some stuff that just doesn't fit Fridays," Jeremy said. "I might do a solo project one of these years. If I do, I'll ask you to play."

"Sounds great," Garrett answered.

"We'll see you guys bright and early next Wednesday. We're flying out at ten," Andy Walker reminded everyone. "The crew is leaving on Monday."

Jeff slapped Jeremy on the back. "It sure was thoughtful of whoever runs the SoHam airport to lengthen that runway to accommodate larger jets. We don't ever have to use Midway or O'Hare again."

"We are getting spoiled now. Remember when we first started?" Jeremy asked. "We used the van and a trailer and had to set up our own gear."

"We've come a long way. I could never go back to the old days," Jeff said.

"Hey! I bet we could write a song about that," Kenny mentioned.

The guys looked at Kenny and shook their heads.

"Well, it could be interesting," Kenny replied. "Maybe I'll save it for a solo CD down the road."

Chapter Seventeen

"Do the twins get frequent flyer miles for going on tour?" Liz Hammond asked while she held Kevin in the nursery at church.

"Not this time," Emmy said. "We're using Mr. Robertson's 737. We're not flying commercial at all."

"Must be nice to fly everywhere."

"It's better than taking a bus, but even flying gets old real quick." Emmy sighed as she changed Heather's poopy Pull-Up. "All the airports look the same after a few days. How can you make such a smelly mess? You need to tell me if you have to go potty," Emmy said as she wrinkled her nose. "Go find your father."

Liz let baby Kevin wrap his fingers around her little finger. "Is the band going to Hawaii this time?"

"I wish! At least that airport is different." Emmy heard Kenny talking to Heather and Isabella in the hallway.

"When are you guys leaving? I know it's this week."

"Wednesday morning, so we have three days left at home. Then we will be living out of suitcases most of the week."

"But you will be home for Sunday, right?"

"Yes." Emmy nodded. "No shows on Sunday, Monday or Tuesday. At least we can be home for part of the week."

"Are the other guys bringing their families?" Liz asked as she grinned at Kevin. "You are such a cutie."

"Not every week, but I imagine at some point the plane will be full of kids. I'm the only wife who has to be there every night."

"Tyler said that The Only Hope is playing every Saturday with you guys for the whole summer. Why just on Saturday?" Liz asked.

"The Saturday shows are festivals that run from like noon until whenever. The Only Hope is one of the bands that play. I think they play in the middle of the lineup."

"Are you singing for them?"

"I'm doing three or four songs, but most of the set is just the guys. I'm doing a few songs with Kenny, too. It's like the best of both worlds. I get to sing with my band without having to do a whole show. Then I can do a couple songs with Kenny."

"Do the guys miss having Ryan in the band?" Liz asked as she rocked the baby in her arms.

Emmy thought about Ryan for a few seconds. "I think the guys have adjusted, but I kinda miss him. For the concerts. I didn't mean I miss him personally even though we were friends. Kenny tried to get Jennifer a spot on Saturdays, but she already had a tour booked."

Liz handed Kevin back to Emmy. "I will be praying for you and Kenny."

"Thanks, Liz. We'll be back in time for church, but I don't know how often I will sing with the worship team. I won't be around for rehearsals." Emmy secured Kevin in his carrier, grabbed the diaper bag and walked out into the hall.

"Hey, Emmy! How are you?" Christopher Braun asked as he approached.

Emmy set Kevin and the diaper bag on the floor. She opened her arms for a hug. Christopher hugged her and even lifted her off of her feet.

He set her down and smiled. "You're lookin' good. How have you been?"

"Good. Busy," she said. "This is Kevin Michael."

Christopher leaned down to look at her son. "He still looks adorable." He straightened up. "I've been rather busy the last few months, but I've made it to church when I can."

"That's good. Where is Elena? Is she in her class?"

"Victoria and her parents have her today."

"Kenny's tour starts Wednesday. We're flying everywhere." Emmy caught Christopher up on the latest news.

"I better run. Kenny has the girls somewhere in the building," Emmy said.

"Do you need some help with the baby?"

"Sure! You wanna carry him, and I'll take the diaper bag."

They found Kenny, Heather and Isabella in the music suite talking to Chase and Tyler.

"Here you are." Emmy grabbed Kenny's hand. "I ran into Christopher."

Christopher shook hands with the guys while holding

Kevin's carrier. He smiled at the girls, but they drew back and hid behind Kenny.

"Do you have plans for lunch?" Emmy asked Christopher.

He nodded. "Sorry, but I do. I have to pick up Elena, and we're going to help my parents celebrate their anniversary."

"Some other time perhaps?"

"I'd love that, Emmy."

"Maybe we can have you and Elena over and invite Randy and Vanni, too," Kenny suggested as he took Kevin Michael from Christopher.

"That would be cool," Emmy said.

"I gotta run. Have a safe tour," Christopher said and then left.

"Are you ready to head home, Em?" Kenny asked.

"I'm ready."

Chase and Tyler made noises and funny faces at Kevin trying to make him smile.

Emmy shook her head. "You guys are dorks, too. He's not even three months old."

Carson and Caden were fighting as Diane answered her phone.

"Will you please knock it off? Carson, let Caden play with that truck. Hello."

"Did I call at a bad time, Diane?"

"Hey, Rory. No, the boys were fighting over a toy truck. What's up?"

"Would you be interested in dinner and a movie tomorrow night?"

"I'm not sure I can get a babysitter on such short notice," Diane said. She frowned at Carson and he gave the truck to Caden.

"Maybe we could do something different. Something the boys would enjoy. Do they like Burger Bob's?" Rory asked.

"I've never taken them there. You know, I think I could get a sitter for tomorrow. I'd like to go out. I'm bored of staying at home every night."

"Great! Could I pick you up at six?"

160

"Sure," Diane answered and sighed because Caden lost interest in the toy truck. "I'll be ready."

Rory arrived exactly at six with a bouquet of flowers.

"These are for you, and I bought two toy trucks for the boys. I hope that's okay."

Diane grinned as she took the flowers. "I might keep the trucks and let them have the flowers."

Carson came running into the living room. "Why are you here? I thought you were Aunt Emmy's friend."

"Carson! Be polite, or else I will take away your new toy," Diane warned as she handed him Rory's gift.

"Did you buy this for me?" Carson asked.

"Yes, and I brought some flowers for your mother."

"Thanks for the toy. Mom hates flowers!" Carson said as he ran out of the room.

Rory looked at Diane. "Is that true?"

"No, I once told Carson that I didn't like daisies, so he thinks I don't like any type of flower."

"Is the babysitter here, or do we need to wait?"

"She's here. Let me tell her we're leaving, and I'll be ready to go."

Diane let the babysitter know she was leaving. They walked outside, and Diane saw his car in the driveway. "Is that the same Camaro you had in high school?"

"I can't believe you remember that," he said. "It's not the same one, but it's the same year. A 1993 Z28. I picked it up in St. Louis for a pittance. I restored it and had it painted the same red as my old one."

"I remember a lot of girls in high school would choose their dates because of the car they drove. I did. Glenda Matuzak and I went out with some guys because one of them had a Maxima or something. Actually, it was his parents car now that I think about it."

"I don't think having a Camaro hurt my chances with the girls." He opened the door for Diane and then got in and started the car. "Where would you like to eat?"

161

"Rory, would you be upset if I offered to buy dinner?" Diane asked.

"Why would I let you buy?"

"Has Emmy ever mentioned anything about a trust fund?" Diane asked as she stared at his profile. *You look better now than when we were kids.*

"Not that I recall. Why?"

Diane explained about the trust.

"Holy... I swear I didn't know. Please don't think I did, and I only asked you out because of your money."

"I believe you."

"Yeah, I knew Emmy was loaded, but I just assumed it was because of Kenny."

"So, you'll let me buy. I think I can afford it easier than you. I know you probably make decent money since you're a manager, but... whatever."

"I don't know what to think," he said seriously. "This might just damage my male ego past the point of recovery."

Diane looked at him.

"I'm kidding! You can buy tonight, and if we go out again, I'll buy. I can afford Burger Bob's."

"I haven't been to a Burger Bob's for months. Could we go there?" Diane asked.

"Seriously?"

"Why not? We can pretend we're back in high school."

They spent two hours in the Burger Bob's and didn't make it to the movie.

"Should I take you home now, Diane?" he asked as he checked the time.

"Might as well. I have some ice cream and a store-bought cherry pie at home. Would you care for some?"

"I'd love some," he said with a smile. "I'm used to store-bought pies. Mom never baked a pie in her life. I don't think she knew how to bake anything."

Diane paid the babysitter and got the boys tucked into bed.

"Are you ready for dessert?"

"Sure. Do you have any coffee?" He followed her into the

kitchen. "Stainless steel appliances. Those aren't cheap."

"I'm careful with my money, but it but it is nice not to have to worry about where the money's coming from to pay the bills anymore."

"Do you think you'll ever go back to work?" he asked while looking at the artwork on the fridge. "Nice coloring."

"Not until both boys are in school all day. I'd like to find something. Maybe real estate." She got out the pie and ice cream, pointed and said, "The coffee's in that cabinet."

Rory made the coffee and grabbed two mugs from the tree by the coffee machine. They sat at the kitchen table, ate their dessert and drank a few cups of coffee.

"I should get going, Diane. I've been here for over an hour, and I have to work in the morning."

She walked him to the front door. "I had a pleasant evening. Let's do it again soon." She kissed his cheek.

Rory and Diane began dating once or twice a week and talking on the phone almost every day. They decided to keep their relationship a secret from Emmy and Kenny as long as possible. The boys looked forward to his visits, and he tried not to spoil them. After dating for close to a month, Diane let him spend the night.

"You have to leave before the boys wake up," she told him as they got ready for bed.

"I will."

A week later, Rory helped put the boys to bed.

Carson asked. "Are you going to spend the night like Uncle Fernando used to?"

"That depends on whether your mother invites me to," Rory said as he looked at Diane.

"If you do, I want pancakes for breakfast, please."

"Go to sleep, Carson. I will make breakfast for you in the morning." Diane kissed him on his forehead.

"Yuck, Mom! I'm too big to be kissed in front of Rory."

"Go to sleep."

163

Diane turned off the light on but left the door open partway. "Coffee?"

"Yes, please," Rory said.

They sat on the brown leather couch in the family room and drank their coffee.

"Does Emmy know about us now?" he asked.

"I don't think so. I haven't mentioned anything. I actually haven't seen or talked to her since the tour started. You? I know you email her."

"Nope!"

Diane moved closer. "Do you remember when we were sixteen?"

"That was a long time ago, but I do remember."

"I was messing around with Owen. Which is the biggest regret of my life, by the way."

"Understandable."

"I knew you had a crush on me, but I blew you off because you were my age. I was only interested in older men."

"Diane, you don't have to tell me about your previous boyfriends or anything."

"I wasn't going to." She grinned for a moment becoming serious. "Can I ask you something?"

"You can ask me anything."

"I know you and Emmy used to sneak around and do... stuff. Did you ever do anything I should know about?"

"Are you asking if I ever kissed her?"

"More than that. I don't care if you kissed her or made out."

"Emmy and I were friends. I know I didn't always treat her like a friend, but when we were alone, I did. And to answer your question, I never kissed her back then or anything else."

"You sure?"

"We did some things that are just between me and Em, but I didn't sleep with her like you did with Owen."

Diane sat up straight. "That was a low blow. I already told you I regret that."

"Sorry. Forgive me, please?"

"You're forgiven." *I wonder just what you did with her. I*

know about Grafton's wild drinking parties, and I know you took her to a couple of those.

Rory said, "I think we need to tell Emmy about us before she finds out on her own. I don't want her to be mad at me."

"We don't need her permission to date."

Rory nodded. "I know, but I kinda hinted that we might, and I sorta asked for her permission."

"What did she say?" Diane asked as she snuggled against him.

"She told me not to get you pregnant."

"Did she really?"

"Yup!"

"Wait until I see that little stinker."

Rory confessed in an email to Emmy that he and Diane were dating. Emmy read the email while in San Francisco one night, but kept the information to herself.

"Just remember what I asked," she emailed back.

Rory read her message and thought about how to respond. "I learned my lesson about being careful a long time ago," he whispered as he typed a reply and then added, "Not sure if I should mention this or not, but Diane was asking if we ever let our relationship get physical. I said we were just friends."

Later, Emmy read his email and replied back, "You better not tell her about playing football with those guys that one time. I never should have let them tackle me, but I kinda liked it when you did."

Chapter Eighteen

"Do I smell coffee?" Emmy asked as she rolled over in bed. She stretched her arms over her head and yawned.

"I thought you might like breakfast in bed today since it's a special day." Kenny sat on the edge of the bed with a tray.

"What time is it?"

"A little past eight," he answered.

"Why did you let me sleep so long? I have tons of laundry to do today." She threw back the covers and started to get out of bed.

"Whoa! Hang on there!" He held her down. "I started the laundry already. Did you forget today's your birthday?"

"I know it's my birthday, but so what? It's nothing special. It's just another birthday. They come around every year." She tried to keep a straight face, but eventually grinned. "Thank you, sweetie. What else do you have for me?" She sat up.

Kenny set the tray on the nightstand. "Coffee, and one of those chocolate muffins you like so much and your favorite flavor of yogurt. Pina Colada."

"Um-mm! I know those muffins are full of bad stuff, but I do like them."

Kenny peeled the paper wrapper off of the muffin and held it up so she could take a bite.

"Are you going to feed me?" she asked and then giggled.

Mary walked into the bedroom carrying Kevin. Heather and Isabella scampered over to the bed and used the cedar chest to climb onto it.

"Daddy feeding Mommy!" Isabella pointed.

"Come here, my sweet babies." Emmy held out her arms.

"Do you know what today is, girls?" Kenny asked.

Isabella nodded. "Uh-huh."

"Mommy's birt-day!" Heather said. "I want some cake."

"This is a muffin," Emmy explained as she let Heather, and then Isabella, have a bite.

"Birt-day cake," Heather said and took another bite.

"Happy birthday, Emmy." Mary moved to the opposite side

166

of the bed and placed Kevin on his belly close to Emmy.

He lifted his head and smiled at his mother.

"Good morning, my little man," Emmy cooed. "Are you hungry?"

Kevin made little laughing noises at Emmy and then rolled over onto his back.

"Hey! Did you see that?" Kenny pointed. "I've never seen him roll over before."

"He's done it a few times from his stomach onto his back, but I haven't seen him flip from his back to his belly." Emmy picked him up and positioned him. "We can both have something to drink. Would you hand me the coffee, please?" Emmy asked Kenny.

"It's still kinda hot," he warned.

"It's supposed to be hot, silly."

Heather and Isabella lost interest in being on the bed as soon as the muffin disappeared. They scrambled down and ran out into the hallway.

"I'll entertain them." Mary watched the girls turn down the hallway toward their playroom.

"Thanks, Mary." Kenny opened the yogurt and spoon fed Emmy.

She grinned at Kenny. "I could get used to this kind of treatment."

"Yeah, well, don't expect it every day."

She finished the yogurt and coffee and moved her legs over the side of the bed, while Kevin contentedly nursed. "I'll take care of Kevin if you sort the laundry for me. I need clean clothes for tomorrow." She finished the coffee and handed the mug to Kenny.

"Sorted, huh? Do all the different colors need to go in a separate pile?" Kenny took the tray and headed out of the room.

"You're such a dork." Emmy rolled her eyes. "Didn't your mother ever show you how to do laundry?"

"You know I'm joking. I've been doing my own laundry for years." He blew her a kiss. "Happy birthday, Em."

Later, Emmy walked down the hall and peeked into the playroom at the girls on her way to the laundry room. She stopped in the doorway and asked, "How are you doing with the laundry?"

"Three more loads to go, I think." He motioned to the piles of clothes on the heated ceramic floor. "Maybe we should buy a bigger washer and dryer for up here? We've got the room."

"No way! These cost us a fortune. We'll keep using them and the ones downstairs until they self-destruct." She picked up one of her tops and moved it to the pile of her underwear. "You need to use the delicate cycle for this pile. Would you mind if I go for a run?"

"Go ahead, but be careful on the trails. It rained last night."

Kenny was putting clothes into the washer in the downstairs laundry room when Emmy returned from her run. He looked at her and laughed. "What happened to you?"

"I slipped on that big hill past Mr. Robertson's place and slid on my butt to the bottom," she explained. "And don't you dare tell me you warned me."

"Take those clothes off, and I'll put them in with this load."

She removed her t-shirt and shorts. "I have to take another shower."

"Tony called."

"What did he want?" Emmy asked.

"He said he was coming over to return the pack-and-play they borrowed."

"When?"

"Now, I guess." Kenny shrugged.

"Crap! I don't want him to see me like this," Emmy said and then dashed out of the room and upstairs.

By the time Tony arrived with the pack-and-play and Noemi, Emmy had showered and gotten dressed again.

"Happy birthday, brat."

"Thanks."

He grinned.

"What's so funny?"

"Did you have a good run?" Tony asked and then laughed. "Kenny told me what happened. That would have been fun to see."

"You've seen me in my underwear before, creep!"

"What? No, I meant sliding down the hill." Tony saw the

168

package of muffins on the island.

"Then never mind, and you can have one."

"Did you ever think about what could happen if you fall and break a leg? You could be lost out there, and we wouldn't know where you were," Tony said and then took a large bite out of the muffin.

"Those aren't supposed to be bite-sized."

"I know."

"I know you guys would look for me if I didn't come back." Emmy bit her lip. "You would, wouldn't you?"

Tony swallowed the rest of the muffin. "I suppose we would after a few days."

"You're a creep. Are you having a party for Peter's birthday?"

"Yeah, but not until Saturday. Can you believe he's going to be five already?" Tony said while eyeing another muffin.

"He's getting so big," Emmy said and then shook her head. "Save some food for us, you pig."

Todd Delaney moved along with the 30,000 other people filing into Jay Rosenbaum Stadium in Omaha, Nebraska, on Saturday. He listened to the comments of excited fans and shook his head. "These people aren't anything special," he muttered under his breath. He tugged his baseball cap lower over his eyes and shuffled along. Once inside the stadium, he slowly worked his way as close to the stage as he could manage. "I don't know if I will be able to stand here all day, but I want to see Colasanti again." He noticed a couple of people staring at him and smiled.

"Who are you here to see?" a high-school-age boy with a severe acne problem asked.

The girl with long, dishwater blonde hair next to him said, "We're hear to see Emmy Colasanti and her band."

Delaney stared at them for several seconds and then responded, "Me, too. I actually went to high school with her."

"Yeah, right," the boy said as he rolled his eyes. "Are we supposed to believe that?"

"It's true. We went to Roosevelt High in South Hampshire.

169

We were pretty tight for a while, but then she dumped me."

They looked at Todd and tilted their heads.

"I'm not making it up," Todd said. "I lived in the same neighborhood and we used to walk to school together."

"Does she know you're here?" the girl asked.

"No, we haven't seen each other for several years. I'm hoping to stay close enough to get her attention. She might let me come backstage."

"Do you live here in Omaha?"

Todd shook his head. "I'm here working on a construction project. After it's finished, I'll head back to SoHam. I own a company there."

By the time Emmy and The Only Hope Band hit the stage three hours later, Delaney had worked his way to the barrier separating the crowd from the stage. He watched Emmy from his position to her right. "How can a slut like you become a big deal?" he whispered to no one. "Yeah, maybe you can sing, but you wouldn't be anything if it wasn't for your rock star husband." He watched the entire set and then worked his way through the crowd to a refreshment stand. He walked through the crowd for another hour and then left the stadium. "I'm going back to Texas," he muttered. "I know I can always find a job there while my brother and I wait for a big score to come along."

The members of Fridays At Five waved to the crowd a final time and walked off the stage.

Kenny saw Emmy and asked, "Are you ready to head home?"

"Yes, I can't wait to sleep in our bed."

They landed in SoHam three hours later about the same time Todd Delaney was leaving Omaha for the drive to Texas.

Chapter Nineteen

"Is John meeting you here, or what?" Sloane asked Tony while she waited for her coffee to brew.

Tony shook his head. "I'm suppose to meet him at the end of his driveway. We're going to run on the street first and then head into the woods."

"Don't get lost." Sloane touched Tony's bicep and smiled.

"That sounds like something the brat would say," Tony said as he grabbed a bottle of water from the fridge. "No wait. She would tell me to get lost in the woods."

"You're right about that. I'm surprised Emmy hasn't been running with you guys on the days she's home."

"She wouldn't be able to keep up. We're stepping up our pace. If we were taking it easy, she might keep up."

"I suppose she has more important things to do than exercise with you guys."

Tony checked the time on the microwave. "I gotta run. See you soon." He kissed Sloane and rubbed her lower back. "I should mow the yard this afternoon."

"I promised Peter and Dotty they could go swimming at Emmy's house later."

Tony paused and asked, "Should we go ahead and put in our own pool? Does Emmy ever complain about all of us using their pool?"

"She never complains, but I wouldn't mind having our own one of these days," Sloane answered.

"I'll look into the costs before I head to Olivet."

Tony and John would report to the campus of Olivet Nazarene University for the opening of the Chicago Bears training camp in one week.

John waved when he spotted Tony jogging down the winding driveway. "I was about ready to wake you up."

"I've been up since six," Tony said. "Benjamin was fussing, so I got up and brought him back to bed with us."

"Kristen has been letting Grace sleep in our room," John said as he stretched out his legs.

"She will be spoiled if you keep doing that. How's the knee doing?"

John straightened up, laughed and asked, "The knee feels better than ever. Do you mean Gracie or Kristen?"

"Both, I guess. I know Gracie will be spoiled. Sloane is pretty adamant about not letting the kids sleep with us. Sometimes Dotty will sneak downstairs and sleep with Mama."

After stretching for several minutes, the guys took off at a moderate pace.

"Hey, I was talking to my brother Kirk the other day, and I mentioned how all the kids call your mother Mama. He thought it was kinda strange nobody calls her grandma or something like that."

Tony replied, "I asked her once if she wanted the grandkids to call her something different, but she didn't mind being called Mama. It's weird. All the kids, mine, yours, Emmy and Kenny's, I mean, call us uncle. My kids don't call me uncle."

"I get it," John said and then laughed. "They will grow up thinking they're all related."

"Emmy's girls call Kenny's parents Gra and Me-maw, but I think they call Emmy's mom Grandma. I think they called her dad grandpa," Tony said. "It's cute."

"I called my grandparents different names," John added.

"When I was a kid, I called my maternal grandparents Nonna and Nonno. They spoke Italian to each other, and I picked it up."

"What about your father's parents?"

Tony shrugged and said, "I don't remember my other grandfather at all. Mama says I met him, but I don't remember it. He died before my father."

"Was he old?" John asked as they passed Mr. Robertson's house.

"He was eighty, I think. Nonna Bertucci died when I was in first grade. I kinda remember her."

"My grandfathers died back in the nineties, but my grandmothers are still alive. I don't get to see them very often since they live in Florida now."

"Other than my father, my relatives have lived long lives," Tony said.

"I suppose we have good genes. Are you ready to do some sprints?" John asked.

"Loser buys breakfast?" Tony asked.

"Sure," John said as he took off.

An hour later Tony walked into the kitchen.

Mama turned around holding a spatula and asked, "Why are you so filthy?" Then she flipped over the pancakes.

"We were running through the woods," he answered. He looked at his muddy shoes and saw the caked mud on his legs. "Maybe I should use the hose and clean up before Sloane sees me."

"Can I run through the mud with you, Papa?" Peter asked.

"Maybe not, Peter."

Sloane entered the kitchen and placed Benjamin in a highchair. "He might still be hungry." She looked at Tony, sighed, shook her head, turned around and walked out of the kitchen.

"I'm going to clean up outside," Tony said.

Peter and Dotty giggled.

"Papa is in trouble," Peter said and Dotty nodded.

"See what happens when you play in the mud," Mama said as she stacked the pancakes on a platter. "Who's hungry?"

She helped Noemi Claire, who was not quite two and a half years old, by adding butter and syrup to her pancake and then cutting it into smaller pieces.

"We can do our own, Mama," Dotty said.

"Okay, but try not to make a mess," Mama cautioned.

"I'll be back in a minute," Tony said.

"Would you like some pancakes, too?" Mama asked.

"Yes, please."

"You can have some if you don't make a mess," Peter said. Then he and Dotty giggled again.

Later that afternoon Tony finished mowing the yard, put his riding mower in the shed and walked up the steps to the deck. Peter and Dotty were playing in the backyard. Ben and Noemi were taking naps. Sloane was sitting on the deck enjoying the sunshine.

"Have you seen Scout?" Sloane asked.

"I saw her earlier," Tony answered as he wiped the sweat from his face. "Why?"

"She usually stays close to the kids if they're outside." Sloane looked around. "There she is."

A moment later Peter ran up the steps onto the deck, pointed at Scout and said, "Scout smells funny. She stinks really bad. Come and see."

Tony followed Peter and immediately realized what had happened. "She's been skunked again!" he shouted. "Tell Mama to fix some of that vinegar stuff and get out the tomato juice."

"Don't let her in the house or on the deck," Sloane hollered. "Peter, Dotty, do not pet Scout until your father cleans her up."

Tony shrugged. "Why do I have to clean her? I did it the last time."

Sloane smiled and said, "Yes, and you did a great job. Keep her away from the kids, and I'll fix the vinegar and water. I'm not sure if we have any tomato juice."

"Fine," Tony said in resignation. "See if we have any bones left from those steaks. I read where that helps eliminate skunk breath."

"Do we have skunk breath?" Peter asked.

Tony shook his head.

Thirty minutes later, Tony finished brushing Scout. "There! Now be a good doggy and leave the skunks alone. You can have this bone if you promise to be a good girl."

Scout barked twice and wagged her tail.

"Can we chew on bones, Papa?" Dotty asked. "That would be more fun than brushing our teeth."

Tony smiled, picked up Dotty and held her close. "Have I told you how much I love you lately?"

"I wuv you, too, Papa," Dotty said as she kissed Tony's cheek. "Can we go swimming now? I want to tell Heather and Isabella about the skunk."

"I suppose so," Tony said. "Maybe Scout can chase all the skunks over to Emmy's house."

174

Chapter Twenty

"Man, it's humid today. We'll probably get a thunderstorm later," Jeff said as he removed his baseball cap and ran a hand through his sweaty hair. "What are you working on?"

Kenny sat on the black leather couch in the control room of Steward Music Group's Studio Two with a clipboard and a pen. "I'm trying to come up with the title for this thing. It has to have the word chronicles in it."

"Aren't we going to call it *Street Chronicles*?"

Dave entered the room and caught the last part of the conversation. "I don't think we should use the word street in the title of this CD. What about city?"

"I thought about that, but I also thought about this." He stood up and showed the clipboard to the guys.

"Urban Chronicles. I like it," Jeff said.

Jeremy and P.J. arrived and the guys voted to call the new CD *Urban Chronicles*.

"Okay, now that we've settled that, I have two new songs to go over," Kenny said.

"Do we need more songs?" Jeremy asked.

"Don't we have thirteen tracks already?" P.J. asked.

Kenny nodded. "We do, but these tracks fit the theme of the CD. I wrote them last year, but needed to tighten up the lyrics."

"Let's listen to them and see what we think," Jeff said.

Kenny opened a case and removed a Martin acoustic guitar. He played "Stand By The Power" first and then played "How Can You Live."

"Those are really good," Dave said. "We have to add them to the CD."

"I agree," Jeremy said. "Can we add them without removing any of the other tracks?"

Will Consoli spun around in his chair and answered, "It's not like the old days when the songs had to fit on one side of an LP. We can fit up to eighty minutes on a disc."

"I don't want to drop any of the tracks," Kenny said as he shook his head. "I think they're all strong."

"Then let's get them recorded. I want to be finished recording by the time we leave on Wednesday," Jeff said. He stood up and entered the large room where the band recorded.

Eight hours later the guys sat in the control room and listened to both new tracks.

"What do you think?" Will asked.

"We could polish them up a bit tomorrow, but I think they're almost there," Kenny said.

"You're home early," Emmy said the next afternoon as she read the sales ads from the *SoHam Herald*. "I thought you might be there until eight or nine."

Kenny hung up his keys, set his wallet on the desk, walked over to the kitchen island where Emmy sat and rubbed her back. "Why would you think that, Em? Don't you know we are professional musicians?" He snapped his fingers and said, "We can finish a couple of tracks just like that."

Emmy slapped her forehead, sighed and said, "My bad. I forgot you guys are a rock band. The tracks don't have to be good. They just have to be loud."

"You're so funny. Where are the girls?"

"They better be taking naps."

"Is Mary here?"

"Upstairs." Emmy pointed without taking her eyes off of the Sainsbury's sale ad. "Should I run to the store? Sainsbury's has hamburger on sale if you buy five pounds or more. It's the good stuff with less fat."

"You shouldn't make a special trip just for that. We're leaving tomorrow," Kenny said while he walked around the island to the fridge and pulled out a bottle of water.

Emmy smiled and said, "That is so sweet, Kenny. You're volunteering to go so I can stay home and finish the laundry."

Kenny sighed and then shrugged. "You set me up."

Chapter Twenty-One

Ronald Delaney opened the door to his one-bedroom apartment, tossed his keys on the counter of his small galley kitchen, stepped into the living room and saw his brother sleeping on the couch. He shook his head, walked over and kicked the threadbare couch. "Get your ass up. It's four o'clock. Have you been sleeping all day? I've been slaving away hauling dirt back and forth in a wheelbarrow. You better not expect to stay here much longer if you don't get a job."

Todd shrugged his shoulders to get the kinks out, turned over and stared at his older brother. "I told you I had a line on a construction job. Chill out. This is Saturday."

"Yeah, some of us who live in the real world have to work on Saturday."

"Are you gonna cook tonight?"

"If you want to eat, you can cook your own supper," Ronald said. He walked back into the kitchen, opened the fridge and grabbed a beer. He stood there, finished it and opened a second one.

Todd stood up and twisted his head back and forth. "My neck is still sore from the punch I took at the bar two nights ago."

Ronald peeked around the corner. "You're lucky I was there to back you up. That guy had a hundred pounds on you, and it wasn't fat."

"I could have handled him."

Ronald snorted and walked up to the couch. "God! Will you take a shower already. I'm gonna have to buy another couch when you leave."

"Yeah, like this one didn't reek before I arrived," Todd said and then shuffled off to the bathroom. He emptied his bladder without bothering to close the door.

Ronald didn't even notice.

Todd took off his white t-shirt, sniffed it and tossed it at his duffel bag. He grabbed another t-shirt, smelled it, decided it was clean enough and put it on. "Did you hear anything from your buddy about that shipment of laptops and gear?"

"Yeah, it's coming in Monday night. He said the driver just sits in the cab while the grunts unload the trailer. We can made sure a load of them get lost in transit if you get my drift."

"Yeah, then how are we gonna unload the crap? Did you ever think about that?" Todd asked as he grabbed a beer.

"I know a guy who will give us decent money, and he knows not to ask any questions."

"Do you have anything we can carry just in case we need to convince someone we mean business?" Todd pointed a finger at Ronald and pulled the trigger.

"This is Texas."

Two days later, Ronald and Todd drove away from the warehouse in Ronald's battered, half-rusted-out 1996 Ford F-150.

"Did I tell you it would be easy or not?" Ronald said.

Todd glanced over his shoulder and stuffed his handgun down the back of his jeans. "Just don't get pulled over for speeding until we can dump this stuff off with your fence."

"We'll be there in ten minutes."

An hour later Ronald counted the cash again and handed half of it to Todd. "Don't blow it all on coke and booze."

"Yeah, looks who's talking," Todd said as he counted the wad of bills.

"And another thing, if you don't have a job before the end of the week, you're outta here. I don't care where you go as long as it ain't my apartment. I ain't responsible for you."

"I haven't needed you to take care of me since we were kids," Todd said. "Can we stop and get more beer. I drank the last one for breakfast."

Ronald returned home on Friday afternoon, saw Todd sitting on the couch drinking a beer and yelled, "Did you leave the apartment today? You were supposed to go down to that bar and see about the janitor job. Did you?"

Todd shook his head. "Hell no! I ain't busting my back for no scumbag redneck for minimum wage. I got a line on a construction job that pays cash."

"That's what you said when you got here. I ain't running no charity boarding house here, Todd. This was your last chance. I want you out of here by the morning."

"Fine! If that's how you feel, I'm gone. I ain't staying where I'm not wanted."

"Hey, little brother, that guilt-trip stuff might have worked ten years ago, but it ain't working now. I gave you almost a month, and you haven't contributed a wooden nickel to the upkeep of this place."

Todd laughed as he looked around. "I wouldn't pay a nickel to rent this dump."

Ronald walked over to the corner of the living room, picked up Todd's duffel bag, walked up to Todd and shoved the bag in his chest. "You don't have to. Get out now!" Ronald hooked his thumb at the door. "Come back and see me sometime when you can't stay more than ten minutes."

Todd started to argue, but saw the look in his brother's eyes and kept his mouth shut.

"You can have a beer for the road," Ronald said.

"Yeah, thanks for nothin'."

Todd stuffed the rest of his clothes in the bag, grabbed his keys and walked over to the door. He paused and faced Ronald. "Where am I supposed to go?"

"Buy a map, follow the directions to hell, turn left and keep going."

Chapter Twenty-Two

"I'm sorry to bother you on a Sunday, but are you busy?" Rory asked over the phone around five in the afternoon.

"I'm not busy. Kenny and the girls are visiting his parents. Kevin Michael is taking a nap with Mary. I was about to make myself a sandwich and a garden salad. Rather boring."

Rory hesitated, but then asked, "Would you be able to get away and meet me to talk? We could grab dinner somewhere if you want."

Emmy bit her lip as she thought about his offer. "Is there something serious you need to talk about?"

"It's pretty serious, and since you're my only friend..."

"You have other friends, Rory."

"I know a few guys, but I would never talk to them about important stuff. If you can't, that's okay."

"I will need to be back by seven thirty or eight."

Rory sighed and asked, "Where should we meet?"

"I'll pick you up at your place, and we can decide."

Emmy let Mary know she would be gone and then left.

Rory answered the door and smiled. "That was quick."

Emmy walked past him into the apartment, tossed her purse and keys on the end table next to the couch and sat down. "I'm a fast driver. Tell me what's going on."

"Should we go out to eat first?" he asked as he turned off the TV.

"I haven't had a decent pizza in ages. Could we order one and have it delivered?"

"I suppose. Is that your way of tactfully saying you don't want to be seen with me?"

"It's not that, but sometimes people recognize me now. I'd rather avoid having our picture on the front of some tabloid in the Walmart."

"Okay, I usually order from Kerry Lynn's Pizza. Is that all right with you?"

"Of course. We went there once a long time ago with some of your friends."

"You actually remember that?" he asked while looking for a menu in the kitchen.

"Yeah. I remember sneaking out and climbing in the window around midnight," Emmy said with a grin.

"Yeah, I remember helping you climb in. Was Diane home, or was she with Owen?"

"She wasn't home, but she was probably with Craig. What kind of toppings do you like?"

They decided on the toppings and added mozzarella sticks to the order. Rory called it in and offered to pay for it.

"I'll let you, since you invited me over here."

"Should I ask if Kenny knows where you are?" Rory asked as he pulled some cash from his wallet.

"I texted him, but haven't heard back. I told Mary I would be home by eight, and I have my cell phone if she needs to call."

"How is Kevin Michael doing?" Rory asked. He sat on the other end of the couch and looked at Emmy.

"You don't have to be afraid. I'm not going to kiss you again," she said. "Kevin Michael is doing great. He's such an easy going baby. He doesn't fuss a lot and is always happy."

"That's good. How old are the twins now?"

"They're over two and a half. You know that. Are you trying to avoid talking about whatever's on your mind?"

He chuckled but then nodded.

"You can talk to me, Rory. We were always able to talk to each other in the old days."

"You make it sound like it was a hundred years ago, Em. It wasn't all that long ago."

"Not if you're talking in geological terms."

He tilted his head and stared at her.

She waved her hands and said, "If the Earth is billions of years old... never mind. What's going on between you and Diane? Is the..."

"I'm not talking to you about our sex life," Rory said emphatically.

"We don't have a sex life," she said and then giggled.

Rory stood up and paced back and forth in the fifteen-foot-
181

wide room. "You know what I mean."

"Sit down and talk to me." Emmy patted the couch and turned sideways with her feet under her. "Do you still like my hair this short?"

"It looks good on you. Makes you look more mature," he said and then sat down.

"Good answer. I'm thirsty. Got any beer?"

"Yeah, do you want one?" He stood up again and walked around the couch into the open kitchen. "I need one."

"I'd rather have water or a Dr Pepper."

"I've got both."

"Water, please."

Rory brought the water and a beer.

"How are you getting along with the boys?" Emmy asked and then took a drink of water. "I'm assuming they know you spend the night."

"I get along great with them. Caden was a little shy at first, but now he's opened up. Carson is more outgoing. He doesn't see it as a big deal that I'm there."

"Do they ever talk about Craig?"

"Not much and I never bring him up."

"Does Diane put him down in front of the boys?"

Rory shook his head. "She's pretty good about that. If I was her, I would be talking crap about him."

"You don't talk about your ex very much," Emmy said as she adjusted her feet.

"You got that right," Rory said. "Next subject."

"Are you gonna ask Diane to live with you?"

Rory looked around the apartment and chuckled.

Emmy reached out and smacked his leg. "I meant are you gonna move in together. Most likely at her house."

"We haven't talked about it. I'm pretty sure that would be a mistake. I'm sure we are better off with our own place."

The pizza arrived, and Rory set it on the coffee table.

"Do you need to say a prayer?" he asked.

"I can if you don't mind."

"Go ahead."

"Lord, thank you for this food, and please help Rory with whatever's on his mind, since he won't tell me. Amen."

Rory stared at her for a moment. "Is that your way of putting me on a guilt-trip?"

"Is it working?"

He shook his head as he grabbed a slice of pizza.

"It was worth a shot." Emmy opened the mozzarella sticks. "I like their dipping sauce."

A few minutes later Rory asked, "Are you finished, Em?"

"Do you want the last mozzarella stick?"

"You can have it," he said as he waved. "I'll save the rest of the pizza for breakfast."

He put the three slices in the fridge. "You thirsty again?"

"Could I have a Dr Pepper?"

"Sure." Rory grabbed the pop and another beer.

"Thanks."

He sat down, took a long drink and placed the bottle on the table. "Can you see me and Diane together ten years from now?"

"Can you?"

"Don't go playing shrink with me," he said with a shake of his head. "Answer the question."

She took a deep breath before answering, "Sorry, but I can't."

"Me either. It's too bad because I really adore the boys."

"Give it some time. Diane isn't the easiest person to live with."

Rory laughed for a moment and then said, "I can't believe you're actually telling me to keep working on our relationship. We aren't married."

"Hey! I'm not saying I think it's all right to live together or even to fool around, but it happens."

Rory glanced at the clock. "I don't want to kick you out, but it is almost eight."

Emmy stood up. "Did we get anything accomplished? Did we even talk about whatever was on your mind?"

"Yeah, we did, Em."

He hugged her and she left.

183

"You made it back," Kenny said as Emmy walked into the kitchen. "How did things go with Rory?"

Emmy set her purse and keys on the desk, walked up to Kenny, took his bottle of water and drank deeply. She handed back the bottle and answered, "I think he and Diane are having some issues in their relationship."

"What kind of issues?" Kenny asked and then finished his water. "Did you discuss their lovelife?"

Emmy shrugged and made a face. "Not specifically. Not details or anything. Let's sit in the family room to talk."

Kenny followed her down the long, wide hallway, and they sat in their leather recliners facing the fireplace.

Emmy put her feet under her and said, "Rory really cares for the boys, but I'm not sure he and Diane are meant to be together."

"Why do you think that, Em?"

She leaned back against her recliner and closed her eyes for a moment. "Oil and water."

"Do you mean oil and vinegar like a salad dressing?" Kenny asked while grinning.

She shook her head. "No, oil and vinegar go together. They mix well. Oil and water never mix. You know what I mean?"

"I understand."

"He asked if I could see them together in ten years, and I said I couldn't."

"Can you see us together in ten years?"

She leaned over and touched his arm. "I can see us together when we're eighty-years-old and half blind."

Chapter Twenty-Three

"I still think you need to tell Kenny about this," Elly Colwell said to her husband while on the way to see Dr. Samid Ekanayaka.

Carter Colwell turned into the parking lot and parked their 2005 Honda CR-V next to an older Chevrolet sedan. "I'm not going to mention anything unless I have to. For all we know this mole could be nothing."

She rubbed his shoulder and said, "Or it could be something serious."

"I prefer to look on the bright side," he said.

They got out of the car and peered at the upper floors of St. Bart's.

"Emmy will be upset if she finds out you've been hiding this. She will say she could have been praying about it," Elly said as they walked into the three-story medical building.

"Which floor are we going to?" Carter asked.

"Third floor," she replied.

They rode the elevator to the third floor and entered the office.

"May I help you?" the receptionist asked with a cheery smile.

"My husband has an appointment. His name is Carter Colwell."

The receptionist checked her computer and said, "Yes, I need you to fill out some forms, please."

Elly took the clipboard and they sat in two comfortable chairs facing the large TV mounted on the wall.

"I'll fill these out since you conveniently left your reading glasses in the car."

She spent a few minutes filling out the forms while he watched a video about skin cancer and new methods of prevention and treatment.

"Do you know of anyone in your family who has ever had skin cancer?" she asked.

He rubbed his jaw for a moment before answering, "I think

185

my grandfather Colwell died from some form of cancer, but I don't remember any specific details. I can't think of anyone else who had cancer."

"Your parents had heart issues, but they lived into their eighties," she said while checking a few boxes. "What about strokes?"

"Parker had a mild stroke last year, but he's doing pretty good," Carter said about the middle of the three Colwell brothers.

"That reminds me. I heard from Thomas last week. He and Elsa are going to Ireland for a vacation. He wanted to know if we were interested."

"Are we?" Carter asked. "Are Parker and Clara going?"

"He didn't say, but I imagine they will be."

"When?"

Elly ticked some more boxes on the form. "This fall. He didn't give a more specific time. No one has ever had a mental illness in your family, right?"

"Not unless you count my great-great-great grandfather's desire to become a gold prospector."

"Lots of people did that back in the day."

Carter laughed and shook his head. He said, "Not in the swamps of Virginia. He claimed he had a secret treasure map and didn't want to go all the way to California or Colorado."

"I'll check no, but only because there's no option for maybe."

Fifteen minutes later Dr. Ekanayaka was peering closely at the dark mole on the back of Carter's right shoulder. "I don't think it's anything for concern, but I want to take a biopsy just to be sure."

"Do it," Elly said with authority.

Dr. Ekanayaka nodded.

"What about that thing on his forehead?" Elly asked later after the biopsy procedure. "It's gotten a big larger."

Dr. Ekanayaka took a look using his lens. "This is nothing serious. It can be removed using cryotherapy."

"What is that?" Carter asked as he flexed his shoulder.

The doctor shrugged and said, "I freeze it and it falls off in

186

a few days. Quick and painless. I can do it now."

"That wasn't so bad, was it?" Elly asked a short time later as Carter buttoned his shirt.

"Better than going to the urologist," he said with a grin.

"We will call you with the lab results," Dr. Ekanayaka said. "If it's benign, there is no need for a follow-up."

"And if it's not?"

"We will cross that bridge when we get to the river," he said and then left the examining room.

"Do you want to grab lunch?" Elly asked while they walked out to the CR-V.

"We haven't been to Darby's lately. Would you like a hot dog and a root beer?"

She smiled and took his arm. "Can we sit in Kenny and Emmy's booth?"

"If it's free."

"Will you share some fries with me?"

"I think I can afford two orders of fries," he said and then kissed her.

"Who was on the phone," Carter asked as he sat in his recliner in the living room reading a book on Friday.

"The doctor's office. The biopsy was negative," Elly answered.

"Negative, huh? Is that good or band?"

She smiled and said, "It's good news. It means you don't have skin cancer."

"Good. Then we don't have to say anything to Kenny and Emmy," he said and then resumed his reading.

Chapter Twenty-Four

The summer tour flew by, at least Emmy thought so.

"I can't believe we're flying back to SoHam for the last show already," Emmy whispered to Kenny as she nursed Kevin. "I've never been on a tour where time passed so quickly."

"You've never been on a tour where we flew everywhere," Kenny said as he glanced over at Heather and Isabella, who slept peacefully. "We slept in hotels every night, so that makes it easier."

"It must have cost the organization a fortune to fly and stay in hotels."

"You know Mr. Robertson let us use the jet for nothing, right?"

She nodded.

"We had to pay the expenses, of course."

"The ticket prices have gone up a lot over the last few years."

"Tell me! Part of it is just the economy. Promoters need to make a profit. The price of everything is so high. The merchandise is more expensive. I remember going to concerts when I was a kid and buying a t-shirt for five bucks. Now they're twenty-five for the cheap ones."

Emmy grinned and said, "I remember some of those concerts and the t-shirts."

"Yeah, you would wear them until the writing would fade away to nothing," Kenny said.

"So, you guys are still making a profit, huh?"

"Yeah, Every place was sold out."

"What about the fall?" Emmy asked as she moved Kevin to her shoulder.

"Smaller indoor venues. Tickets have been going fast."

They landed in SoHam and were driven home to catch a few hours of sleep.

"We need to get to the stadium early, Em," Kenny said as he stretched his arms over his head.

"What time?"

"We have to be there at three. We have to do the meet and greet, and a couple of interviews with local radio people."

"I have to make sure I leave enough breast milk for Kevin Michael."

"We should give Mary a large bonus. She does much more than she should," Kenny said.

Emmy grinned. "I already did."

Kenny had purchased a hundred tickets for friends. He and Emmy greeted many of them backstage. Emmy shielded her eyes against the sun and eventually spotted Rory and Christopher.

She headed toward Christopher, Randy and Vanni first. "Hey, guys! Are you enjoying the show so far?"

"Yeah, Em, that first band really rocked," Randy said.

"You mean the two brothers who play acoustic guitars and sing folk songs?" Emmy asked.

"Yeah! One of them even broke a string," Randy said and then laughed. "What time does The Only Hope go on?"

"Not until seven."

"Oh, too bad. Vanni and I have to get home to take care of Stephen," Randy teased. "We won't get to see you sing."

Emmy looked up at Christopher. "You better stay."

"We're staying, Emmy," Christopher assured her.

"The Only Hope is getting better and better," Randy said before he led Vanni away. "Will you be at church tomorrow?" Randy asked over his shoulder.

"I'll be there." Emmy smiled and looked up at Christopher. "Are you here by yourself?"

"If you don't count Randy and the other thirty thousand some people," he said as he grinned.

"That's not what I meant." She bit her lip.

"I didn't bring a date, Em."

"Did you ask anyone?"

"Nah. I didn't bother."

"There are plenty of single women at church."

"I know, and someday I will find the right one for me."

She squeezed his arm. "I keep praying that you will."

"Thanks, Emmy. I'll see you tomorrow."

She turned, spotted Rory in the same place she saw him earlier and walked over to him.

"Hi, Emmy, is this the right spot?" He looked up at the large sign listing the years of the state championships won by the St. Raymond's Crusaders football team.

"I figured it would be easy to find you here."

Rory looked around. "Where's Kenny?"

"He and the guys are doing radio interviews at the moment."

"I saw Kristen and John earlier. Is Tony here?" Rory asked.

"He and Sloane aren't here yet, but they're coming later. Sloane's parents are visiting."

They sat on a wooden bench to continue talking.

"How are things going between you and Diane? Any better than three weeks ago when we talked? Or shouldn't I ask?"

He waited a few seconds before replying. "Pretty good. In fact, not bad at all."

"Tell me everything!" Emmy's eyes sparkled. "And wipe that silly smile off your face. I don't need details of your sex life."

"Everything?"

"As much as you can."

"The boys are getting to know me. I played catch with Carson the other day. He's not very coordinated, but he's getting better. Caden was afraid of me at first, but he's coming along."

"They were both shy with Fernando at first, too," Emmy said. "Are you and Diane getting along all right? I don't mean to be nosy, but I care about you guys."

"We actually are. There is an attraction between us that surprised me."

"Get out!" Emmy poked his arm. "You have always been attracted to her."

"She never felt the same."

"Does she now?"

"You could say that."

"You better be careful," She poked him in the side. "Have you talked about moving in together?"

He shook his head. "We haven't talked about that anymore.

190

I can't see it happening anytime soon."

"That's probably for the best," she said.

He looked into her eyes. *Is there still an attraction between us, Em? I know we can never act on it if there is, but I think we still have feelings for each other.*

"I should get back, Rory. Do you need a ride home later?" She bit her lip as soon as the words left her mouth.

"Thanks, but Diane and the boys are coming for your set and the Fridays show. I caught a bus here."

She stood up faced him and said, "Let me know if she doesn't make it here for some reason. You can text me if you need a ride. I'm leaving as soon as Kenny and I do 'I Will Be True To You.' I want to beat the traffic out of here."

He touched her hand tenderly and replied, "I'll let you know one way or the other, Em. Break a leg."

"Why?"

"Is that what you're supposed to say?"

"Maybe back in the old days." She laughed and waved. "Later, Rory!"

"I still like coming back here and doing one last show to finish the tours." Kenny said thirty minutes later. He held Emmy's hand while they munched on veggies in the crowded room under the east side of the stadium.

"I never get tired of performing here." Emmy crunched a baby carrot as she glanced at the peeling paint on one of the concrete walls.

"Performing?" Kenny tilted his head. "You never used to think of singing in that way."

"I know. I still do it to share my faith, but I know people expect a performance." She shrugged. "I guess I can do both."

"I've seen you 'perform.' I'd even pay money to watch you."

"You're goofy," she said and then giggled.

"No, I really would." He nodded.

"I could sing for you later."

"What do you mean?"

"After the show when we're getting ready for bed."

"I like that idea," he replied while raising his eyebrows.

191

"What are you guys talking about?" Andy overheard part of their conversation. "Or shouldn't I ask?"

"Nothing, cuz!" Emmy put a finger to her mouth.

"I know you better than that." Andy put his arm around around her shoulders. "Just make sure you behave when you're onstage."

"Would it be awful if I kissed him on stage?" Emmy asked while she grinned.

"Just make it a quick one," Andy said.

Fridays At Five walked off the stage at eleven. The guys were handed towels by Frankie and his crew and headed to the SUVs to be driven home.

"Great show!" Jeff slapped Kenny on the back. "It does feel good to be home, but Frances showed me her honey-do list. She's always coming up with something to renovate. By the time we're finished, there won't be an original piece of lumber left in the old place."

"That's what you get for buying an older home," Dave said and then laughed.

"I could never live in a glass and steel house like you." Jeff pictured Dave's ultra modern home.

Kenny grinned and added, "I'll talk to you guys later. I think Emmy might have a surprise waiting for me."

P.J. shrugged. "Are you guys ever going to realize life is not always a honeymoon?"

"I hope not." *I want to be on my honeymoon when I turn eighty.* Kenny smiled and slid into the back seat.

Emmy was already home. She left as soon as she sang her last song with Kenny. Rory had texted that Diane made it to the show and he wouldn't need a ride.

Chapter Twenty-Five

"The bus just picked up Peter," Tony said as he walked into the kitchen. "I'm going to get John, run Dotty to preschool and head to practice." He kissed Sloane and smiled at Emmy. "See ya, brat."

"Don't forget to wear your helmet. Your brains are already scrambled enough," Emmy teased back.

"You're such a riot, Emmy." Tony grabbed Dotty's coat and backpack from the mudroom and handed the coat to Dotty.

Dotty put on her coat by herself and said, "Bye, Mommy. I'll draw a picture for you today."

Tony attempted to help Dotty with her backpack.

"I can do it, Papa," she said and then pushed his hand away. "I don't need any help. I'm big now."

"Yes, you are, pumpkin. Give Mommy a kiss."

"Noemi and Ben are still sleeping, Mommy. I'll see you after school. Bye, Auntie Em." Dotty kissed them and held Tony's hand as she walked out.

"I will pick you up, Dotty. Do a good job today and stay on green."

Emmy waved at Dotty and made a face at Tony. "What did you mean?" she asked Sloane.

"If she behaves, she stays on green and gets more privileges."

"I would be on whatever color the troublemakers are on," Emmy said and then finished her coffee. "I can have one more cup but that's it."

"I can't see my feet anymore," Sloane complained to Emmy as they refilled their coffee mugs. "I feel as big as a whaling boat. Let's go sit in the family room. I need to get off of my feet."

"Why a whaling boat?" Emmy asked. "Are they bigger than other boats?"

"I don't know. That was the first kind of boat that came to mind." Sloane sat down on the family room couch. "I am so tired of being pregnant."

"Well, you don't have much longer, and this will be the last

193

time," Emmy consoled her. "I love that we can have sex without any possibility of me getting pregnant."

You're so lucky. We haven't told anyone, but Tony didn't get snipped. "At least I only have three and a half months to go."

"That's still a long... Oh, you were being sarcastic, huh?" Emmy realized.

"You got it, Emmy. I hope I still fit through the doors by then. I will be bigger than Tony and John put together."

"No you won't." Emmy shook her head. "You won't be any bigger than when you had Benjamin."

"Ha! When I got married, I weighed a hundred and forty pounds. I'll never see that again. I'll be closer to two hundred than one-forty."

"You used to play basketball at Olivet. You could start exercising again."

"You are so smart, Emmy. Why didn't I think of that? I'll just add that to my daily schedule. Let's see. Yeah, right after laundry, cleaning the house, taking care of the babies, paying the bills..."

"I get the picture, Sloane. Don't be mad at me. I'm only trying to help." Emmy got up and started to leave.

"I'm sorry, Emmy. Please don't go. I'm just having a pity party." Sloane patted the couch, so Emmy sat back down. "I look at you, and I get jealous. You don't look any different than you did when you got married."

"I do so!" Emmy grinned and touched her chest.

"That's beside the point. I bet you still fit into the jeans you wore in high school. I think I will be wearing maternity clothes for the rest of my life."

"No you won't."

"What if Tony hates me for getting fat? What if he leaves me for another woman?"

"Sloane! Enough of this crap!" Emmy raised her voice. "Tony is not going to leave you. He loves you, and he loves his family. So, get over this pity crap, and get off your butt. Let's go for a walk around the neighborhood."

"Who's going to watch the babies?"

"Isn't Mama here?"

"Yes, but..."

"No buts about it. Mama needs to feel needed. If you don't let her take care of the kids, she will be lost."

"Sometimes I feel like I'm taking advantage of her."

"Ha! Have you ever seen anyone take advantage of her?" Emmy asked.

"No, I suppose not."

"That settles it. I'm going to ask her to watch the kids." Emmy strode purposefully out of the room and found Mama sitting in her rocking chair reading a book. "Mama, could you help Sloane for an hour or so?"

"Of course, I'm not doing anything," Mama said. "I've been trying to read this book, but I just don't understand it."

"What's it about?" Emmy asked

Mama held up the book to let Emmy see the gruesome cover. "Some girl who is obsessed with a woman who married a vampire or something. I just don't get it, but it's so well written. The characters are so interesting."

Emmy pointed to the cover. "That's some big teeth and a lot of blood. Sloane and I are going for a walk."

"Good. She needs to be more active. She's been too lazy if you ask me. She's in perfect health, and there's no reason for her not to be doing her normal routine. You're a good friend to her," Mama said and then smothered Emmy with hugs.

"Dotty said that Noemi and Ben are still asleep, but I thought I heard them playing."

"I will go check on them. I like taking care of the kids better than reading."

"Do you think I need a jacket?" Sloane asked.

"I wore one for my run, but it's getting warmer. I'll taking mine with, but might not need it," Emmy said.

Are you rubbing it in that you get up early enough to go running? "I'll take one with me." Sloane grabbed a lightweight jacket.

They walked down the winding driveway to the street.

"Which way should we go?" Sloane asked.

"I always go past Kristen's." Emmy pointed to the right. "If you go that way, you end up at the security shack."

"We are going to walk, right? I don't feel like running."

"I didn't do any running when I was six months along, either," Emmy said. "We can walk."

Sloane stayed to the edge of the street as they walked.

"Emmy, this isn't a sidewalk. You should walk over here like me."

"I'll move if I hear a car coming." Emmy looked behind her but didn't budge out of the middle of the street.

"Do you think we will ever have sidewalks?" Sloane asked. "We are incorporated into SoHam. The city might require them one of these days."

"Mr. Robertson has talked about a paved trail along this street. Asphalt, I mean. There's enough room on your side."

A gust of wind blew some leaves along the street.

"Can you believe it's fall already? Some of the leaves in our front yard have already turned colors." Sloane looked back and could just see the top of her house through the trees.

"I love the colors, but we have so many trees close to the house."

Sloane looked to her left in the direction of Emmy's house. "Don't you guys have leaf guards on the gutters?"

"I'm pretty sure we do, but I imagine one of these years they will need to be checked. It's a long way up to them. Kenny will never climb up there. I would do it, but he probably wouldn't let me."

They walked past John and Kristen's property and came up to Andy Walker's driveway.

Emmy grinned and then said, "Let's see if Andy's home. I want to bug him."

"Have you been in his house?" Sloane asked.

"Sure, haven't you?" Emmy walked on the brick pavers that lined the edge of his long driveway.

"Tony has, but I haven't."

"It's a big house, but he doesn't have anything on the walls. I tease him about hanging pictures all over one of these days."

196

Emmy ran up to Andy's front porch and rang the doorbell like a machine gun.

A few seconds later, he opened the door. "What do you want? I'm not buying any candy or whatever you're selling to raise money for your high school band."

"Oh, please, mister! It's only a dollar for a candy bar, and I have to sell fifty of them." Emmy sounded just like a high school kid. "Please! Please! Please!"

Andy saw Sloane walking up the drive. "Hi, Sloane. Are you with this kid? She's trying to sell me some candy."

"Hi, Andy. Wow! That's a steep driveway."

Emmy brushed past Andy. "Sloane wants to see your house since you've never invited her over."

"I've invited her over, but she's never... never mind. Please, come in, Sloane."

"I'll show her around," Emmy said as she pulled Sloane into Andy's den.

"Would you like something to drink, Sloane?" Andy offered as he scowled at Emmy.

"I'll take one of those fancy root beers you always have around," Emmy said.

"I didn't offer you anything, cuz."

"I'm fine, Andy. I'm sorry for barging in like this."

"No problem, Sloane. I'm used to her showing up unannounced. I had to change the code on the garage to keep her from just walking in. Men do need some privacy at times."

"This is his den, obviously." Emmy pulled Sloane along wide hallway. "His master bedroom is through there, but I won't take you in there."

Andy shook his head. "Thank you for that, Emmy."

"He's got a huge bathroom with a whirlpool tub."

Emmy dragged Sloane through the living room, dining room and finally into the family room.

"Notice anything?" Emmy asked.

Sloane touched the white wall. "Do you mean aside from there not being anything on the walls?"

"I told you about that." Emmy looked down. "Andy hates

carpeting. He doesn't have any in the whole house. Not even upstairs in the spare bedrooms."

"I see."

Emmy grinned up at Andy and asked, "Can I show her the basement?"

"Go ahead. I'm going back to work. I was in the middle of contract negotiations when I was rudely interrupted."

Emmy galloped down the basement stairs and waited for Sloane. "There are pinball machines here." She scurried around a corner and pointed. "In there is his media room. Big screen TV, home theater sound. The whole bit."

"Just like Kenny's."

"Yeah. You have to see this room." Emmy opened a door, turned on a light and waved. "This is the vault."

Sloane stepped into the room. "Holy smokes! I've never seen so many records and CDs."

"He has over ten thousand of them. He built all the racks and all the stuff is alphabetized."

"It's a perfect home for a bachelor," Sloane said as she followed Emmy upstairs.

"We're leaving! Thanks for the tour, Andy," Emmy shouted as she headed to the front door.

"You're welcome. Come back again sometime, Sloane." Andy spun around in his leather office chair. "Make sure you close the door, Emmy."

"I will." She closed the door and machine gunned the doorbell. She jumped down the steps and waved at Andy in his den.

"That's enough walking for me, Emmy. I need to get back and check on Noemi and Ben."

"I'll walk with you every day if you want," Emmy offered.

"I'll see."

"Hey, Emmy! Christopher Braun's on the phone and needs to talk to you. I think it's pretty important," Kenny hollered up the stairs on Saturday morning.

"Okay, I'll get it," Emmy answered. "Hi, Christopher. How

are you? Everything all right?"

"I'm all right, Emmy. I'm sorry for calling so early on the weekend."

"That's all right. I've been up since six, but I'm still in my pajamas," Emmy said while laying on her belly with Kevin beside her.

"You know Elena has been sick for a while and the doctor got some test results back yesterday."

"Do they know what's wrong with her? She doesn't act like she's sick, but I know there's something wrong from what you told me."

Christopher waited a second and then answered, "She has Crohn's disease, Em. A mild case, but still."

"I don't know a lot about that, but it's got something to do with the intestines, right?" Emmy asked as she sat up.

"Yes. The doctor described the symptoms and what we can do to lessen the effect of the disease. It's rather unusual for someone Elena's age to have this. I guess part of it is genetic, but there are other causes," he explained.

"What can I do to help?"

"Would you be willing to pray for Elena sometime. I know you're busy with your own family, but..."

"I will pray for Elena and you right now." Emmy rolled off of the bed and knelt beside it.

"You don't have to pray right now, Em."

"Why not? There's no better time than now."

"Should I hang up?" Christopher asked.

"No, you can listen and you can pray, too. Where is Elena?"

"She's actually sleeping on my lap. I'm sitting in my recliner."

"Good. Put your hand on her head," Emmy instructed.

"Okay, I'm doing that."

"I'm going to start. You can pray along if you want. You can pray silently or out loud. God hears our prayers no matter what form they take."

"I'm not real good at praying, Em. I don't really know how

to use that flowery language like some people at the church."

"That doesn't matter," Emmy said. "I don't speak good Christian-eze either. I just talk to God like we're having a regular conversation."

"I'll try."

"Dear Lord," Emmy began. "You already know about Elena's condition, and we're asking if you would heal her. We know you can do all things..." Emmy prayed for several minutes. Christopher prayed silently on the other end of the connection.

"... so if you choose to heal her, or just make her life as normal as possible, we thank you. Amen." Emmy paused. She couldn't hear Christopher. "Are you still there?"

"I'm here, Em." His voice cracked. "Sorry, but I started to cry."

"That's perfectly all right. You love Elena, and this is something difficult to deal with. I would be bawling my eyes out if one of my babies was sick like this. I cry if they get a runny nose," she said and then bit her lip.

He laughed for a moment. "You're funny, Em. Most of the time Elena seems perfectly healthy. One would never suspect anything was wrong with her. I'm hoping she can lead a normal life by taking this medicine."

"Sometimes kids will outgrow stuff they have." Emmy waited for a few seconds and then continued, "Did I ever tell you about the time I almost died?"

"What? No, never. What do you mean? When was this?" Christopher asked.

"When I was ten or eleven months old, I can't remember for sure now, but I had this thing called Myocarditis. It's like a virus that attacks your heart. I had this and was in the hospital for a couple weeks. I guess everyone was worried about me..."

"No kidding!" he exclaimed. "Your parents must have been scared to death. Oh, sorry. Bad pun."

"They were and Mr. Robertson told me that Grandpa actually cried. I guess he never cried, but he did in front of Mr. Robertson."

"I'm sure your grandpa loved you very much."

200

"Anyway, I got over the disease. Duh, I guess you know that since we're talking on the phone. Mom and Dad had to keep an eye on me, but I had a fairly normal childhood. At least health wise. It might not have been normal in other respects, but that's beside the point. I'm rambling, huh?"

"A bit, but that's all right. I never would have guessed you were that sick."

"The doctors told Mom and Dad that it was like a miracle or something. One day I was real sick and then almost overnight I was a healthy baby again."

"Do you think God cured you, Em?"

"I think He had His healing hand on me. He had a purpose for my life, and it wasn't to die from that disease."

"That's a good thing. I would have never known you."

"God has a plan for all of us. Sometimes it's our own fault if we don't follow His plan. I suppose it's always our fault. He knows what's best for us. I know I never really planned to be a singer, but God gave me my voice. Duh, I guess he gives everyone their voice."

He chuckled and then said, "I know what you mean, Emmy."

"I kinda resisted becoming a singer, but now I'm glad I did. Oh! Kenny and I were talking to Liz and Tyler the other day. We got on the subject of college and stuff. Tyler didn't start out at Olivet. He was going to some other college. I can't remember which one, but that's not important. Sorry, I'm rambling again."

"I don't mind. Go ahead and ramble."

"Tyler planned to be either a pharmacist like his dad, or a physical therapist. He figured either way he could help people, but during his last year of high school, he felt God calling him to be a preacher. Tyler said he resisted for over a year before he finally decided to follow where God led him. That's why he's a pastor at our church today." Emmy paused to catch her breath. "There! I'm done rambling."

"I'm so glad I called you, Emmy. Not just for the prayer, but to listen to you... ramble."

"You're welcome!" she said and then giggled. "I better let

you go so I can feed Kevin. He's waking up, and he will be hungry."

"Thanks again, Em. I'll see you on Sunday."

Kenny came upstairs. "What's up with Christopher?"

Emmy waved her hands around as she told Kenny the news.

Kenny grabbed her hands. "Slow down, baby. You can explain everything while you nurse Kevin."

The Bears began the season on Sunday night in Indianapolis against the Colts and their outstanding quarterback, Barden Earnshaw.

"Okay, the kids are all asleep. We can watch the game in peace," Emmy said as she plopped onto the couch.

"I never get to watch a game in peace with you around," Kenny teased. "You yell and scream and carry on like some crazy fan."

"I do not!" she insisted.

The game started and within two minutes, Kenny was proven correct.

Emmy jumped up and yelled at the TV. "Bertucci, get the lead out! Can't you read the signs? You know Earnshaw uses play action all the time." She looked at Kenny.

"Told you so," he said as he grinned.

She sat down, crossed her arms over her chest and didn't say another word until the Colts kicked a field goal to take an early lead.

"Who is this new guy playing quarterback for the Bears?" Kenny asked. "What happened to Bobby McMullen?"

"He signed a big contract with Seattle. The new guy is Kyle Maynard. He came from Florida State a couple years ago. He's supposed to have a cannon for an arm, but he needs to learn how to read defenses faster."

"The offensive line needs to protect him better. Those ends for the Colts are quick. Maynard is always on the move."

"Yeah, he's got happy feet."

Kenny looked at her. *Whatever that means.* "What

happened to Bishop, the running back?"

"They cut him. Remember last year?"

"Are you asking in general, or about football specifically?" Kenny asked.

Emmy glared at him before explaining. "His stats dropped off big time. Running backs don't last long in the NFL. Four or five years and they're history."

"Maybe the new guy will be better. What's his name?"

"Dante Setta. He's a rookie from the University of Illinois. I don't know much of anything about him. He runs kinda upright and he doesn't look all that fast."

"He looks pretty fast right now, Em!" Kenny pointed to the TV. "He's going to score!"

"Go! Go!" Emmy shouted as she jumped to her feet and waved at the TV.

Kenny pulled her back onto the couch. "He fooled the Colts with his speed that time."

"Maybe he has deceiving speed like Tony."

Later in the game, John Randolph scored on a twenty-yard pass reception.

"John told me his knee feels better than ever," Emmy said. "The cut he just made kinda proves he's back."

"He did fake the safety out of his jock," Kenny said.

The Bears beat the Colts by seventeen, but lost the next two games. They beat Philadelphia at home to end September with an even record. John proved to himself that his knee healed completely. His twenty-four receptions and five touchdowns led the team.

Chapter Twenty-Six

After taking the month of September off, Fridays At Five resumed the Street Chronicles Tour with a special opening act, The Only Hope. Emmy and her band would open every show on this leg of the tour.

"Mary, are you ready?" Emmy asked. "I'm heading downstairs with Kevin Michael. Kenny and the girls are already waiting."

"I'm sorry it's taking me so long. I want to make sure I have all the girls' favorite books. They will be disappointed if I don't. I can't find *Grandpa and the Three Lost Lonely Lions*. Have you seen it?"

"Oh, sorry. It's in my room. I read it to Isabella this morning. I'll grab it and meet you downstairs."

Once again Mr. Robertson allowed Fridays At Five to use his charter 737 for the tour. One by one, the SUVs arrived at the SoHam airport delivering the various band members. At one o'clock the jet lifted off and the Fridays team headed to Denver.

Emmy and Mary got the kids settled and then sat down for a break.

"This will be your roughest tour yet, Mary. I know we're flying, and that makes it easier, but we won't be home until the end of November."

"I thought we would be home for two days after Halloween." Mary reminded Emmy. "The second and third of November."

"You're right, but that won't be much of a break. It will just be enough time to catch our breath."

Mary grinned and then said, "At least all the shows are indoors."

"We won't have to worry about rain like we did in Oklahoma City this summer. I thought we were going to be blown away."

By the time the pilots landed at Denver International Airport, the support crews had been gone for over a day. The caravan of trucks and buses had arrived at the Pepsi Center in the early morning hours.

Andy Walker walked up to Kenny and Emmy. "Just talked to Ralph. Everything is set at The Can."

"The Can? What's that?" Emmy asked.

"That's what locals call the Pepsi Center."

"Why?"

Andy shook his head. "I don't know. Maybe because it looks like a can."

"Why does it look like a can?" Emmy deliberately pestered Andy.

"You're killing me, you know!" Andy said. "Stop grinning at me like that."

Emmy asked, "Will you still love me even if I act like a diva?"

"No, I will kick you off the plane and make you travel on the bus with the crew."

"I'm sorry you aren't coming to the show tonight, Mary," Emmy said later after they had checked into the hotel.

"It's all right. Kevin will be better off at the hotel. He's probably just got a runny nose and will be fine tomorrow."

"I'm glad we're in Denver for two nights. That might help the kids adjust to the traveling." Emmy kissed Kevin, but he didn't wake up. "We have to get over to The Can for soundcheck. Call me if you need anything. Frankie will always know where we are."

"I actually got Frankie to smile at me once. He even talked to me for five minutes." Mary held up her hand and extended her fingers.

"He must like you because he doesn't usually talk to people."

"I'll leave a light on for you guys, but I'm sure I'll be asleep when you get back."

"Are you sure you don't mind sharing a room with the girls and Kev?" Emmy asked again. "You could have a room of your own."

"I would rather be with you guys and the kids."

"Too bad this place doesn't have suites with three bedrooms." Emmy waved goodbye and hustled out the door.

She met the guys from The Only Hope in the lobby.

"'Bout time, Emmy," Bobby O'Connor teased. "We were getting ready to leave without you."

Adam Vicini shook his head. "Don't listen to him, Em. He just got down here a few seconds ago. He was flirting with those girls over there."

They piled into the waiting SUV and headed to the venue.

"Give me some room!" Emmy said as she sat between Boyd Goldman and Perry Johnstone in the middle seat.

The guys crowded against her and laughed. "You don't need much room, Emmy," Boyd teased.

"Are you guys gonna tease me the whole tour?"

"What? We never tease you, Emmy," Bobby said as he smiled at her from the front seat. He rapped out a beat on the dashboard with his drumsticks.

The driver hit the brakes as a taxi suddenly cut in front and stopped. Boyd moved an arm in front of Emmy.

The driver looked in the rearview mirror. "Sorry about that, Ms. Colasanti. Denver taxi drivers sometimes forget how to drive. They're almost as bad as the ones in New York."

"It's okay. I'm just glad you're driving and not one of these guys," Emmy replied with a grin.

The driver pulled around the taxi. "We're almost there. Just six more blocks."

Adam sat with Sean DelSasso, the newest member of the band, in the back seat. He whispered, "The guys will tease Emmy for a few days, but then they'll leave her alone."

"I still have a difficult time thinking of her as a celebrity," Sean whispered back.

"Don't let her hear you say that. She would smack you."

"She looks like a kid in those jeans and that sweatshirt."

Emmy giggled as Boyd touched her knee through the hole in her jeans.

"She acts like a kid, too. Especially on the road when she's away from the older guys."

"Boyd! Stop trying to tickle me." Emmy shoved his hand away.

"Should we take up a collection and buy you a new pair of jeans, Emmy? These are kinda worn."

"They're comfortable. Not all of us spend a fortune on clothes like you do. How much did this designer leather jacket set you back?" Emmy asked.

"Not as much as you might think. I got it for five hundred," Boyd said.

"You spent five hundred dollars for a jacket!" Emmy stared at him. "Are you nuts?"

"No, he's just a clothes hound," Perry said and then laughed hard enough to shake his entire body.

The driver pulled into the venue and everyone piled out. Emmy saw Nelson Grapella talking to Ty Dalicandro, one of the other Walker Management employees.

"Hey, guys! We're here," she shouted and waved.

Ty walked over with their backstage passes. "Since this is a FAF tour, you need to wear these at all times. Their security is a lot tighter than you might be used to."

"Does Emmy have to wear one, too?" Bobby asked. "Would Kenny throw her out if she didn't?"

"Behave, Bobby." Adam shook his head.

Ty kept a serious expression on his face when he told Emmy, "Mr. Walker insisted that she wear one, or else he would personally toss her out on the street."

Emmy's jaw dropped. "Did he really say that?"

"Yes, Ms. Colasanti, he did."

"Wait until I see him! I'll let him know who's the boss." Emmy walked away and then heard the guys laughing behind her. "I knew you were joking. Cousin Andy would never be mean to me."

"I'm sorry, Ms. Colasanti. Mr. Walker threatened to fire me if I didn't tease you," Ty apologized.

Emmy frowned. "Are you going to keep calling me Ms. Colasanti? We are going to have trouble if you do."

"Do you mind if I call you Emmy?"

"That's much better," Emmy said.

Bobby walked up behind Emmy. "Oh, Ms. Colasanti,

would you mind if I check out the merchandise area?"

"Keep it up, Bobby, and I will smack you," she warned. "Why do you want to check out the merchandise? Did you hear that some pretty girls are working?"

"I just want to make sure they have your CDs and other stuff set out," Bobby said with a straight face.

"Get out of my sight, Bobby. Just make sure you're around for the soundcheck." Emmy shooed him away and then looked at Boyd and Perry. "Did you guys tells him there would be pretty girls at the table?"

"We might have mentioned that, Em," Boyd admitted while shrugging his shoulders.

"You guys are so bad to him. One of these days he will get even."

Nelson handed Emmy a cell phone. "Andy needs to talk to you."

"Hey, cuz! What's the idea of throwing me out on the street?"

She could hear Andy laughing.

"You better be wearing your all-access pass when I see you."

"Where are you?" Emmy swiveled her head back and forth. "Can you see me?"

"No, I'm with the headliner band in the VIP lounge. Too bad you guys can't come up here," Andy said and then laughed again.

"If you want to be allowed to see the girls and Kevin, you better tell me where you are. I want to talk to Kenny." She put a hand on her hip as she continued to look around for Andy and Kenny.

"I'm sorry, but access to the band members is limited to family only. Are you a family member?" Andy asked and then touched her shoulder.

Emmy jumped a foot into the air. "You're gonna get it, Andy."

He opened his arms to hug her. "About time you got here, cuz. You have ten minutes to get ready for your soundcheck."

208

Nelson took back his phone and called Ralph Glissman. "Are you guys ready for Emmy's soundcheck?"

Ralph surveyed the stage before answering, "Give us fifteen."

Thirty minutes later, Emmy and the band started their soundcheck. Twenty minutes after that, they were backstage again.

"Emmy, the wardrobe room is over here, and your dressing room is number four. The guys can use five." Ty led her to the wardrobe room.

"Hi, Sara." Emmy smiled at the middle-age woman ironing a suit for someone. "How are things?"

"First day of the tour. We're working out a few kinks. I have your clothes on that rack against the wall. Do you know what you'll want to wear tonight?"

"I'd like to wear these jeans and a clean t-shirt, but Andy would probably kick my butt if I did," she said. She walked over to the rack, flipped through a few dresses and then pulled out one of her favorites. "Would this one look all right?"

"Yes, dear. That color complements your eyes. Not that anyone can see them in this place."

"Thank you, Sara. I'll be by later to pick it up."

"No need. I'll put it in your dressing room for you. How are those babies, by the way? I bet the twins are getting bigger."

"They are. They will be here tomorrow night if you want to see them."

"I'd love to see them again."

Emmy left and checked out her dressing room. "Oh, that's sweet." She saw a bouquet of red roses on the dressing table. She read the card. " To the most beautiful woman in the world. I love you more and more every day." *Where are you, Kenny?* She left the dressing room and spotted Ty Dalicandro. "Ty!" she hollered and he turned around.

"Do you need something, Emmy?"

"Have you seen Kenny. I haven't seen him anywhere."

"He and the guys just headed to the stage for their soundcheck. You should find him there. Do you want me to show you the way?"

"That's all right. I'll find it." She turned to leave but then stopped. "Do you remember the name of his assistant on this tour?"

"She's brand new. Her name is Jana Cordell‚ and I believe I saw her following Kenny to the stage. I could call her if you'd like."

Emmy shook her head. "No, I don't want to bother her. I'm sure she has enough to do already."

She headed to the stage and saw Kenny talking to Frankie Hanna. She looked around and walked toward a slender young woman with long curly hair, much like hers used to look.

"Hi, Jana! I didn't know Kenny hired you for this tour."

"Emmy! It's so good to see you." She hugged Emmy. "Isn't this amazing? Just last week I was set to start working for my father, and then this position opened up."

"It's not an easy job," Emmy said.

"Your husband warned me about that," Jana said and then looked around. "I didn't expect there to be so many people working. This is rather chaotic."

Emmy shrugged and said, "This is pretty normal. You'll get used to dodging through guys."

"Where are the girls and the baby?"

"They're back at the hotel tonight. Kevin has a runny nose, so Mary and I thought it best to let them stay in tonight. They wouldn't get to bed until much too late otherwise."

"I heard Mary took this semester off. We used to have lunch two or three times a week along with some of the other students from church."

"Did you put the flowers in my dressing room?" Emmy asked.

"Yes, did you like them?"

"They're gorgeous. Thank you."

"Kenny told me what to write on the card. I hope you don't mind. He was kinda busy earlier. The meet and greet lasted longer than it should have."

"I don't mind. I hope he doesn't make you work too hard."

"Oh, he's so sweet. He makes sure I'm all right. He

210

apologizes every time he needs something, as if it wasn't my job to look after him."

Kenny and the guys finished their soundcheck and he came over to talk to Emmy. "I see you ran into my new assistant."

"You didn't tell me you hired Jana."

"I didn't? Sorry. It was such a last minute thing. I guess I thought I told you, but I forgot."

"Thank you for the roses."

"You're welcome. How was Kevin doing when you left?"

"His nose was still running."

"Did his feet smell?" Kenny asked. "Get it? Nose running. Feet smelling."

Emmy shook her head and looked at Jana. "He's such a dork. I hope he doesn't drive you nuts with his corny sense of humor."

"I don't think he will," Jana said.

"Are you ready to grab a bite to eat, Em?" Kenny asked.

"Yes, I can hear my stomach growling. Can you hear it?"

Kenny put his ear to her belly. "Sounds like a volcano."

Emmy looked at Jana, and they both shrugged.

"Total dork, Jana."

Later, after eating, Emmy went to her dressing room to prepare. She got dressed and took a few minutes to read her Bible and pray.

Adam Vicini knocked on Emmy's dressing room door. "Are you dressed, Emmy?"

"Yes, come on in."

He tried the door. "I can't. It's locked."

"Oh, sorry, I guess I locked it." She opened the door and let him in.

Since Ryan Lederer's departure to join his wife's band, Adam had assumed more of a leadership role in The Only Hope.

"We've got ten minutes, Em. Are you ready to go over the set list one last time?"

"Okay." She looked at the printout Adam handed her. "We really can't make any changes because that would mess up the light guys and the computer techs, right?"

211

"They would adjust."

"I think we'll be okay. Kenny is going to play on 'Yolanda's Song' and the next two." Emmy handed the printout back. "How's Bobby doing? Is he nervous?"

Adam chuckled and then said, "He's always nervous before a show. I'd be more worried about him if he wasn't."

"He'll be fine once we start. He'll just look for the cute girls in the audience. How does Boyd feel about playing with Fridays? He wouldn't tell me."

"He's worried that he'll screw up something, but he knows those four songs inside out. Don't worry about him," Adam assured her.

"I'm not worried. I remember a verse that kinda says something about who can add a single minute to your day by worrying. I trust Jesus to take care of us."

Adam knew exactly what she meant. "That's Matthew 6: 25-27."

"How can you remember all those verses. I try, but I just can't."

"I just happened to read that chapter a couple of days ago."

"If everyone is ready, we need to take a moment to pray." Emmy checked herself in the mirror one final time. I guess I look all right.

Emmy gathered the guys in a huddle and prayed.

"All right! Let's go have some fun!" Bobby shouted.

As they got closer to the stage, they could hear the crowd stomping their feet.

Emmy bit her lip and grabbed Adam's arm and held him back while the other guys followed Nelson and Ty to the side of the stage. "I'm scared," she whispered.

"Don't worry, Em. I think they're ready for us. That's why they're making so much noise."

The house lights went dark, and the crowd roared even more. The guys took their positions, and Bobby counted off the first song.

"Here's your mic, Emmy." Frankie Hanna handed it to her.

"I'm nervous for some reason, Frankie."

212

"Don't be, sweetie. You're going to knock 'em dead."

"Thanks." Emmy waited for a moment and then ran out onto the stage. She heard the crowd but couldn't see them because of the lights.

Kenny joined Frankie just out of the crowd's view on stage right. "Look at her, Frankie. She's even more amazing than before."

"You're right, boss."

"Wow! They nailed that cue. Their light show is almost as good as ours."

"You both have come a long from from the early days."

Kenny slapped Frankie on the back. "Thanks to you, and the other guys."

"Yeah, I got to get back to work. I still have to train that new guy, and he's got to change the strings on the '55 Gibson."

"See ya in a bit." Kenny smiled as Frankie headed back behind the stage. *I think that might be the most talkin' you've ever done, Frankie.*

Kenny joined Emmy for three songs, and then headed to his dressing room to change.

The Only Hope finished their forty-five minute set, and headed backstage.

Ty handed out towels to the guys, and Jana took care of Emmy.

"Did Kenny tell you to look out for me?" Emmy asked after Jana handed her a bottle of water.

"He thought you might want a woman to go back to your dressing room with you instead of Ty or Nelson."

"He is such a loving husband."

Emmy and Jana zigzagged though the backstage throng and made it to her dressing room.

"Sara brought in some fresh tops and a couple pair of jeans for you to wear. She said that if you want something different to tell me, and I'll run and get them for you."

"These are perfect. I'll wear that top and these are new jeans." Emmy changed clothes and freshened up. "Do I look all right?"

213

"You look stunning," Jana said.

"No," Emmy said and then giggled. She asked, "I meant are these jeans too tight? I don't want the local guys to stare at my butt."

"You look fine, and they're gonna stare no matter what."

"I could dress like a nun," Emmy said with a smile. "Come on! I want to be at the side of the stage when Kenny's show starts. I heard they have a new opening number."

"Okay, but I need to see if he needs anything first," Jana said.

Emmy followed Jana to the green room where the guys were hanging out.

"Do you need anything, Mr. Colwell?" Jana asked.

"I'm good, Jana, and you don't have to call me that just because Emmy is with you."

"I didn't want her to think I was being too familiar," Jana replied.

"I understand, but please, call me Kenny. Everyone else does."

"We got about fifteen minutes," Andy announced, and then he noticed Emmy. He winked at Jana. "Hey! How did you get in here? This is a restricted area. Do I need to call security?"

"Andy! Are you gonna throw me out?" Emmy grinned up at him. "Don't you remember me?"

"Where is your pass, young lady?"

Emmy touched her chest. "Ooops! I must have left it in my dressing room. I'll go get it."

"You stay right there and don't move! Jana can go find it."

Jana scurried back to Emmy's dressing room, retrieved the pass and brought it back. She walked in and saw Kenny kissing Emmy.

"Oh, sorry. I should have knocked first."

"Don't be silly," Emmy said. "I was just kissing this guy who claims to be a rock star of sorts. He's a pretty good kisser, so maybe I'll spend the night with him."

"You guys are too funny," Jana said and then laughed.

214

The tour continued non-stop for the month of October. The two day break flew past, and the band held a small press conference to celebrate the release of the *Urban Chronicles* CD. They left the Steward Music Group office and headed right to the airport for the trip to Cleveland to start the second month of the tour.

On the morning of November twenty-sixth, the Fridays At Five machine rolled into Los Angeles for the final four shows of the tour. Emmy carried Kevin Michael into the hotel suite.

"Kenny will you take care of feeding the girls? I'll take care of Kevin, and then I want to eat. I'm starving."

"Didn't you eat any breakfast?" Kenny asked as he helped Heather and Isabella remove their coats. "What would you like for lunch?"

"French fries!" Heather said.

"Nuggets!" Isabella replied.

"McDonald's it is!" Kenny said as he laughed.

Emmy rolled her eyes. "You guys can eat fast food. Mary, Jana and I will eat healthy."

By now Jana Cordell had been hired as a full-time assistant for both Kenny and Emmy. She would turn the Colwell guest house into a home office for both bands.

Jana found the room service menu. "I'll call after you have Kevin settled."

Later, Kenny and the girls ate their fries and nuggets as Emmy, Mary and Jana toyed with their chopped salads.

"Would you like a fry, Em?" Kenny asked with one sticking out of his mouth.

"No, thanks. I'll stick to my salad." Emmy wrinkled her nose at him. "Holy cow! I forgot to check to see if the Bears won on Sunday. Do you know?" she asked Kenny. "I can't believe I forgot."

"You've been rather busy, Emmy," Jana remarked.

"They beat the Rams in St. Louis," Kenny answered. "Frankie told me."

"What's their record now?" Emmy asked and then took

215

another bite of salad.

"Six and five. They play the Vikings in Minnesota Sunday night. Do you wanna go to the game?"

"Not if it's in Minnesota."

"I'm glad we don't have to fly anywhere from here but home," Mary said. She rested her chin in her hand and sighed. "I've had enough flying to last for ten years."

"I kinda feel the same, but this was all new for me. I'll be glad to get home, but I've had a blast," Jana said. "And I got paid, too!"

"You should tell them about that time you were gone for over a year," Emmy suggested.

Mary and Jana both looked at Kenny.

"Were you really gone for a year?"

"It was more like a year and a half. Back in '97 and '98. The early days of the band."

"How did you travel back then?" Jana asked.

"Stagecoach!" Emmy teased.

"We started out using a van, and then moved up to a bus. We played all over the world. If we weren't playing or traveling, we were in a recording studio."

"How did you survive, Emmy?" Jana asked.

"I dated Derrick and Tony."

Jana tilted her head.

Mary explained, "She dated Kristen's brother Derrick for a few months before she met Tony."

"Are you talking about Tony Bertucci?" Jana asked.

Emmy nodded.

"But you guys act like brother and sister at church."

"We do now, but we actually dated for about a year. At one point, I thought we would get married."

"But he's so much bigger than you!" Jana exclaimed. "He would squash you." Jana blushed and put a hand over her mouth. "Sorry."

"He didn't," Emmy said. "He used to pick me up and put my feet on the ceiling. He's so strong, and I didn't weigh that much."

216

"You still don't, Emmy," Mary said.

"You should write a book about your life, Kenny. I'd love to hear about how you and Emmy met, and fell in love, and all that," Jana said as she waved her fork around. "I bet all your fans would buy a copy."

Kenny shook his head. "Maybe someday someone will do that, but not yet. I want the kids to have a normal life."

Yeah, like this is normal. Emmy thought. *They fly all over the place and live in a big fancy house. That's not normal. I just hope they don't get too spoiled.*

Emmy joined Kenny and the guys onstage for their encores on Saturday night. She danced around the stage as she sang the Beach Boys' classic "Fun, Fun, Fun" with Kenny and Jeff. They took a bow after that song and ran off as the house lights came up.

"This has been a fun tour, but I want to get home. I miss my bed." Emmy held Kenny's hand as they headed to the SUV that would take them to the airport.

"I agree. It's been a hectic two months, but it flew by."

"Are you making a bad joke?" Emmy asked and then giggled.

"Not intentionally, but I guess I did."

Emmy and Mary got the kids into bed while Kenny brought in the luggage.

"Thanks, Mary. I am so glad to be home. I'm going to sleep for a week."

"You might need to wake up once in a while to nurse Kevin," Mary said.

"Oh, just set him on my chest. He'll figure it out."

Emmy headed to her bedroom and collapsed onto her bed. By the time Kenny came upstairs, she was sound asleep.

"You are really worn out, baby." He removed her shoes, pulled back the covers and picked her up.

"Will you undress me? I'm too tired to move."

"Are you too tired to..."

"You are a dork, but I love you."

217

Chapter Twenty-Seven

"Tony, I think it might be time," Sloane said while sitting on the edge of the family room couch with her knees spread.

"Are you sure? Maybe it's those hip things again." Tony stood in front of her holding Ben upside down.

"These are not Braxton Hicks contractions. I can tell the difference. We need to get ready to go."

"Tony! Put Ben down this instant. You shouldn't carry him around like that." Mama waved a finger and scolded. "Did I hear you say it's time, Sloane?"

"Yes, and I haven't packed my bag yet." Sloane tried to get up but sat right back down.

"I took care of that last week. I had a feeling you wouldn't make it to your due date. Take Emmy for example. Doctors aren't always right. They're just practicing. I'll call your doctor and see what he says."

"Do you need help getting up?" Tony asked after setting Ben on the floor.

"No, I can manage." Sloane pointed. "You better grab Ben before he breaks something."

"Benjamin Alexander! No! That's Daddy's toy." Tony grabbed the remote from Ben, who surrendered the remote but picked up one of Dotty's dolls.

"No, Ben! That's mine. You can't play with her."

Ben waddled over to Noemi. She held her dolly tightly to her chest and pushed Ben down. Ben got back on his feet and jabbered at Noemi.

"Come on, Ben. We can play with my trucks," Peter offered. "You don't want to play with them. They're girls."

Ben sat down on the floor, picked up a truck and threw it over his head. It hit Noemi in the head, and she began to bawl.

Peter rushed over and looked at her. "You're all right, Noemi. Ben didn't mean to hit you."

Mama rushed back into the room. "Your doctor said to go to St. Bart's. He's already there delivering another baby."

"Will you be okay, Mama? Should I call Emmy and see if

she can come over to help watch the kids?"

"You take care of Sloane. The kids and I will be okay. I don't need anyone's help."

Tony helped Sloane into the Envoy, and they made it to St. Bart's in plenty of time.

A nurse walked up to Tony. "Mr. Bertucci? Is that how you pronounce it?"

"Yes! That's me. I'm Tony Bertucci."

She handed him a hospital gown, cap and paper shoes. "Put these on quickly and follow me."

Tony put the cap on backwards, only got one arm through the gown and hopped on one foot trying to put on the paper booty.

"Is she having the baby already?"

The nurse turned around, laughed and said, "You have a couple of minutes. Do you need help?"

"I can manage."

Fifteen minutes later Tony held his infant son in his arms as though he were made of thin glass that might shatter with the slightest movement. "What are we going to name him?"

"I thought we agreed on Howard Beckett," Sloane said and then sighed. *I really hate that name.*

"We did, but the more I think about it, I just can't imagine calling him Howard when he's two or three. Howard is a name for an old man."

"Are you sure? We told your mother," Sloane said.

Tony shook his head. "I'm sure. Mama will understand."

"Oh, thank God! I agree totally, but I was afraid to tell you. I know how close you were to your grandfather."

"I still like Beckett for a middle name. We could call him Beck for short."

Sloane shook her head. "Not gonna happen."

"We don't have to decide right now. We can take another look at that list of names we liked."

"You need to call Mama, and tell her to call everyone. Tell them if they want to see the baby in the hospital, they better hurry because I feel like I'll be ready to go home tonight," Sloane said as she closed her eyes.

219

The nurse took the baby from Tony and set him in his crib. "You have a healthy son, Mr. Bertucci. He has a good set of lungs for sure."

"Thanks! I have to call my mother."

"Go right ahead. We will look after your wife and son. That's what we do here," she said as she grinned.

"Hello, Mama! Can you hear me?"

"Ssssh! Be quiet. Papa is on the phone." Mama waved at the kids and they settled down. "Did Sloane have the baby already?"

"Yes! He weighed seven pounds and eight ounces and he's twenty-one inches long."

"How is Sloane? I can hear the baby crying. He sounds healthy."

Tony chuckled and answered, "He is healthy, and Sloane is ready to come home tonight."

"No! Surely they won't send her home that soon."

"I think she will be home tomorrow. I'm going to stay here tonight. Will you call Emmy and Kristen for me?"

"Certainly," Mama said. "Are you still going to name him Howard?"

"Would you be terribly disappointed if we didn't?"

"Good gracious no! I loved my father, but Howard is too old-fashioned a name for a boy these days. Do you have another name picked out?" Mama asked. "I'm sure Emmy and Kristen will want to know."

"We still like Beckett for a middle name, but we're not sure about his first name. Tell the brat we're going to call him Emmett after her."

"You aren't really, are you? That's too many 'etts'. Em-mett and Beck-ett. That doesn't sound right."

"We're not going to name him Emmett. I wanted to tease Emmy."

"You can do that yourself. I'll tell them you and Sloane haven't decided. Call me if you need anything."

"I will. I love you."

"I love you, too, son." Mama hung up and looked at the

220

other kids. "You have a new baby brother."

"Good! I already have enough sisters," Peter said.

"When is Mommy coming home?" Dotty asked. "I want to see the baby."

"She might be home tomorrow. You play together and don't fight. I have to make some phone calls."

Mama called Kristen first and then called Emmy.

"Hi, Mama. How are you?" Emmy balanced the phone on her shoulder as she spread some Sabra Chipotle Hummus on a flour tortilla shell. "I was just thinking I should call you. We've been so busy since we got back from the tour. Maybe I could bring the girls over later so they could play with Dotty and Noemi. How is Sloane? She called yesterday, and said she felt like a blimp."

"Well, she doesn't feel like a blimp anymore," Mama said and then grinned.

"Did she have the baby already!?" Emmy dropped the butter knife to the floor and shouted into the phone. "Did she? Did she?"

"Yes. They have a healthy new son. Tony called me a few minutes ago. He said if you want to see him, to come on up."

"What room is Sloane in?"

"You know he didn't say."

"That's okay. I can find out at the hospital." Emmy waved at Kenny. "Thanks for calling, Mama. I'll talk to you later."

"What's up, Em?" Kenny asked as he walked into the kitchen from the hallway.

"Sloane just had the baby. Will you watch the kids? I want to run down to St. Bart's." She handed the tortilla shell to Kenny.

"I got it covered." He looked at the tortilla shell, sniffed it and made a face. "How can you eat this stuff, Em?"

Emmy called Kristen, and they drove to St. Bart's together.

"Did you talk to Tony?" Emmy asked.

"Not yet. Mama called me."

"I only talked to her for a moment. I wanted to get to St. Bart's as fast as I could."

"I understand that," Kristen said as she held onto the door for support."

"I'll get us there in one piece," Emmy said as she floored it.

They parked in the deck and rushed up to the information desk.

"May I help you?"

"We need to know which room Sloane Bertucci is in. She just had a baby," Emmy answered while bouncing on her toes.

The volunteer checked the computer, found the room number and handed Emmy and Kristen their visitor passes. "Room 4012. Do you know how to get there?"

"Yes! That's the same room where I had Kevin." Emmy pulled Kristen toward the elevators. "Hurry up! I want to see the baby."

"Slow down, Em. He isn't going anywhere."

Emmy sprinted out of the elevator and raced around the corner and skidded as she slowed down to enter room 4012.

"That was quick," Tony said as Emmy rushed into the room.

"Hi, Sloane. How do you feel?" Emmy asked as she looked at the baby sleeping peacefully in his crib.

"I'm fine. That was the easiest birth I've had," Sloane answered.

"Hey! Aren't you going to ask how I feel?" Tony asked as he grinned.

Emmy turned and looked up at him. "No! You didn't just have a baby, dork."

"Brat." Tony saw Kristen walk into the room. "Hi, Kristen. Did you tell John?"

"Of course. I want to see... What are you going to name him?" Kristen stood on the opposite side from Emmy and cooed at the baby. "Please say it's not Howard."

"No, we changed our minds."

"Thank God!" Kristen sighed. "So, have you decided on a different name?"

"We're going to call him Emmett Beckett in honor of the brat," Tony said with a straight face.

"What!?" Kristen looked at Sloane.

Sloane shook her head.

222

"Really?" Kristen knew he was joking. "That's a lovely name. Emmett Beckett Bertucci. It has a nice flow."

"Are you really?" Emmy asked.

"No! Fooled you."

Emmy poked him in the ribs. "You're a stinker."

"You didn't name your son Tony," Tony replied. "Tony Colwell would make a good name."

"I'm never naming a kid after you," Emmy said while staring at the baby.

"Will you guys knock it off." Sloane rolled her eyes. "We have a short list of names, but I have one that I like best."

"What?" Tony asked.

"I think we should name him Taylor. Taylor Beckett Bertucci."

"I like that!" Kristen and Emmy both said.

"You mean Tyler like Pastor Tyler from church?" Tony looked at his son. "Won't that be kinda confusing?"

"No! Taylor. It's different than Tyler, you goof," Emmy teased.

Tony tilted his head and whispered the name several times. "I like that, too, Sloane. It's a whole lot better than Howard... or Emmett," he said. He grinned at Emmy.

She responded by sticking out her tongue.

Chapter Twenty-Eight

Sloane stood at the foot of the bed with a fussing Benjamin in her arms. "Tony, it's only five days until Christmas and you promised Peter you would find a tree today. You need to get up. He's downstairs waiting for you."

"I will." Tony yawned and stretched his arms over his head. "What's wrong with Ben?"

"I told him he couldn't go with you. He wants to do everything that Peter does. Could you take him and explain why he can't go?" Sloane set Ben on the bed, turned on her heels to check on baby Taylor.

Tony held out his arms. "Come here, buddy."

"Me go, Dada!" Ben shouted over and over.

Tony hugged Ben and then tickled him. Ben stopped crying and laughed as he squirmed to escape.

"Peter is going to help me find a Christmas tree. We have to hike through deep snow."

Ben stared blankly at his daddy.

"You don't have a clue, do you?" Tony said and then laughed. "Maybe I could bundle you up and take you along. Let's ask Mommy."

Tony carried Ben on his shoulders into the nursery.

"Maybe I could take Ben with us. I could carry him. What do you think?"

"And after you find a tree, how will you carry Ben and the tree? Did you expect Scout to carry him?"

"Of course not."

Sloane asked the obvious question. "Do you expect Ben to walk back?"

Tony rubbed his stubble of beard. "I'm sorry, Ben, but I guess you'll have to stay with Mommy."

Later, Tony bundled up Peter in his windproof snowsuit. "There! You look like the little brother from *A Christmas Story*," Tony said. "Can you move your arms?"

Peter moved his arms in circles.

Mama closed the refrigerator door and laughed. "Peter, you

remind me of the robot from the old TV show *Lost In Space*."

Tony tilted his head. "What?"

"Never mind. It's before your time." Mama looked out the kitchen window. "Do you think it's too cold to take Peter?"

"Hah! He'll be fine. It's thirty degrees already and supposed to hit forty this afternoon. Besides, we'll only be gone for an hour. I spotted the perfect tree two weeks ago, but I want to pretend we're searching the woods for the right one."

"Don't keep him out any longer than that" Mama checked Peter's boots and Gore-Tex mittens.

"Can you see?" Tony re-positioned the stocking cap that covered Peter's entire face.

"Thanks, Papa, I can see better now."

"Let's go! We have a mission to accomplish. Come on, Scout."

Tony led the way through the heated garage and out the back service door while carrying his saw over his shoulder. Scout charged past Tony in search of a rabbit to chase.

"Try to follow where I walk, Peter. Some of the snow is drifted."

Peter looked up at the jagged teeth of Tony's saw. "Okay, Papa." Peter squinted in the sunshine but didn't feel the drips from an overhanging icicle land on his shoulder.

Scout ran back and forth and buried her nose in the snow at times.

Within a couple of minutes, they climbed a short hill and entered the woods at the back of the property. For ten minutes they wound their way up and down the hills and left and right through the different types of trees as Tony looked for the perfect tree.

"How about that one, Papa?" Peter pointed.

Tony checked it out. "It's kinda short, and do you see how it looks like some of the branches are missing on this side?"

Peter stared at the tree. "I get it now. We need a humongous tree!"

Tony laughed. Scout barked and wagged her tail. Peter kicked the snow at Scout.

"Scout girl, find me a stick and I'll play fetch with you."

225

They entered a clearing of about thirty feet in diameter.

"How much farther? There were lots of trees back there." Peter turned around and pointed.

"We're looking for a very special kind of tree, Peter. It needs to be about ten feet tall with symmetrical branches."

"What are cemetery branches?"

"Uh, I mean trees that are shaped kinda like a pear only a whole lot taller."

Peter looked up as he hopped over a small drift. "Papa, it's snowing again."

"I think we're going to have a white Christmas this year." Tony's breath hung in the air like a mist as he trudged through the snow making a path for Peter to follow.

"Can we get a really big tree like that one?" Peter raised his hands over his head as he pointed to a forty foot tall Blue Spruce.

"It has to fit in the family room, remember?" Tony spotted a tree at the edge of the clearing and pointed it out to Peter. "How about that one? It's looks pretty good. It's the right height, and the branches look even on both sides." Tony walked around the tree as Peter caught up. "I think this one will be perfect."

Peter trudged through the foot-high snow to get closer to the tree. "It looks really big, Papa. Can you cut it down?"

"Just watch me! You need to stand over here, so you're safe!" Tony moved Peter out of harm's way. *This should be safe. You're twenty feet away from the tree, so it can't possibly fall on you.* "Stand right here for you, okay?"

Okay, Papa." Peter saw Scout running toward him with a small stick. "Scout! Here, girl!"

Scout ran up to Peter and dropped the stick. Peter picked it up and threw it as far as he could. Scout dashed through the snow, grabbed the stick and brought it back to Peter.

"Good girl, Scout. You keep Peter occupied while I saw this thing down." Tony sawed it down in a flash like he was Paul Bunyon. He turned to see Peter fall on his back in a snowdrift.

"Scout! Come and find me. I'm hiding."

Tony laughed as Scout jumped back and forth over his son. "Peter, I need you to help me carry the tree, okay?"

226

Peter scrambled to his feet and raced through the snow toward Tony. Scout ran between his legs and tripped him.

"Are you all right, buddy?" Tony asked as he helped Peter to his feet.

"I'm okay! Can I hold your saw?"

"I don't think so, Peter. It's too heavy for you." *And Sloane would kill me if she found out.*

They walked over to the tree.

"We can do this every year, Peter. We can make it a family tradition."

"I like that plan." Peter tried to lift the tree. "It's heavy. It must weigh a million hundred pounds."

Tony picked up the tree by the stump. *It is heavier than I thought. I'll have to drag it back.*

Peter helped him carry it back to the house by holding on to a small branch. By taking a direct path back to the house, they were home in five minutes.

"We made it, Peter. Thanks for your help," Tony said as he removed Peter's stocking cap.

"I really helped, right?" Peter took off his mittens, grabbed some snow from the tree, made it into a ball and threw it at Scout.

Scout shook the snow off of her fur. Tony and Peter took off their coats and boots in the warm garage.

"Let's get this inside, Peter." Tony grinned as they carried the tree through the kitchen past Sloane and Mama.

Sloane sat her Christmas mug on the counter hard enough to spill some coffee. "Tony! You're getting snow and pine needles everywhere."

Tony shrugged. "Sorry, Sloane. I'll come back and clean it up."

"You better believe you will." Sloane shook her head. *At least the floor's ceramic.*

"Sorry, Mommy. We'll clean it up later, but right now I have to help Papa." Peter lifted the tiny branch he was holding even higher. "Look what we're doing, Mama! I'm carrying this humongous tree."

"I can see, Peter." Mama smiled. "It's almost Christmas,

227

Sloane. Let the boys have their fun."

Tony set the tree up in the corner of the family room to the right of the fireplace. Peter handed him the hammer and stayed out of the way. Scout sniffed the tree and then lay down on the floor in front of the crackling fireplace.

"There! Now Mommy and Dotty and Noemi can decorate it." Tony stood back to check the tree. "What do you think? Does it look okay to you, Peter?"

"Uh-huh! Can I help decorate?" Peter pulled a strand of lights from one of the four green plastic tubs.

"Let's let the women folk do that, Peter. We men can watch while we drink our hot chocolate." Tony grinned as he walked past Sloane.

"Hey, buddy boy, the tree's leaning to the left." She poked him in the side and laughed. "And I'm not making any hot chocolate for you men." She emphasized men as she ruffled Peter's hair. *Peter will love helping you find a tree every year. You can be such a loving teddy bear at times, Tony.*

Tony looked back at the tree. "It looks all right to me," he said while leaning to the side.

"I will make hot chocolate for everyone after the tree is finished," Mama said as she pointed to the tree. "Fix it."

Tony's shoulders slumped, but he straightened the tree. He looked at Sloane for approval.

"Much better." Sloane nodded. "Will you bring in the ladder, please? We will need it to reach the upper part."

"Be right back."

"Come on, girls. Let decorate it." Sloane opened the plastic tubs filled with ornaments, lights, unopened boxes of tinsel and strands of popcorn.

Tony brought in the ladder.

"Thank you." Sloane kissed Tony.

"Yuck! Kissing again." Peter made a face.

"Peter, we might as well help with the decorating. No one will be able to reach the top except us." Tony positioned the ladder against the tree.

"Do not let Peter climb that ladder," Sloane said.

"I wasn't going to," Tony replied.

An hour later everyone stood back and stared at the tree.

"The lights aren't blinking." Sloane pointed out. "That one strand is supposed to blink."

Tony checked them, and they started blinking. "Loose connection."

"I put up all these ormanents, Papa," Dotty said proudly.

"Or-na-ments," Sloane corrected her. "You and Noemi were a big help." Sloane pulled a strand of popcorn from Noemi's hair. "Please don't eat this, Noemi."

"The hot chocolate is ready," Mama announced. "That's a beautiful tree." Mama looked at the very top. "That angel is almost thirty years old. I remember when I bought it."

Sloane put an arm around Mama's shoulders. "Thanks for letting us use it."

"You're welcome, dear."

A few minutes later, everyone sat in the kitchen sipping hot chocolate.

"I have marshmallows in mine." Peter showed Dotty and Noemi.

"Me, too!" Noemi held up her cup.

"Okay, but you have to sit at the table to drink your cocoa." Mama sat Noemi on her booster seat next to Ben's high chair. "Be careful. It's still a little hot."

Tony held up a mop. "It's all cleaned. Can I have my hot chocolate now, please?"

Sloane inspected the kitchen floor. "Thank you, Tony." She reached up and kissed him.

"Yuck!" Peter grinned. "Mommy and Papa are kissing again."

During the previous weeks, presents began to fill all the closets and other storage spaces in the house. Mama, Sloane and Emmy gathered on Saturday night to wrap and tag all the gifts. Tony's job was to keep the kids upstairs until bedtime.

"Where did you get this tree?" Emmy asked. "How much was it?"

"Free! Tony and Peter found it in the woods out back," Sloane explained. "We will never have to buy another tree."

"Peter sure picked a perfect tree," Emmy said and then giggled. "I love all those red and green ornaments." She straightened out some of the strands of tinsel. *I bet Noemi did this part.*

"Are all the kids asleep?" Sloane asked from her recliner when Tony returned.

"All of them except for him." Tony pointed to Taylor and then picked up a gift and shook it..

Sloane rolled her eyes. "Will you stop snooping through the presents?"

"Can't I just look around?" Tony held up a rather large gift. "I should put this under the tree. I think it's for me."

"No, Tony, you can't put any presents under the tree until Christmas Eve," Emmy said. "If you put them out now the kids will ask why Santa Claus has been here early. They know that Christmas isn't until next week."

"Taylor Beckett doesn't know," Tony joked as he watched Sloane nursing him. "Aren't there any presents for me that Santa Claus has sent out early?"

"You are worse than the kids," Sloane said and then sighed as Taylor spit up on her. "I told you if you were good Santa Claus would have something for you."

Tony grinned at Sloane. "Do you think he has something for me tonight? I have been very good."

"Ha!" Emmy laughed as the twins ran into the family room followed closely by Kenny. "Not that good! Besides, it's too early for you guys to... you know. You have to wait for at least a month. You are incorrigible."

"Are you afraid to say it in front of the girls?" Tony teased as he scooped up Heather and Isabella.

Emmy poked him in the arm and made a face. "I'm going home. Come on, girls. We have to make dinner for Daddy, and I have to feed Kevin Michael."

"Thanks for helping out, Emmy. I appreciate it." Sloane crinkled her nose. "Did you make another mess?"

230

"No," Emmy said before giggling.

"Not you! I meant Taylor." Sloane sniffed his diaper and made a face.

"No problem," Emmy said. "You were only in the hospital for a day and a half. Don't forget. Mama helped out, too."

"Not even good enough for a kiss?" Tony tried again.

"Maybe," Sloane said and then shook her head. "Now leave me alone. I've got to change another messy diaper."

Tony helped Emmy and Kenny by carrying Heather out to the van.

"So, you guys can clinch the division if you beat the Packers Monday, and then win down in Houston, right?" Emmy opened the sliding door and tossed the diaper bag inside.

"If Minnesota wins both of their remaining games, we'll be out of the playoffs. Unless Atlanta loses their last two games. Actually, there are a bunch of teams still with a chance to make the playoffs. It's going to come down to the last week of the year to see who's in."

Kenny strapped Isabella into her car seat while Tony helped Heather.

"Then we better hope they lose tomorrow."

"Thanks for helping out, Em. I wasn't serious about... you know"

"Sex!" she said with a grin. "I know. See you at church in the morning."

Later, after fixing a late dinner for Kenny and getting three kids in bed, Emmy called Kristen. "I swear I don't know who's worse Tony or the kids! He is more anxious for Christmas than ever. It's a good thing their game is on Monday night."

"John is not quite as bad as Tony, but the two of them together, I tell ya. Do you want me to wrap Kenny's present, or are you gonna come over and do it?"

"How about I come over Wednesday, and we can do all the wrapping then. I don't want to see another gift until then."

"Okay by me."

"Did I tell you what the girls have been asking?"

"No, what, Em?"

231

"They have been asking, 'Mommy is today the day Jesus was born?' and I tell them 'No, girls, you have to wait until Thursday to open presents.'"

"That's sweet."

"Isa said something else I thought was cute. She said, 'I don't need any presents, Mommy. I have enough toys and dollies.' and I answered, 'I know you do, Isa, but you have been my best little girl this year, so I think Santa will bring you at least one present.' And then her eyes sparkled and she grinned and said, 'Do you think so, Mommy? Do you really think so?'"

"She is so precious, Em. I'll talk to you later."

Chapter Twenty-Nine

The week passed by and Wednesday night arrived. Sloane finally got the kids to bed after an hour of baths, putting on jammies, brushing teeth and reading stories. She kissed them all good night, tucked them in and then headed downstairs.

"All right, Santa, get busy. They're finally down for the night."

"Okay, Mrs. Claus, I'll get busy," Tony said and then grinned.

Soon a mountain of presents surrounded the tree. Tony and Sloane were looking at the tree when she heard soft footsteps on the back stairs and looked to see who was out of bed.

"Dotty, why are you out of bed? Get back upstairs."

Sloane didn't want Dotty to see the presents in the family room already.

"Mommy, I forgot to put out cookies for Santa Claus. I need to put them out so he doesn't get hungry."

"It's all right, Dotty. I will take care of the cookies for you."

"Okay, Mommy. Santa Claus likes the chocolate chip ones with extra chips that Mama made yesterday. Make sure you put plenty of cookies out, all right?"

"I will, honey. Give me a kiss and go back to bed."

"Good night, Mommy, and tell Papa not to eat all the cookies by himself. You can have some, too, Mrs. Santa."

Sloane raised her eyebrows.

"Don't worry, Mommy. I won't tell the babies." Dotty giggled as she ran upstairs.

At six o'clock in the morning Sloane felt a tug on her arm.

"Mommy, Mommy. Santa was here last night. I think we should get up and see if he brought you anything. Come on, get up!"

"I'm getting up, Dotty. Where is Noemi?"

"Mommy," Noemi said softly.

"Noemi, why are you in bed with us?"

"Dada said I could cuddle."

"Is Peter awake?" Sloane asked Dotty.

"He's downstairs getting breakfast ready."

"Oh, no!" Sloane elbowed Tony. "Will you get up and make sure Peter isn't eating ice cream for breakfast like last year, and I think I hear Taylor crying. Where's Ben?"

Ben heard his name and did his Frankenstein imitation as he walked over to the bed.

"Look at you, Ben!" Sloane said as she grinned. "You're walking like a big boy now."

"Come on, girls, let's go see what's going on downstairs, and let Mommy get dressed. Dotty, will you help me put a fresh one on your baby brother?"

"Okay, Papa. I can change him by myself if you want me to."

"Maybe I should do this one. It might be kinda messy." Sloane sat up on the edge of the bed and picked up Ben. "Thanks, Dotty, but he's a little small for you to change his diaper."

"I'll run downstairs and find Peter." Dotty ran out of the room and scrambled down the stairs.

Tony made it downstairs with Noemi and Ben a few minutes later and found Peter and Dotty eating cereal.

"Look, Papa, no ice cream just chocolate syrup and milk on our cereal."

"That's good, Dotty. Ice cream is not for breakfast, is it?"

"Here's some hoops, Noemi, and some booberries," Dotty told her little sister.

"All right now does everyone want some spinach and liver and rutabagas for breakfast?" Tony asked with a straight face.

Peter made a face. "Yuck! I don't want that stuff whatever rooterbagers are!"

"Aw, come on, you guys have never had liver and spinach for breakfast. You might like it."

"I'll try some, Papa, if you will eat it with me."

"Don't say that, Dotty," Peter warned. "You know Papa will eat anything."

"Ben! Don't put the whole banana in your mouth. You might choke." Tony took it away, broke off a piece and handed it back to Ben.

234

Sloane came downstairs after reading her devotional book and saying her morning prayers.

"Mommy! Papa is trying to make us eat spinach and liver for breakfast," Peter complained.

"And rooterbagers, too!" Dotty added.

Sloane shook her head at Tony. "Really!? Are you ever going to grow up?"

Tony smiled at Sloane as he took another spoonful of Breyers ice cream out of the carton.

Over at the Colwell house, Kenny made breakfast for everyone.

"Are you sure you don't need any help, son?" Mom Colwell asked.

"I got this. You could see if Emmy needs any help. Mary is already gone. She's spending the day with her family."

Dad Colwell filled his coffee cup again and sat at the island reading his paper. "Elly, let him do his thing. Just as long as he doesn't burn the bacon."

"Breakfast is ready!" Kenny announced a few minutes later.

Emmy and Mom got the girls in their booster seats after a brief struggle. Emmy placed Kevin Michael in his high chair. "Here's some mashed banana for you to either eat or play with."

Kenny brought everything to the breakfast nook.

"Something smells good! I hope we're not too late for breakfast," Andy Walker said as he walked up to the girls and kissed the tops of their heads. "I brought Charles along with me. I hope that's all right."

"There is enough food for everyone," Kenny said. He smiled and shook Charles' hand. "Merry Christmas!"

Breakfast took almost an hour, and then it was time for presents and a story. Emmy read Luke 2:1-20 to the kids.

Kenny said, "Now it's time for presents!"

"Kenny, be patient, and I'll see if Santa left a present for you," Emmy said and then kissed him.

"We brought presents, too," Andy said while holding up a

large festive bag. "Oh, am I not supposed to say that?"

"It's all right. I don't think they understand the Santa Claus thing yet." Emmy took the bag from Andy and set it under the tree.

Emmy acted as Santa and passed out presents for the kids. They took turns opening gifts and every time Isabella opened a present she squealed, "Oh, Mommy, thank you. It's just what I always wanted!"

Back at the Bertucci's, Mama made it out to the family room. "I'm sorry I stayed in bed so long. I guess I needed the rest."

"You deserve it, Mama," Tony said.

"What time did they wake you up, Sloane?"

"I think it was six, and, at this rate, I figure we will be through opening presents around Easter Sunday."

"These are for you, Mama." Dotty showed Mama a pile of presents as Ben played contentedly with an empty box. Peter tossed his new football in the air and tried to catch it. Noemi dressed her new dolly. Taylor dozed in his playpen.

Dotty asked Papa, "Did you share the cookies with Mommy, or did you eat them all?"

"Dotty, I didn't eat them. Santa Claus did."

"That means you ate them all, didn't you? Why didn't you let Mommy have any?" Dotty asked as she made a face.

"She wasn't hungry, Dotty."

Tony looked at Sloane, and she shrugged her shoulders.

"She told me she wouldn't tell the babies. Oh, I think she meant you, too," Sloane teased. "I'm sorry if I spoiled it, baby, but there really isn't a Santa Claus. I hate to have to tell you."

Tony kissed Sloane as Kristen walked into the room, carrying Gracie.

"What are you guys doing?"

"Nothing." Sloane pushed Tony away.

John walked in with a bag of gifts. Zachary followed along with a new red fire truck.

"Did Santa Claus come to your house, too, Uncle John?" Peter threw his football at John, who didn't catch it.

"He did, Peter, and everybody got presents except for

236

Auntie Kristen. She was a bad girl this year, so all she got was a lump of coal."

"I'll give you a lump on top of your head," Kristen warned.

"Nice hands!" Emmy said and then giggled as she walked in behind John with Kevin on her hip.

"I have my hands full," John claimed.

"Yeah, what was your excuse for dropping that sure touchdown in the last game?" Emmy teased.

"You better be careful, brat, or John will get after you." Tony picked up Peter's toy football and handed it to Kevin. "Uncle Tony's is going to tackle you." He picked up Emmy and Kevin and carried them toward the couch.

"Don't you dare throw me on the couch while I'm holding the baby," Emmy hollered.

"I wouldn't think of it." He set Emmy on the couch and tickled Kevin.

Kenny walked in dressed in a red and green striped sweater with a Santa Claus face on the front. "Merry Christmas, everyone!"

Emmy shook her head and explained, "His grandmother gave him that hideous sweater, and he insists on wearing it. Doesn't it make him look like a dork?"

"I think it looks very festive," Mama said. "But maybe a bit dorky."

"I have presents for all the kids," Kenny said.

After another hour of watching kids open presents, the grown ups exchanged gifts with each other. John handed Emmy a small package with a card.

Emmy read the card and began to cry as she hugged him. "John, I will always remember this as the first Christmas we shared together as Christians. The best present I got this year was last month when you gave your heart to Jesus."

"Even if I still go to St. John's?"

"Jesus doesn't mind if you go there as long as you have a relationship with him."

"Isn't this a wonderful life!?" Kristen announced without making it sound too corny.

Several days later at the Colwell house, Kenny, Tony and most of the kids were in the family room playing with Peter's football.

Emmy, still in her pajamas and open robe, heard the commotion, and stood in the open entryway with her hands on her hips. "Stop horsing around. You'll wake Kevin and baby Taylor. They're still sleeping, and I wish I was, too. Tony, you are playing too rough with the kids."

"Maybe I should play with you instead, brat."

Tony chased Emmy down the hall. She slid in her white socks and squealed childishly as he caught her, threw her over his shoulder and brought her back to the family room.

"Put me down! Put me down this instant, you creep!" Emmy hollered.

"Okay! If you insist."

Tony dumped her onto the couch and promptly sat on her.

The kids gathered around and watched.

"Let me up you big ox," Emmy hollered as she tried to push him away.

"Don't hurt my mommy," Isabella screamed.

"I would never hurt your mommy, sweetheart." Tony lifted up, allowed Emmy to escape and then sat down. He picked up Isabella and held her on his lap.

Emmy stood up and kicked Tony's shin. "Ow! That hurt." She jumped up and down while holding her foot.

"Serves you right for kicking him, Em." Kenny walked up behind her and kissed her cheek.

"I think all the kids should climb on Tony and tickle him," Emmy suggested as she stuck out her tongue at him.

The kids squealed and Peter and Dotty climbed on top of Tony. Kenny and Emmy helped the younger ones.

"We're going to tickle you, Papa!" Dotty said as they all giggled.

"Oooh! That tickles so much." Tony laughed as the kids tickled him. "I think your daddy should tickle your mommy instead of kissing her. What do you think, Isabella?"

She grinned and glanced at Kenny.

238

Kenny put an arm around Emmy's waist and tickled her. They lost their balance and tumbled to the floor.

"Stop it! No, not there!" Emmy hollered as she laughed. "Kenny, you know how much it tickles behind my knees. Not my feet!"

"We want to help Uncle Kenny tickle Aunt Emmy," Peter said.

"Me, too!" Dotty squealed.

Kenny sat on Emmy's legs while Peter and Dotty tickled her feet through her white socks.

"Kenny, I give up! I give up! Make them stop, please."

"Will you kiss me if we stop tickling you?" Kenny asked as he smiled.

"Yes, but I won't enjoy it."

She finally got them to stop. Kenny kissed her all over her face, and she kissed him back.

"Am I still the most beautiful girl in the world?" Emmy asked Kenny while flat on her back.

Tony looked at her and laughed. "You might be the prettiest brat in the world."

Sloane moved next to Tony and poked him in the side. "You need to stop teasing her so much."

"Yes, and you always will be," Kenny answered Emmy's question.

Isabella got on her knees by Emmy's head and whispered, "Why are you always kissing Daddy?"

"It's because I love him, Isa."

Isabella looked at her very seriously for a moment and then asked, "How long are you going to 'wuv' Daddy?"

Emmy smiled and said,

"Forever... Isabella... Forever."

Check out these other titles by the author

The Emmy's Story Series

1. We We're 'posed to Get Married
2. One Of The Guys
3. A New Friend
4. Did You Like the Ravioli Tonight?
5. Completely and Forever: A Wedding
6. It's Time To Go!
7. How Difficult Can It Be?

The Annie Mercer O'Dell Series

1. Roosevelt High

Stand Alone Books

1. Growing Up In Kinmundy Junction
2. Grandpa, Lions and Kitty Cats: A Collection Of Short Stories For Children Of All Ages